Title
Author: Neil Connelly
On-Sale Date: March 26, 2019
Publication Date: April 2019
Format: Jacketed Hardcover
ISBN: 978-1-338-15775-8
Retail Price: $17.99 US
Ebook ISBN: 978-1-338-15776-5
Ages: 12 & up
Grades: 7 & up
LOC Number: Available
Length: 320 pages
Trim: 5-1/2 x 8-1/4 inches
Classification: Sports & Recreation / Martial Arts (F)
Social Issues / Physical & Emotional Abuse (F)
Religious / Other (F)

ARTHUR A. LEVINE BOOKS

An Imprint of Scholastic Inc.
557 Broadway, New York, NY 10012
For information, contact us at:
tradepublicity@scholastic.com

BRAWLER

ALSO BY NEIL CONNELLY

BRaWLER

NEIL CONNELLY

ARTHUR A. LEVINE BOOKS
AN IMPRINT OF SCHOLASTIC INC.

Library of Congress Cataloging-in-Publication Data available

ISBN 978-1-338-15775-8

10 9 8 7 6 5 4 3 2 1   19 20 21 22 23

Printed in the U.S.A.   128

First edition, April 2019

Book design by Phil Falco

I dedicate this book to my astonishing siblings:

For my eight older sisters, who provide an easy and honest answer to the question, "Neil, why are your female characters so resourceful and strong?"

And for my brother John, who surely has similar influence on my tendency to work with male protagonists that have powerful emotions and a deep concern for doing the right thing.

*T*here was a time when I could see the future, not that it did me much good. My visions came when they wanted, never giving me more than a fleeting glimpse of what was to come. They never offered enough detail or advance warning for me to win great fortunes or sidestep catastrophes. Take for example the very first one I ever had, back in fourth grade, when we lived in the yellow rent house on Seventeenth Street. That was the Tuesday night when my mom asked my father one too many questions about the Civil War and all our lives got ripped to shreds. It's a pretty crappy gift that lets you know trouble's coming for the ones you love most, but doesn't give you the chance to save them.

As the years passed, I'd see flashes now and then, but during my high school wrestling matches, the visions came on strong. My opponent would start to lean forward, or shift his foot just so, or an eyebrow would twitch — and my opening would become clear. That's when I knew with absolute certainty what was about to occur, in that split second before that next move, when I'd sweep his leg or hit a fireman's carry or headlock him so hard the whole gym would rock when his shoulders slammed the mat. Coach Gallaher said it was my intuition, that I was just visualizing the move before I did it. But it felt like way more than that.

One of these mini prophecies came to me in the state

semifinals against Tony Dunkirk over in Hershey. This was the bout that was supposed to put me into the state championship for the second year running. Five minutes before go time, I was getting into my zone, black hoodie tucked over my head, earbuds in place. Rather than stretching with the other wrestlers warming up, I was by myself along a wall, pacing back and forth like a panther or leopard in a cage. In one fist I gripped my secondhand MP3 player, boxy with a lightning-cracked screen. Music is one of the things that helps me stay even. Vintage rock 'n' roll works the best — Led Zeppelin, Black Sabbath, even Van Halen (but only before David Lee left. Don't talk to me about Sammy Hagar). These were the bands my mom loved back in high school, and this was the heavy metal music she played on our nighttime drives around Harrisburg's beltway when I was a kid, circling the city in her blue Subaru. Waiting for my match to begin, alone in the shadows along that wall, I listened to AC/DC's lead singer Bon Scott scream about riding a highway to hell, something about being on his way to the promised land.

Between songs, I glanced up from my MP3's fractured glass and saw Shrimp hightailing it through the other wrestlers, all jumping rope or bouncing lightly. With his bleached blond hair and pink skin, Shrimp tends to stand out. As he closed in on me, I plucked one earbud free just in time to hear him say, "Coach G, everybody, we're all over by mat three. You're like second on deck."

"I know when I'm in the hole."

"Ain't you gonna warm up more?"

"I'm warmed up enough for Dunkirk."

Shrimp shook his head and folded his skinny arms, looked away. A sophomore with more attitude than talent, he only goes about ninety-three pounds despite an addiction to Happy Meals. I'm in the unlimited class and tip the scales at 235. That's two and a half Shrimps, a fact I remind him of now and then. He turned back to me. "C'mon man. Don't make the same mistake you did in Bethlehem."

At the Christmas City tournament, it's true, I got a little lazy in the second period. I was rocking Dunkirk in a cradle and he managed to drop a foot down, push back into me enough to tilt us so my one shoulder grazed the mat. Everybody flipped like I was going to get pinned. I recovered quick and fifteen seconds later added one more win to my undefeated streak. Dunkirk raised a stink, claimed the ref didn't call me pinned as part of some conspiracy. Later, I heard he was going around calling me a cheat. He was all bluster though, no real threat.

Shrimp swallowed and said, "Look. Your mom's getting kind of upset."

With that, I told him, "Let's go." That lady's gone through enough for me.

As I followed Shrimp into the main part of the arena, the three mats stretched out before us in a way that reminded me of a three-ring circus. The stands weren't packed like I knew they would be for the championship bouts the next day, but there were still a ton of people in the audience, maybe four thousand. Wrestling's a major deal in Pennsylvania, a place with a long tradition of coal miners, farmers, and steelworkers where fathers still want their sons to be able to kick a little ass.

While we cut along the bottom row of bleachers heading for the far mat, I could hear the little whispers of folks as we passed. "That's MacIntyre." "What a mess." "Wouldn't want to be on the wrong side of that dude." "Waste of talent."

I know why people think the way they do, like they know the real me. They've read the same online articles I have, the ones with titles like "Undefeated, Unsportsmanlike, and Unacceptable" or "Why PA Wrestling Doesn't Need Eddie MacIntyre" or my favorite, "MacIntyre — Brute Boy!" (Mom says that nickname stuck because of my boyish face, especially the baby-blue eyes that reminded her of her dad.)

Those writers — all failed athletes you can bet — casually mention my record, 54-0 my junior and senior year. They all point out how I breezed through states last year and was the #1 favorite to win again. They all bring up the fact that my sophomore year, I got kicked off the team at Bishop McDevitt High School for violent outbursts. They call me a loose cannon.

Who knows, maybe what my mom says is true and I play into the image a bit too much. I'm no monster. But I'm not upset that people are wary of me, that some think I'm a bit nuts. People don't want to mess with a guy who could be sort of crazy. True or not, those stories keep me safe. Out on the mat, when some other guy is trying to rip my head off, that's when life makes the most sense to me. In the ebb and flow of combat, I'm in control. It's not just the occasional prophetic vision I get, though that doesn't hurt. Even when some opponent pulls an unexpected move, I can react to it. I'm not in the dark. I'm not smelling mothballs.

As Shrimp and me came up on the mat where I'd be wrestling soon, I saw Dunkirk's familiar shape ahead of us. He was facing away from me, getting last-second advice from his coach. I was trying to think of something to say to get in his head, but then just as we neared I heard him tell his coach, "Ever hear about that freak's dad? No wonder he's so screwed up."

This caught me by surprise, kind of stole my breath, and I lost the urge to drop a cute crack. Instead I just barged into him, hard enough to drive Dunkirk into his coach, who threw me a dirty look I happily returned without breaking stride. Folks in the crowd caught this little interaction and a bunch rose up, hollering crap like "Cheap shot!" and "Hothead!"

I stopped and turned, ready to take on a rowdy fan or Dunkirk or anybody who wanted to challenge me. But a hand gripped my shoulder from behind and I glanced back to see Coach Gallaher. "Save it for the match," he said. He and Shrimp ushered me away, past the scorer's table to where a little gang of Camp Hill Lions was gathered. My fellow wrestlers — LeQuan, Carson, Tyler — rose up on their feet. Behind them, my mom stood too, running a hand nervously through her long black hair streaked with white. Her thin eyebrows were bunched up and her expression nervous, like my winning wasn't a foregone conclusion. Life had taught her to expect disaster.

"Don't be so worried," I told her.

The buzzer sounded behind us as that match came to a close. The wrestlers shook hands and the ref raised the winner's arm. The loser huffed off, sagging. After a quick shuffle, two new wrestlers hustled to the center of the circle, crouched into position, and waited for the whistle. I was on deck now. Next up.

"You need a drink?" my mom asked, holding up a water bottle. I wasn't thirsty, but I took a swig anyway.

"You got to get warm and loose," Coach Gallaher said. "Jump some rope?"

I waved the suggestion away. "I'm all good," I said. "I got everything covered."

Pacing along the wall, I'd been working a few things out in my head, how I wanted this match to go down. I didn't just want to win. I wanted to put on a show.

And I wasn't only thinking of the fans. I knew for a fact that a half dozen college recruiters were in the audience, waiting with iPhones to record the infamous Eddie MacIntyre, to capture firsthand evidence of the Brute Boy in action. I'd been contacted by colleges as far away as NC State and Oklahoma. But I had reasons to stay local, so I was more interested in the offers I'd received from Lehigh and Penn State. These were the two best wrestling schools in the state — and both with decent programs in criminal justice. Something about the idea of being a cop appealed to me, somewhere on the far side of all this.

I stepped up onto the first bleacher next to my mom and scanned the crowd, looking for the face of one of those recruiters, but I didn't see them. One short guy about six rows up might've been a new one, from Pitt or Scranton. He smiled at me kind of crooked, like we knew each other. I stared at him and his Coke-bottle glasses, which along with his greasy dark hair made him seem like a nerdy troll. I didn't like how those buggy eyes drilled into me.

My mom reached out and took my hand. "Be safe, okay?"

I looked down at her looking up at me, her thin face, sunken cheeks, the right eye aimed my way but her left locked to the side. This lazy eye makes it look like she's perpetually checking to be sure no one is coming, like she's never sure she's safe. That eye is one more thing I can never fix.

"Tell that to the Dunkirk. He's the one that needs to be worrying."

At this, there was a loud whomp behind me, and I spun to see a kid in a blue singlet squirming on his back, mounted by his opponent, who'd clearly just stuck him. The ref smacked the mat, signaling a pin, and I unzipped my hoodie. "Game time," Shrimp shouted, smacking me on the shoulders.

I headed for the mat and Coach Gallaher swung in front of me, slapped my cheeks a few times to get the blood going. "Keep it simple. Don't forget the goal: advance to the finals."

I had no doubt that I would win, but as I trotted onto the mat and took my stance in the center circle, I focused on my other objective: I was going to humiliate Dunkirk. Make him pay for his insults by putting on a display of my talents so impressive it would silence all critics — this was the future I had carefully plotted.

For a while, my plan worked to perfection.

Off the whistle I shot in low instead of locking up like we big boys in the upper weight divisions tend to. This caught everyone off guard, including Dunkirk, so I scooped up a single leg and dumped him with ease, then scrambled on top for my two-point takedown. Stunned as he was, it wasn't hard to break him down from all fours to his belly. Chest pressed between his shoulder blades, I slid in a quick half nelson, my hand snaking under his armpit and latching on to the back of his head. At that point it's simply a matter of mechanics, just like a lever. As I spun to the side and cranked, Dunkirk slowly rotated to his back. All this time I was calm, patient, and methodical. Completely in control.

With Dunkirk's shoulders exposed, the ref started sweeping his hand to signal I was earning back points. I got my four, shimmied my chest back onto his chest, sunk the half a bit deeper, and shoved into him like a bulldozer. I could see one shoulder blade flat, and the other was inching closer to the mat. I ignored Dunkirk huffing and straining. The ref, a grandpa-looking guy with a crown of white hair and a shiny bald top, was belly down and right there, cheek pressed flat, whistle held loosely in his lips. He even lifted his right hand, ready to slap the mat and advance me into the finals. I was half an inch away from a first-period pin and had power to spare.

That's when I eased back and let Dunkirk up.

Sometimes in a match, a takedown artist will let a guy up if he's way behind and is convinced he can't turn him for back points. But in that situation, which you see a lot, the guy's not on his back like Dunkirk was, certainly not on the verge of getting stuck. I can say with some certainty that none of the four thousand fans in attendance — and you can bet they all were watching me at that moment — had ever seen a wrestler in a command position like me — a half nelson ratcheted tight, his opponent all but pinned — suddenly climb off him and return alone to the center of the mat.

Dunkirk reacted first, rolling to his belly and rising to an uneasy stance. It was like he thought he missed the whistle. The ref was slow to call the one-point escape, but then everyone kind of stared at each other, uncertain of what they'd just witnessed. Dunkirk glanced at his coaches. The ref looked over at the scorer's table. I stole a peek at the crowd, all wide-eyed and confused. Then I went back to work.

I feigned another single leg and Dunkirk overreacted, shooting his hips back so far he almost fell. But then he overcompensated, leaning forward so much that he was wide-open for an ankle pick. My right hand on his neck, I stretched down and blocked his right ankle, then toppled him sideways for another two points. This time I instantly let him up, only to pounce the moment he was on his feet, basically tackling him for a third takedown. It wasn't even a move. Half the stadium cheered. But I heard something else mixed in — boos.

As Brute Boy, I'd grown used to some in the crowd being against me, so it didn't do much to rattle my cage. I stayed focused, riding Dunkirk hard with a gut wrench, one arm cinched around his stomach. All the fight was out of him already, and he rolled pretty easy. But after just a couple seconds, I released him again, even saying, "I'll just take two this time."

The first period ended with the score 12–3. I knew I'd have to pace myself, since if I got ahead by 15 they'd stop the match, a mercy rule. I didn't want it to end too quick. While Dunkirk, on his knees, tried to gather himself and think of a way out of this nightmare, I circled him, hands on hips, glaring his way. I glanced over at my corner, where Shrimp was giddy with excitement and Coach Gallaher looked a little serious. He held both hands palm down and said, "Take it easy. Easy."

To start the second period, Dunkirk had choice and picked down position, settling on his hands and knees. Following the grandpa ref's instructions, I genuflected at Dunkirk's side, right arm circling his waist, left hand gently on his elbow. In front of us, the ref bent low, looked me in the eye and said quietly, "Just wrestle now, okay, son?"

"You ain't my father," I shot back.

Instead of blowing the whistle, the ref straightened and raised one hand, his fingers curled in a C shape. He announced, "Caution green. Unsportsmanlike conduct."

"For what?" Coach Gallaher shouted. No one else had heard me. In wrestling, you don't talk to the man in the striped shirt.

The ref bent once more, raising an eyebrow to see if I wanted to challenge him again. I eased my cheek onto Dunkirk's back.

Off the whistle I let him up, giving him the escape, then swooped in to lock up like heavyweights normally do. Standing, we pummeled, working our arms inside each other's and banging chests like rams battering horns. Finally I got what I wanted, both arms inside his. I locked my hands tight and squeezed, administering a textbook bear hug. Dunkirk made a little "ugh" sound, which only inspired me to crush him a bit more. I could feel his ribs grinding inside my grip. With some effort, I hoisted his body off the mat, rendering him all but helpless.

Whenever you've got an opponent in that kind of vulnerable position, the ref always says something like, "Careful now," and grandpa ref was no different. It's your responsibility to return your opponent safely to the mat. From the dominant position I was in, I could easily sweep a foot and dump us sideways, drive us both straight ahead into the mat, or even get fancy and flip backward, executing a wicked move I picked up at a summer camp at Kutztown called a suplex. This last option was my plan. I'd end the match in spectacular fashion. I'd hoist him high and arc my spine while twisting, spin our bodies in midair and slam him flat on his back, plant his shoulders deep and hard in an instant pin.

But when Dunkirk made that little "ugh" sound, and I knew I was hurting him and completely in control, I didn't see a reason to change things. After a few seconds, the ref said, "You got to do something with that."

I ignored him and crunched a little harder. Dunkirk was weak, and I hated him for it.

Five seconds later, the whistle blew. I let Dunkirk drop and turned to the ref, who held up a single finger. "One point red. Green — unsportsmanlike conduct."

"What for?" I asked, as the crowd reacted with a scattering of applause for the penalty.

The ref ignored me and motioned us both to the center of the mat. Dunkirk looked pale and woozy. He was dead on his feet, but I didn't square off against him. Instead I faced the ref. "Explain that call."

"Face your opponent," he said. "Ready to wrestle."

I stood with my hands posted on my hips, and I heard Coach Gallaher and Shrimp shouting. Even my mom was yelling at me now, but this ref's attitude was hacking me off. "Really," I said. "Tell me what I did."

Instead of telling me though, he blew the whistle to start the clock. Dunkirk, groggy as he was, still wasn't dumb enough to miss such a chance. I had my back to him, and he jumped in behind me, locked his hands around my stomach and tried to pick me up. Everybody clapped but I just slid my right foot back inside his, hooking his ankle and blocking his lift. "Give me a break," I said.

I hunched us forward, and he leaned in hard. With my fingers, I tried to break his grip, but it was tight and his hands were slick with sweat. I thought of hitting a switch, dropping quick to the right leading with an arm, letting my weight swing me around behind him. But then Dunkirk shifted his head, settling his face along my right rib cage, and that's when one of my prophetic visions arrived. I saw what was about to happen with perfect clarity, the purest dream you can imagine.

Almost magically, my right arm rose up, and I angled it down and back, driving my elbow into Dunkirk's mouth. I felt a crack on impact and he shot backward, releasing me and tumbling to the ground.

The ref whistled a stoppage. Dunkirk writhed on the mat, cupping both hands to his face. As his coach rushed out and bent at his side, grandpa ref raised a hand and awarded him another point for unsportsmanlike conduct, then gave me a harsh look. But I didn't care about points. It was 16–5 now. Big deal. I was safe and in control.

When I scanned the crowd, most folks were booing or giving me the thumbs-down. Coach Gallaher was standing with his arms crossed, clearly not liking what he was seeing. Shrimp and the other guys on the team were clapping, but even they looked a little shocked. Behind them, my mom was looking my way, one eye fixed on me and the other cocked to the side, and I wasn't really sure what I saw in her face. Weariness or disappointment. Maybe both. I turned away.

My eyes fell down to the mat, where they locked on to what I took at first for a tiny white stone. I bent to pick it up and saw a sharp edge and little flecks of blood. One of Dunkirk's teeth. Didn't suck to see that. I held it in my palm, the spoils of this war, and then with everybody watching, I strutted over to the huddle of people around his crumbled form — the kneeling ref, Dunkirk's coach, some lady trainer with a first aid kit. They had Dunkirk sitting up now, elbows draped over his knees, and the trainer was holding a cloth to his mouth. When she took it down, Dunkirk's bloody mouth looked raw and nasty, a glistening wound. His top lip was split and you could see the open space where that front tooth had been. I tossed it to him and said, "Consolation prize from states."

For added dramatic flair, I turned away from him as I dropped that line, so I wasn't facing grandpa ref when he sounded his whistle. This confused me though, because time had already been stopped. I looked back and saw him crossing his wrists over his head, walking calmly toward the scorer's table. He leaned in and talked with some official in a tie. They nodded as one and then the ref moved to the center of the mat. He raised a hand signaling a third unsportsmanlike conduct penalty against me, then walked over to where Dunkirk still sat crouched and bleeding. Reaching down, he took Dunkirk's wrist and raised it in victory. The auditorium exploded in applause.

Standing on the mat, I felt stunned and sort of numb. Coach Gallaher put his hands on my shoulders. "Come on," he said. "We need to go sit down."

I shrugged him off and advanced on the ref. "What the hell!?" I said. "What kind of crap is this?" He just shook his head and I demanded, "What did you just do?"

Now he looked at me. "I didn't do anything. You got yourself disqualified son."

Maybe it was that word. I don't know for sure. Maybe it was the adrenaline or the crowd booing or how the ref looked at me, like I was a failure. But right then, I lost control. I didn't consciously think anything, and I sure didn't have a vision of any kind. I didn't even feel the fingers of my right hand tightening. I just saw the ref's face widening in shock and my clenched fist swinging up, punching him flush just under his jaw. His head snapped back as he stumbled three steps, then collapsed.

The arena went silent. Even the other two matches stopped. For a few heartbeats, nobody moved. Grandpa ref was flat on his back, still. The lady trainer who'd been tending to Dunkirk scrambled over a few feet and leaned above the ref's face. She cradled his head. I looked around at the crowd, and four thousand people stared back, all of them with accusing eyes. Nobody was applauding anymore, and nobody needed to boo. I knew full well what I'd done, and I knew the consequences. In an instant, all my dreams were snuffed out.

So it seemed kind of sick, but perfect too in a way, when I heard a single person clapping. He was right there in front of me, maybe a dozen rows above my mom. My father stood, the only one on his feet in the whole auditorium, and he smacked his big, rough hands and whooped with excitement. He was wearing the same outfit as last time I saw him seven years back — just that one time Mom convinced me to go — the one-piece orange jumpsuit of the Fort Indiantown Gap Correctional Facility. I knew this wasn't some sort of vision, that this was only my twisted imagination. But I could see him all the same, real as can be, and I knew for sure that if my father had witnessed what I'd done on that mat, he'd be proud of me. He'd see all this the same way I sure as hell did, proof positive that his boy was just like him.

02

*A*ll weekend, I held my breath and waited for the axe to fall. Saturday night, when Giant Center filled with fans who were supposed to watch me raise my fists in victory, I stayed on the couch and wreaked havoc playing *Call of Duty*, not answering the phone and avoiding the Internet like I had all day. I heated up a frozen pizza and finished *Lord of the Flies* for Mrs. DJ's class, even though I doubted I'd be around for the exam. Just once before I went to bed, I gave in to temptation and hopped online. Turned out Dunkirk won in overtime, 2–0. The wimp was state champion.

When Mom wasn't working that weekend, she respected my silence and gave me my space, but Sunday morning she dragged me to St. Sebastian's for mass, same as always. In the days after my father got locked up, when we were staying at New Hope, my mom quit drinking and traded her bourbon for a Bible. At that particular 10 o'clock mass, I ignored the cold stares from the other parishioners and knelt when I was supposed to and stood when everybody else did, but I didn't beg for forgiveness like I know Mom wanted me to. I decided at some point in my life that God's pretty much going to do what He pleases.

Father Singh read about the time Jesus got mad at the merchants in the temple, overturned their tables in anger and chased them into the streets. This was a Christ I could get behind. But of course the sermon that followed was all about being gentle and the benefits of forgiveness. During the sign of peace, Mom sniffled back tears and hugged me tightly, whispering "Peace" as she squeezed, as if she could press it into me.

After the recessional, we wandered out with the crowd and the deacon asked if we needed a ride. My mom said no and clearly he was disappointed. No doubt he had some words of wisdom he was eager to share.

It's about two miles from the church to our one-bedroom apartment and so, carless, we started hiking home in our Sunday best. Our path led us through some of the nicer neighborhoods in Camp Hill — lots of porches and manicured landscaping. At one intersection she took my hand in hers, like I was a toddler, and on the other side of the street she held it still. I left it there, for her comfort, mostly.

As we walked my mom was quiet, but when she saw an Open House sign staked in a front yard she said, "Come on, for old times' sake?"

It had been years since we'd played this particular game, and much as I wasn't in the mood, I could tell it mattered to her. So I nodded and we headed inside, up the stony steps.

A realtor in a blue dress greeted us in the bright living room with a beaming smile. There were two couches, an enormous TV, and a brick fireplace that rose into the ceiling. Me and Mom nodded our approval. The realtor handed us a colored page of information and reviewed some highlights: The home was a four/two with updated HVAC. The finished basement had undergone radon remediation. "Great," my mom said, though I doubt she had any more idea than I did about what that meant.

The realtor, still beaming, walked us into the dining room (oak table with twelve chairs beneath a silver chandelier) and offered us a plate of chocolate chip cookies. My mom said no. I took two.

A family with young kids came in, distracting the realtor. She excused herself and invited us to look around. We could see the kitchen, but the stairs drew us up into the bedrooms. The walls were freshly painted in yellows and blues, and every-thing was so clean. We could only find a few clues that real people even lived here — a handful of Legos on a bedroom floor, some worn paperback books on a shelf. I lost track of Mom while investigating the Jacuzzi in the master bath, then found her by the bedside holding a framed photo. Over her shoulder, I saw the husband and wife, smiling together. After about ten seconds, I took the picture from her and set it back on the nightstand. "Let's check out the kitchen," I said. "I'm guessing stainless steel appliances, granite countertops."

She looked out the window into a backyard with green grass, shady trees, and one of those expensive play sets that belongs in a playground. The children from that other family arced on the swings while the mom and dad dropped together into a white hammock.

"No," my mom said, not facing me. "This wasn't . . . I think we'll just head home, okay?

"Sure," I told her. She handed me the colored page and turned away.

Somehow we wandered down a second set of stairs that dropped us in the kitchen. I was wrong about the stainless steel, but right about the countertops. As my mom hustled into the dining room, I lingered at the fridge, covered in magnets I imagined they'd collected from a dozen airports: Hawaii. Puerto Rico. The Canadian Rockies. I peeled one off — a green shamrock that proclaimed, *"Ireland!"* — and slipped it into my back pocket. A little sin I could confess next Sunday.

At the front door, the realtor's smile was gone. Clearly my mom had passed. I gave her back the colored information sheet and its six-figure asking price and when she raised her eyebrows in curiosity, I said, "Not quite what we're looking for. This place is a dump."

———

Monday at school, I moved through the crowded hallways like Moses crossing the Red Sea, the mob of students parting ahead of me. Shrimp tried cheering me up at lunch, but I was on edge. It felt like when a guy's about to hit some move but you're not exactly sure what it is. During fifth period, Coach Gallaher found me sitting in study hall, staring blankly at the periodic table for an exam I doubted I would ever take. He came up behind me and clamped a hand on my shoulder. "I'm sorry Ed," he told me. "I did all I could."

I rose and told Coach he had nothing to apologize for. The rest, the somber march to Principal Suskind's office and the notification of my expulsion, news of how I'd have to finish the remainder of my senior year through online classes, all that was a formality. I couldn't picture myself as a cyber kid.

After Suskind ended my high school days with a blank

expression and a signed letter, I was no longer welcome on school grounds. So I couldn't go down to the weight room and burn off some steam, which was about the only thing I was looking forward to all weekend. Instead, when I should have been taking a test on the abbreviations and atomic numbers for the elements, I had to empty my locker into a cardboard box and hike home. I flipped up my black hoodie and hunched against the chill March winds blowing across Fiala Field.

We live in the cruddiest apartment complex in Camp Hill — Creekview Court. (Who the heck thinks a view of the creek is a selling point?) Our place is a drafty one bedroom with a hot water heater that should've been replaced years ago. The same rent money could totally get us a nicer apartment in Harrisburg, but after Bishop McDevitt, I was stuck with public school, and Mom said that meant back to Camp Hill, even if we were cramped. Too dangerous across the river. With her on the overnight shift at New Hope Sanctuary, we take turns in the only bed. Mostly Mom's a day sleeper. Her other job is waitressing at Perkins, typically the dinner till midnight shift. On weekends we fight over who gets the couch, which she insists is too small for me. I don't care if my feet hang over the end.

For years, my master plan has been to pay her back, to make all her sacrifices worth it. But taking care of my mom means a real job, and that means college. I've always been decent at English, likely because of Mom's insistence on a steady diet of library books when I was a kid — lots of Harry Potter, Chronicles of Narnia, Redwall. But when it comes to precalculus, chemistry, the formulas swim in my head. An academic scholarship simply isn't in the cards. Wrestling was my passport to a university and the life beyond, far from Creekview Court, but I tore that up on the mat in Hershey.

As I neared home, I saw two unfamiliar cars outside the red-brick complex. One was a simple white sedan but the other, across the street, drew my attention. It was a gleaming gray SUV with a broken front grille, like a crooked smile. The driver was talking on the phone, leaning out the open window. With a start, I recognized him from the Giant Center, the nerdy troll with the thick glasses. When he saw me looking his way, he hung up the phone and swung out his big door.

But at that same moment, my mom yelled, "Eddie!" and I turned to her waving from the front entrance to our apartment. At her side was a slim black woman I hadn't seen in years but who I instantly knew. A door slammed and I just caught that SUV rumbling off. I didn't care anymore — I was too focused on the notion that I was about to be arrested.

Something in my leg muscles tensed, and I realized I was thinking about making a break for it. But my mom's face beside the cop's made me worried — the puffy cheeks and shiny eyes convinced me she'd been crying — and I didn't want to abandon her in trouble. I approached our front door and set down the box on our ratty welcome mat. The woman extended a hand, and when her slender forearm slipped past the sleeve, I saw the wondrous swirls of ink I'd forgotten.

"You remember Detective Harrow?" My mom sniffled and looked between us.

We shook, my big hand swallowing hers, and Harrow nodded seriously. "Edward," she said. "You've gotten a lot bigger."

I ignored this. She was wearing pants and a nice jacket — dress clothes. "How come you're not in a uniform?" I asked, then glanced out at the curb, lined with regular cars and that white sedan. "And where's your cruiser?"

An array of images — Harrow's holstered gun, the shiny badge, her gleaming squad car — had kept me company many nights since the Civil War.

"I got promoted a couple years back," she told me. She let go of my hand to lift one side of her jacket, revealing a detective's shield.

"What's in the box?" Mom asked.

"What's left of my high school career," I answered. "Suskind pulled the trigger."

Mom caught her breath. Over the weekend, I'd told her this would happen, but she was praying that Jesus might intercede. Framed by our front door, Mom began to cry and Harrow suggested, "Maybe we should step inside, Janice."

Three minutes later at the kitchen table, we all stared at each other over glasses of water no one was touching. I looked away, at the paint-by-numbers my mom had put in Goodwill frames — waterfalls and sailboats. "Art therapy" was another thing she picked up during her reconstruction phase. I glanced back at Harrow and wondered what her deal was.

I remembered Harrow ushering me out of the yellow house, buckling me into the front seat of her squad car. Later, at the station, when I wouldn't stop crying, she rolled up both sleeves and showed me those amazing tattoos that covered her arms, every inch some intricate curling pattern. Together we got a can of warm orange soda from the vending machine, and I drank it sitting in her chair, which creaked if you spun in it. Harrow's the one that hooked us up at New Hope too, where we stayed till Mom got back on her feet. I wasn't sure I'd ever thanked her, let alone told her she'd helped inspire a possible career, but today seemed like a weird time to offer gratitude for good deeds eight years old.

"Why are you here?" I finally asked.

My mom inhaled sharply at my bluntness and Harrow said, "Mr. Benedict and his lawyer visited the station today and completed the paperwork to have charges filed. It would be better for everybody if you came down first thing in the morning to be interviewed."

"Mr. Benedict?" my mom asked.

"The referee," Harrow said, "the one Edward —"

"Am I gonna be arrested?" I asked.

Harrow considered her response. "That depends on your answers. But it's a strong possibility. Even probable at this point."

"Arrested?" my mom said. "What charges?"

"That's up to the DA, but disorderly conduct for sure, maybe aggravated assault."

My mom reached across the table and grabbed my wrist. Harrow added, "Which is a felony."

"That sounds so serious," my mom said as she swiveled her head. Her grip on my wrist tightened. "All this for one punch?"

She was looking at the detective, but her lazy eye stayed fixed on me.

Harrow turned to face her. "Janice, Edward broke Mr. Benedict's jaw. The doctors had to wire it back together. So yes, this is serious." She turned my way. "That's why we've got to play this right. I didn't want to spring this on you, so I stopped by. But in the morning, I could pick you up and bring you down. It looks a lot better. I know one of the public defenders, a man named Quinlan, who'd take your case. He could help explain your story to a judge."

This line made me pause. I wondered just what the story of Eddie MacIntyre was. One thing for sure, I didn't like where it was headed.

Harrow sat back in her chair. "The referee's association has decided to make an example of you, and they can do it. They've got cell phone videos and an arena full of witnesses. If this goes to trial, you'll be looking at jail. Honestly, I'm not sure that can be avoided."

I banged my glass on the table, water sloshing over the top, then stood. I looked away from Harrow, and my eyes fell on the empty refrigerator. Just a week ago, it was plastered with a half dozen letters from top college recruiters. Now the magnets held a couple expired coupons. The *"Ireland!"* on the newest one yelled a suggested getaway.

Harrow calmly took a drink from her glass and stood, her chair scraping the linoleum as she pushed back. "Thank you for the water. I've said what I came here to say. You two need to talk." She left her card with a phone number and made her way to the front door. My mom gave me a desperate look, then hurried after Harrow.

When my mom came back ten minutes later, she found me sitting right where I had been. Without saying a word, she passed me by and went into the bedroom, a minute later emerging in her Perkins waitress outfit. "I'm late for my shift. Kevin's going to give me hell. After, I'll have to go straight to New Hope but you can call me there around ten, okay? We'll talk and figure out what's best. There's yesterday's meatloaf in the fridge."

I nodded.

She bent down so our faces were close. "Eddie," she said, "we'll get through this. We've tackled bigger problems before and we'll do this too, together." Her silver cross dangled from a chain around her neck. After a kiss on my cheek, she said, "It might go a long way if you'd apologize to that ref. Think about it, okay?"

I told her I would and she hustled off, and I was alone.

I felt bad for lying to my mom, making a promise I knew I wouldn't keep. The truth is that I felt horrible for what I did to that referee. I didn't want to hurt some old man, even one who was such a total geriatric jerk. But the notion of calling that guy up and apologizing to him didn't feel like something possible for me, like walking through a brick wall.

My father had taught me that real men never say they're sorry. By this definition, he remained a real man all the way through his trial. My father never once told me he was sorry for what he did, and even though Mom has explained to me over the years that he's apologized to her, that he's a changed man, I know she's just making that up for me.

After I heated some of that meatloaf, I watched TV for a couple hours, but there's only so many repeats of COPS a man can take. *Dancing with the Stars* was on, Mom's favorite, but I had no taste for fancy outfits or upbeat music without her. I went online for a while on the ancient PC that Mom inherited when the women's shelter got a new one last summer. It's a total piece of crap but as the only high schooler who can't afford a phone, I can't complain. A couple dozen emails waited for me, including one from Shrimp asking how I was doing, seeing if I wanted to get pizza at Roberto's or catch the latest MMA on pay-per-view. McGregor was fighting. The other emails were mostly nothing. A couple reporters asking for interviews, a series of recruiters withdrawing invitations to visit campus "with deepest regret."

At 10:30 the kitchen phone rang, surely Mom calling from New Hope. But I didn't know what to say to her, so I just let it ring.

My mind kept flipping through scenarios, trying to visualize the future that might unfold. I wondered what this public defender Quinlan could really do, given the evidence against me. I pictured myself standing before a judge in handcuffs, and him eyeing me up. While I knew it was impossible, I kept fixating on this one image — me and my father in the same prison cell, wearing identical orange jumpsuits, like distorted twins.

I realized with a start that no matter what, whether I went

willingly or in handcuffs, come morning I'd be down at the station. They'd have me. My mom would have to go through the trial and take off work and face all the stares of people who knew the truth. Her son had turned out just like her no-good ex-husband. And my great plan of getting a degree in criminal justice and then the police academy? Gone for good. Let's say I could find another way into college. Would the police academy even accept an application from a convicted felon?

I was debating whether or not to look this up online, to know for sure or hold out some tiny hope in ignorance, when a knock sounded at the door. I startled, picturing the cops. Then I realized it could only be Shrimp. He was a good guy, knowing I shouldn't be alone. But when I pulled back the door expecting my friend, I was shocked to see someone else entirely.

03

"**G**reeting and salutations," the short man said, executing a curt bow with his arms at his sides. "Raymond Blalock, at your service." His glasses magnified his eyeballs, and I recognized him from Friday's match and earlier in the day, the SUV with the cracked grille. He extended a hand and I shook it, giving him a medium squeeze and watching his face for the flinch. His short body was compact, thick, and his skin was oily. "Utterly delighted to make your acquaintance, Edward. There's something I'd very much like to show you," he said, shaking out his freed hand and rubbing it. "Something directly related to an endeavor with mutually gratifying benefits."

With this, he opened his palm toward his gray SUV, waiting like a huge loyal dog at the curb.

I said, "What about that whole 'don't get in cars with a stranger' thing?"

"I hardly qualify as a stranger," Blalock said, shaking his head. "I am an old associate of the family, here to lend my assistance in a time of need. Think of me as a long-lost uncle, a fairy godfather."

"You know my mom?" I asked.

He grinned. "I suspect you know better than that."

I understood what he meant but didn't say anything. Up close, I could see his glasses were dirty and I wondered how he saw through the streaks. Blalock told me, "You bear a striking resemblance to him. Surely I'm not the first to offer that observation."

When I come across people from our old life around town, they often remark on how I look like my father. They say it like it's a compliment. "Whatever," I said to Blalock. "What is it now you need me to see?"

"Just your future, Edward," he answered, chuckling to himself. "Come now. Fortune favors the bold. Unless you harbor some private inhibition against making money."

Instead of responding, I looked around the cramped apartment, which was starting to feel like its own prison cell.

Blalock grinned, rapped his knuckles on the already opened door. "This is the sound of opportunity knocking, young man."

"Screw it," I said. "Let me grab my jacket."

Looking at Blalock behind the wheel, I couldn't be sure he could see over the hood. The car was pretty beat-up but it smelled new, which didn't make sense till I saw the Magic Tree hanging from the rearview mirror. It was yellow and labeled "Vanillaroma." While we headed south on 15, out of Camp Hill, he told me he'd been to a half dozen of my matches over the years. He thought I had an impressive headlock but my endurance waned in the third period, both of which were true statements.

"So Mr. Benedict is intent on pressing charges?" Blalock asked.

I asked how he knew and he said he had his sources.

"There's this detective," I said. "Her name is Harrow and she wants to help me out. Even has a lawyer set up."

"Rule number one pertaining to law enforcement. Their prime motivation is self-interest, the perpetuation of the status quo. Don't delude yourself. Once you enter into an agreement with the system, you are beholden to their policies and procedures."

"What's that mean now?" I asked.

He faced me to say, "Talk to the cops and you take your chances."

I nodded, wondering why he didn't just say that in the first place. He sounded like he swallowed a thesaurus, but he didn't always make sense. I said, "So what would you do?"

"Abandon the world view that's failed you. It's time to strike out on your own."

I had nothing to say, and Blalock let the silence hang. We passed the exit for the mall, then the turnpike a while later. Finally he pulled up a ramp and made a left down a road I'd never been on. He asked me, "Are you familiar with the fighting league commonly known as Brawlers?"

This turned my face. "As much as anybody," I said. "Crazy-ass pay-per-view fights online. Rumor is they broadcast a pirate signal out of upstate New York, maybe even Canada." LeQuan and Shrimp had bragged about catching a bout once, even using his big brother's credit card to place a bet. Shrimp claimed his brother took a cut but he still won $500, though he couldn't produce the cash as proof. Still, he did buy everybody a Happy Meal to celebrate.

"Point of fact is that we are in much closer proximity." Blalock emphasized the *we*. "Brawlers is a highly profitable sports organization, operating with an unconventional business plan yes, but one must adapt to market forces. Though I've had my eye on you for years, there's an emerging situation that, intersecting with your own misfortune, produces an opportunity where a young man with your assets could make a significant contribution and reap substantial rewards."

I spent a while looking out of the window at the rolling hills, trying to decipher his babbling. We left the highway behind and headed into the country. The houses grew farther apart and we passed furrowed fields and silos. Even through the vanillaroma, I smelled something nasty, but I couldn't tell if it was cow manure or Blalock's BS. "By substantial rewards, you're talking about money?"

He nodded. "I'm interested in paying you to do what you do best."

"And what is that, exactly?"

"Kick ass." The blunt language sounded odd coming from him.

"This doesn't sound entirely legal."

"Oh let's not equivocate. This is entirely illegal." Blalock snickered at his own joke. "But illegal endeavors have a tendency to be among the most profitable."

I wondered just how profitable, and a memory from one of those Sunday open houses popped up: my mom slipping off her sandals, dipping her toes in the cool water of a backyard pool. "Not in my wildest dreams," she laughed.

I was sucked back to reality by a rattling sound in the SUV's engine. It was probably a loose bolt on the heat shield or a timing belt that needed to be replaced. Before Mom swore off boyfriends (the electrician/plumber, the scoutmaster/truck driver, the recovering alcoholic/mechanic) I'd learned a few things where I could.

We stayed quiet in the car, and at one point, his headlights caught on the remains of some animal along the shoulder. The roadkill was a few days old. I couldn't tell from the mess of guts and fur if it was a raccoon or a dog.

Eventually, we slowed at the entrance to one particular farm. At the front gate stood a huge guy in a trench coat, huge like a bouncer at a big city club. He looked German or Russian, carved from stone. Blalock lowered his window as we rolled up. When the guard leaned his face in, I saw he wore a black tie and had a crew cut and a square jaw. Blalock said, "We're running behind schedule, Grunt, can we dispense with the formalities?"

In no rush, this Grunt character eyeballed us both, glaring at me over a crooked nose broken more than once. Up close I saw he was older than I'd thought at first glance, and I decided he was no bouncer but an ex-NFL lineman, kicked off the team because he couldn't remember the blocking schemes. The guy was truly enormous. He glanced in the back seat and then, true to his name, nodded and made a guttural grunt. He swung open the creaky gate and waved us through by sweeping his other hand, which I noticed now was holding a shotgun. Blalock, clearly annoyed at the delay, said to himself, "Scintillating conversationalist, as always."

Gravel crunched under our wheels as we approached an old barn, leaning with age and lit from within. Parked outside it were a few dozen vehicles including a Rolls-Royce, a Benz, even a white stretch limo. Blalock explained, "Most of our profits come from the online proceeds, plus we get a handsome cut from the independent gambling websites, all of which are offshore of course. But a handful of high rollers pay a premium to attend the matches in person. This region offers an ideal location, off the grid but within a couple hours of Philadelphia, Baltimore, DC, even New York. For security reasons, we rotate locations, never fighting in the same place twice."

Blalock shut off the engine and got out. I followed. Inside the barn, a crowd of about a hundred people, some standing in the rafters, circled around an open space illuminated with tripod lights. Two college-age guys, shirtless and muscular, were on the fringe. One was tall and lean with a blond head of hair, bouncing on his feet. The other was thick as stump, shorter than me but heavier by 50 pounds, pushing 300 maybe. This bulkier one's skin was deep tan, and tribal tattoos covered his chest and face. He paced back and forth, staring at his opponent.

Blalock saw me looking and said, "That's the reigning champion, Badder. Should you feel compelled to ask him 'Badder than what?' he's got a ready-made response: 'Badder than you.' His real name is Bahadur, which is Maori for fighter, or so he'll tell you."

"How about Blondie?" I asked, checking out the tall guy, who had a raging case of acne. Zits cratered his cheeks.

Blalock said, "Maddox. During the winter he enjoyed a

series of victories but has recently fallen from grace. Bit of a tragic case — past his prime at twenty-two."

Along the perimeter I saw one stationary camera, as well as one hanging from the rafters. In addition, a guy had one hoisted on his shoulder. This must have been how they beamed out the pirate signal, which according to the rumors was untraceable. The bouts were shown just once, live and only to paying subscribers, and then the video disappeared without a trace. You couldn't find old video floating around YouTube or anything. Me and Shrimp had tried.

As we shouldered through the crowd, I saw it was a mix of people. A few guys wore suits and ties and had model-girlfriends at their side. But there was also a fair share of shady-looking characters. Blalock finally wormed his way to the edge of the fighting space, alongside a girl who seemed just younger than me. She looked me up and down, then lifted her chin to Blalock. "This your latest golden boy?"

He said, "Edward MacIntyre, meet Khajee."

She didn't lift a hand to shake, so I didn't either. "Call me Mac," I said.

"Hey," she said back. Khajee's face looked delicate and she was slight — her head barely reached my shoulder — but the way she stood, shoulders back, arms crossed, suggested a certain confidence. She wore a gray T-shirt and jeans the same black as her hair. I imagined relatives somewhere in her family tree were from the far side of the world, China or Japan I guessed.

"So what's Khajee mean?" I asked, leaning into her.

She looked up at me, blank-faced. Her eyes were green, which seemed a little unusual. "What's Mac mean?"

I smiled awkwardly but she kept a stony glance, one I couldn't penetrate.

The tense moment was broken by a single bell that gonged out, like from a church tower. All around us the crowd went wild. As one, they yelled, "No mercy!" and they turned to a guy standing in the loft above, leaning into a railing. Dressed in a white suit, he was bald and wore a neatly trimmed white beard that came to a V-shaped point just beyond his chin. In one hand he held a golden disc and in the other, a padded drumstick. Next to me, Khajee said, "That's Mr. Sunday. He's big into dramatic touches, among other things."

I didn't ask what she meant by that, but saw her glare at Sunday.

He struck the gong a second time and everyone hollered, "Prepare!" The two brawlers faced each other, and you could feel the air crackling now with charged energy.

Sunday seemed to relish all the attention on him. Something, maybe his big hands or his thick chest, gave me the impression that back in the day he was in the military. He hesitated before the third gong, then banged it louder than ever, which triggered the room erupting with "Brawl!" and the fighters launched toward each other.

Just before Badder and Maddox collided, though, they pulled up short with lifted fists, bobbing on their feet like boxers and dancing in a circle. Maddox wore mini boxing gloves, fingers exposed but knuckles padded. Badder's fists were wrapped in colorful rags. They traded a few jabs, testing each other, then Maddox spun a full 360, extending one lanky arm and driving his fist into Badder's tattooed face. The audience oohed.

At my side, Khajee observed the fight with interest but no passion. I'd seen that look before, on wrestlers watching their future opponents, mentally taking notes.

The challenger was quick to follow through, swinging a foot into Badder's gut, doubling him over. But as Maddox stepped in for a swooping uppercut, Badder sidestepped the punch, quicker than I'd expect for a big man. Maddox's follow-through left him exposed, and Badder delivered a ferocious one-two combination from the side, first a right to his ribs and then a left cross to his jaw. Maddox reeled back into the crowd, slumping, and they pushed him forward, back into the ring. Maddox tried another kick, which Badder blocked, and then they locked up like wrestlers, bent into each other. Each poked at the other with short, choppy punches, more annoyances than anything else at that close range, and the crowd booed even this brief lull in the action. In response, Badder crouched and exploded upward, leading with an elbow that caught Maddox flush on the jaw. His back arched as he staggered backward, and he shook his head and blinked his eyes, which had gone starry and blank. His arms were limp noodles. Badder moved in for the kill.

No longer caring about style, Badder flat-out tackled Maddox and they crashed to the floor, scattered with straw. The mob pressed in behind me.

As they tumbled, I was surprised to see Maddox scramble behind Badder. He drove him onto his stomach and slipped his forearms around his neck, then planted a knee on his spine. When he pulled back, he lifted Badder's face to my own, and I could see the champ struggle to breathe. But also, it was clear he was calm, and that's when I knew the tall man was doomed.

Sure enough, Badder took hold of his opponent's elbow and tugged hard, loosening the chokehold. Then he put some sort of arm lock on the wrist he'd freed, and Maddox cried out before rolling off the champ, who quickly mounted him, squatting on his stomach. From his back, the tall man tried to protect his acned face with his forearms, but Badder's position gave him too much advantage. He pounded away at his jaw and pimpled cheeks, even driving his elbows down into Maddox's face a few times. The tall man's hands slumped to his sides, and I scanned for a referee to stop the bout, then realized there was none. This was a place without rules.

Badder rolled him over and propped him up sitting, then knelt behind him, belly to back. He snaked his forearms around Maddox's neck and leaned in close, ratcheting the chokehold tighter. Maddox jerked to life. His body spasmed as he tried to escape, but it was no good. Without air, his cheeks glowed even redder and his eyes went wide. It was like watching somebody drown. He slapped at the straw with his right hand. This was a signal I knew from watching mixed martial arts on TV, even Olympic judo — it was a sign of submission, a universally understood way to say, "I surrender. No more." But Badder didn't seem eager to acknowledge this. Instead of letting go, he cranked a bit harder, sticking out his tongue and bulging his eyes into a mad, taunting grimace.

Finally a chubby guy, maybe Maddox's manager, broke out of the crowd into the fighting space and Badder relented. Maddox's body slumped. Badder got to his feet and stomped the ground a few times, banging his fists into his thighs. Next to me, Khajee glanced at her watch and said flatly to Blalock, "Almost ninety seconds. The over/under was a minute."

When I turned back to Badder, he was striding our way and he asked Blalock, "What's this now? Fresh meat?" He bumped his chest into mine and starred without blinking into my eyes. "You out past your bedtime, Baby Blue?"

Blalock stepped back and put a hand on my shoulder, trying to draw me away. But I stood my ground, raised my chin, and didn't break eye contact. Up close, I was struck by how detailed the tattoos were that covered his forehead, his cheeks, swirling designs making his face a living mask.

Badder eased back a half step, then made that crazy grimace again, with his eyes huge and his mouth open, wide fat tongue extended. "To my people, this means, 'Be warned! I am going to eat you!'"

"You might try," I said, these my first words. "Muscle's a bit chewy though."

Everyone tensed, and then, from above, a voice said, "Not tonight boys. Bahadur, the show's over! Clear out everybody!"

I looked up and saw Mr. Sunday rubbing his bearded chin, studying me.

Obedient, Badder backed down, skulking away. He made sure to actually step over the body of his fallen opponent. As the crowd dispersed, we followed the flow outside, and Khajee said to me, "You sure know how to make friends."

"I got all the friends I need," I replied.

Outside at Blalock's SUV, the three of us stood by the busted grille. I propped a foot on the fender and waited expectantly. Blalock said, "Here are the particulars of my current situation. I've signed for a fight next Sunday, six days from now, but my fighter is no longer in a position to fulfill his contractual obligation."

"How come he's not available?" I interrupted.

Blalock frowned at being cut off. "He contracted the plague. He has jury duty. He joined a monastery. That isn't your concern. The purse is six thousand if you win, two thousand if you lose. I get twenty percent either way. I also cover your expenses."

Forty-eight hundred bucks could at least get Mom in a decent used car. "And after that?"

"If you're half as successful as I suspect you'll be, there will be other opportunities. Some even more lucrative."

Khajee was eyeing Blalock hard, like he was holding back something. I dipped my head in her direction. "And what's her deal? She's my designated cheerleader?"

"Your trainer," Khajee cut in, with more than a bit of heat. "Plus you get to crash on my couch."

I chuckled. "How exactly you think you'd train me?" I asked.

The grin on her face and a mischievous spark of green in those eyes gave me pause. She said, "Like you've never been trained before."

"Agree and I'll drive you back to your place," Blalock explained, "let you gather some essentials before dropping you at Khajee's place." I was still trying to read her expression. Was it warning me? Inviting me? He went on. "Or I can return you to the life you had and tomorrow morning you can roll the dice with the police."

I looked around the barnyard. Almost all the other cars were gone, but the white limo was idling over by the silo. Its engine made a low rumble. I pictured my mom crying through the trial, my fingers tightening around the cold bars of a jail cell. And then, in some hazy alternate future, Mom and me unloading a U-Haul, carrying cardboard boxes into a new home. These images didn't feel like one of my visions — they didn't come with the same certainty the others did. I had to pick a path on my own, without the benefit of clairvoyance.

"Okay," I said, sticking out a hand for Blalock. "I'm in."

Khajee looked away while Blalock smiled and we shook. "Your father would be proud," he told me.

Just then the white limo pulled out, cruising slowly around us like a circling shark. Behind those tinted windows, I wondered just what Mr. Sunday saw.

I'm not afraid of the dark, not like some bratty kid. It's just that sometimes, especially late at night if I can't sleep, I don't like being awake in a room where there's no light. I picture being in that mothball closet, tumbling in the blackness, curled up with my hands clamped over my ears. Nights when my mom's at New Hope and I'm sleeping in the bed, I leave the lamp lit on the nightstand, something I'd never admit to anybody. Maybe it's just habit, but it keeps the waking nightmares at bay.

That first night on Khajee's lumpy couch, I tossed and turned for nearly an hour. Finally I got up and went to the bathroom, conveniently forgetting to turn off the light and leaving the door cracked just enough to spill a white cone into the hallway. After that, the living room wasn't quite as dark. Even so, I only slept in fits and starts, worried about my mom, alone in our home. The note I'd left behind read, "I'll be okay," but I knew that assurance would only do so much against her anxiety. I imagined her crying, and somehow this sound merged with an odd groaning coming from the only bedroom in Khajee's place, down at the end of the slim hallway. Khajee hadn't offered any details about who she lived with, so I wasn't sure what the deal was. Regardless of the source, that sound was hard to ignore, and only my exhaustion finally coaxed me into sleep.

Early in the morning, I woke in the shadows to something cold and wet nuzzling my neck.

I opened my eyes and found a pit bull baring its teeth, inches from my face. It was tan with a white stripe running from its nose up to its forehead and its breath smelled like tuna. Deep in its throat, it growled low. My first thought was, *How did a dog get into our apartment?* Panicked for her, I called out, "Mom?" and shot up to a sitting position. Then I saw the unfamiliar easy chair, the antique boxy TV, and remembered where I was.

I knuckled the sleep from my eyes and smiled. "I'm not afraid of you, doggo," I said. It hesitated, then its stump of a tail wagged and the dog planted its front paws on my knees. It brought its face up to mine and licked me on the cheek. Since I was a kid, I've gotten along better with animals than most people. They tend to make more sense.

Take this pooch for example. Who could blame him for protecting his turf and checking me out? I rubbed the scruff of his neck and head, where my palm rubbed over nubs in the spots where ears should have been. I couldn't see too well in the half dark, but it struck me right away that this dog had been on the wrong end of a fight. I said, "S'okay, boy. I'm no threat. You're a good boy."

"Girl," Khajee corrected, emerging from the bedroom. At the whispered hush of a male voice in the shadows behind her, she paused in the doorway and responded in another language. I decided it was her boyfriend and she was apologizing again for the guy on the couch. A weird smell slid from the room, something antiseptic. The guy asked something, his voice rising in a question, then she said, "Kon mài."

Khajee closed the door and did the morning zombie stumble in my direction, pausing curiously at the lit bathroom. The dog trotted to her side. She bent and patted her head. "I see you met Roosevelt. We call her Rosie."

"She picked the wrong dog to mess with."

"She didn't pick anything," Khajee said, correcting me for the second time in the brand-new day. "She was forced to fight, bred for it down in Baltimore. I found her at a no kill shelter over in Reading a couple years ago."

I've heard of those illegal leagues, people making dogs fight to the death in cages just so they could bet on the action. They beat them to make them tougher, to teach them how to take the pain.

Khajee dumped a cup full of dog food into a silver bowl on the kitchen floor and I stretched, my arms nearly hitting the ceiling of the apartment, even more cramped then the one at Creekview. "I could use some chow myself. Any chance you've got some eggs?"

"After," she said, pouring a glass of water and handing it to me.

I took a drink and asked, "After what?"

"I'm taking you for a run. You got some workout clothes in that bag?" There was more than a hint of challenge in her voice, cockiness too. The duffel I'd hastily gathered the night before, while Blalock's SUV engine rattled at the curb, sat on a patched armchair. It was the only other piece of furniture in the living room besides that square TV, my couch/bed, and a weird corner table crowded with knickknacks. I stepped over to it, and in the dim light from the kitchen, I saw a bronze statue sitting cross-legged, the stub of a candle, a bowl of sand, and some dried flowers.

"A jog sounds good," I told her. "But I run pretty fast."

"Fast doesn't matter," she said. "Far is the thing."

I glanced at the window, still black with night. According to the microwave, it was 4:55. "The sun isn't even up yet."

"So we'll run in the dark."

After I changed in the bathroom, I followed her into the morning, cold enough that I could see my breath. Her place was on the edge of Midtown, less than a mile to the eastern side of the river. Creekview Court — home — was a couple miles off the western bank. Beneath streetlamps, we headed away from the city, following a winding bike path along the Susquehanna that led to Wildwood, a nature park on the outskirts of town. Before the death of her beloved Subaru, which she nursed for years, Mom used to bring me out here sometimes, pack PBJ sandwiches and a bag of pretzels. Later, we rode bikes to get here. We'd wander the paths looking for birds and unusual plants, chasing frogs and turtles into the water. Wildwood offered two traits Mom looked for in any mother/son activity: It was peaceful and free of charge.

I figured Khajee would turn around once we reached the entrance, but she kept going, right from sidewalk to parking lot to forest trail. It was still dark, and I had to follow the sound of her feet scattering leaves, the dark silhouette of her slim frame ahead of me. At one point I joked, "What are you, part shadow?"

She just kept jogging.

We crossed a series of wooden bridges and at one point spooked a couple deer, something Mom would've loved. One magical morning when I was thirteen, we stumbled across a fox and Mom said it was a sign of good luck, that a bright future awaited us. I totally believed her. Finally, Khajee came to a sudden stop beneath the Highway 81 overpass. She turned and regarded me with those judging eyes. I tried not to seem out of breath, but that wasn't easy.

I bent and let my hands settle on my knees. "How long do these matches go?"

"Till there's a winner. That means a knockout or a submission. There are no points, no judges. Most are less than five minutes, but a couple months back, we had two guys go half an hour. Mr. Sunday doesn't like long matches. The longer we transmit, the better a chance of someone tracking the signal."

"Right," I said. "The signal."

Overhead, cars and trucks buzzed by. Through the still leafless trees, the horizon glowed with the initial hints of sun. With that light, Khajee's green eyes shined in the gray morning. She said, "Okay, let me see you ready to fight."

I straightened into a simple sugar foot position, crouching a bit with my left hand extending just past my right, palms open. Her face soured. "Oh yeah, you're a wrestler for sure." It sounded like a verdict.

"And that's a problem?"

"Just hold that pose," she said. Khajee positioned herself directly in front of me. In slow motion, she angled a stiff fist into my chest, right between my hands. Then she leaned back and, balancing on one leg, brought her free foot up to my jaw, tapped it, bent that knee and tapped me in my ribs, under my arms. She hopped once, switched legs, and spun around, then brought her other foot to my knees. After exposing my obvious vulnerabilities, she explained, "Brawlers can kick, punch, use their knees or elbows. You're wide open to a good striker, and we've got plenty of those."

She stepped in and lifted my hands up nearer to my face, pressed my elbows closer together. "Your forearms are shields, okay? Block blows to your head or torso."

I nodded.

With her sneaker, she shoved my forward foot back a few inches. "You need a better foundation, and try to stay on your toes not your heels. You've got to be mobile."

She stepped back and appraised me, not sold but content. Then she said, "Make a fist."

I did like she asked and held it out for inspection. She shook her head. "You don't get into a lot of real fights, do you?"

The truth was, I hadn't. "When you look like me, people tend to make peace or run away."

"Fair enough," she said. "But nobody's running away from Brawlers, at least not without paying the price." I could hear an edge in her voice, but I let it drop. She peeled open my fingers and then, from my pinkie down to the pointer, curled them one at a time into my palm. She smacked the ridge of knuckles where the fingers connected to the rest of my hand. "That's your striking surface."

Next she stood back and held up an open palm. "Jab at this."

I tagged it lightly and she began floating on her toes, shifting backward and sideways. "Again."

I followed her and poked at the targets she put up one after another. She looked at my feet and said, "Don't drag them — lift and plant, touch and go. You probably dance like a rhino."

"I don't dance," I explained. In the half-light, I think I saw her smile.

"When you bring your hands back, fall into that same guard position. Recoil. You'll get counterpunched into next week."

I've always been quick to pick things up from a good coach, and what she was saying made sense for the kind of fight I'd be in. But it was hard. My muscle memory had formed other instincts. After a while she stopped and held up a hand. "Okay, harder now. Hard as you can."

I shook my head at the idea of hitting a woman. "No way."

"You can't say 'no way.' I'm the boss here."

"Nobody is my boss."

Her face sobered. "Don't let Mr. Sunday hear you say that — seriously. Come on, you won't hurt me, I promise. Step into it first with your opposite foot. Plant it and lean forward."

I went ahead and punched her hand, but I held back. Khajee slapped my cheek. "This is no game. Sunday night, this guy you're facing can mess you up, hurt you for real. And Blalock, he might not bring you to any doctor you want to trust. Now do it like you mean it. Don't aim for my hand, right? Aim for a spot twelve inches past it. Drive your first through the target."

"I'm not hitting a girl."

She flicked a foot into my gut, so fast I didn't see it land, just felt the impact. Khajee said, "You sound like a caveman. I told you not to worry. I know what I'm doing."

My cheeks stung and my gut ached, plus my pride was sorely wounded, so I drew back my elbow and let fly. Khajee withdrew her hand as my fist connected, taking all the power out of the blow, but she nodded her satisfaction. We sparred like this for a while, then she paused and said, "Not horrible. You ever kick anyone?"

I smiled. "I took karate at the YMCA back in third grade for a while." Proudly, I took a stance and stepped forward, thrusting my angled foot into the air about waist high.

Khajee's face was expressionless.

"What?" I said. "How'd that look?"

She sighed. "About like third grade at the YMCA should look. Listen, for now, don't kick anybody. Don't even try, okay? We'll stick to other attacks."

I frowned. "Like what?"

She came in close again and tapped my elbows. "These are harder than your fists. Tougher to break too." She bent me into a grappler's stance, so our foreheads were touching. By instinct, I slid into a horse and collar tie-up, one hand on the back of her neck and one loose on her elbow. She slipped that free and drove it up, stopping an inch from my jaw.

I snapped back. "Holy crap."

"Right," she said. "I've seen plenty of guys get knocked out cold by a swift elbow uppercut." She held her hands out flat, palm down, and said, "C'mon. Step into it and drive up, through the target."

We danced around and I tried a few times, but it was awkward throwing elbows instead of fists. "Doesn't feel natural," I told her. Then I wound up a punch and swung a full uppercut into her hand. "That's got more wallop."

"Maybe," she said. "But with that windup it also takes twice as long to deliver. We'll figure out your fighting style over the next couple days. For now, we got to just put together a basic arsenal."

She stepped back and assumed her own fighting stance, swinging her elbows from the side and below, stepping forward and driving her knees up. Timed just right, I realized such a blow could be devastating. In between, she mixed in some standard punches and kicks. She was fluid, graceful. When she stopped, I said, "That's some crazy boxing."

Khajee shook her head. "Not boxing," she said. "Muay Thai."

"Thai?" I said. "Like Thailand? Is that where you're from?"

She shot me a look. "I was born in Wayne, New Jersey, you muttonhead. But my parents were both from Thailand, yeah."

There was a strain in her voice, and it was hard not to take note of the past tense. I mumbled an awkward, "Oh, sorry."

She shrugged. "My folks died a long time ago when I was just a kid. Since then, my uncle's taken care of me. Or I've taken care of him. It's complicated."

I could tell this wasn't a topic she was comfortable talking about, so I didn't press her. Now I knew who was making those sounds in the night. It was my guess there were two beds back there, or maybe she slept on a cot or something.

There was still a tense vibe in the air, and I thought she

might be about to say more, but Khajee stayed quiet, glancing over to some graffiti high up on the underbelly of the bridge. Somebody had gone to a lot of trouble to write "Warriors Rule!" but the sloppy lettering made it look like "Worriers Rule!"

Stiffly, we went back to work on my stance and my striking, and for a little while, we did some of what I'd call mat work. In the dirt, she showed me a few simple chokeholds and how to defend against them. This all came more naturally for me, and as we sparred, Khajee noticed. Sitting across from me, elbows on her bent knees and huffing with exertion, she said, "A good strategy for you will be to get the guy down as soon as possible, then whale on him. Ground and pound, baby. The longer you stay on your feet, the more likely you are to get your clock cleaned."

"Thanks for the vote of confidence."

"Come on," she told me, rising and offering me a hand. "There's a water fountain back by the station. I'm late already."

"Late for what?" I asked.

"School," she said, jogging away from me. "I've got a calculus test in an hour. Got to get home and catch the bus."

This surprised me, as over the course of the morning I'd decided she was older than me, and I asked, "You're still in high school?"

"A junior," she said. That jerked me back to my own reality. In theory, I was supposed to be finishing my semester online, but that wasn't looking too likely now. I tried to push this out of my head as we jogged back to her apartment, through thickening traffic. No point dwelling on a problem you can't fix.

At one point, Khajee led me down an alleyway and paused by a nondescript door, almost hidden by a green dumpster. "We're six blocks from where I live," she said. "Can you remember the way here?"

I looked around and took in a few landmarks, then said I thought I could.

She nodded. "Sunday set up a totally crappy gym in here. It'll open about ten. Mostly all brawlers. You can come lift, fine. But don't spar with anybody."

"Wouldn't it help to practice?"

"I'm the boss," she said. "No sparring till I say. And only with me there. I'll come by after school and check in on you. Other than my place or here, you can't be anywhere else. Blalock said to be sure you understood that."

This made sense. But it sounded boring. "What am I going to do at your house all day?"

She gave me a look that suggested she knew more than I did, but only said, "Last six blocks, we sprint." With that she bolted off, and I did my best to keep pace.

05

When we entered her apartment, my chest heaving, the TV was on and an old man was sitting in the armchair, Rosie curled up at his feet. The dog lifted her head and gave a lame growl, and then the man, thin with wispy gray hair, turned and regarded me with a broad smile. He lifted a frail hand from the blanket covering his lap and waved loosely. "Okay," he said. "Very hello to you."

Khajee chuckled hard and raised an eyebrow his way for some reason. Then she went into the kitchen, shaking her head. She returned with a couple glasses filled with water and passed one to her uncle, saying, "Lung lâyn à-rai kǒng lung nîa? Man mâi dtà-lòk láew ná."

Khajee then turned to me. I took the glass, which was cool on my palm. She said, "This is my uncle. Most folks call him Than. Uncle! This is Eddie."

Than nodded at me and shrunk a bit under her gaze. "Hâi pôo yài lâyn sà-nùk sàk nít. Naai nêe doo òk jà sêr sêr."

Khajee sniffed, and I smelled the faint scent of lemon air freshener. "Were you smoking again?" Khajee snapped, brushing a hand through the air. "Gam-lang kâa dtua ayng róo dtua rěu bplào?"

He grinned and crossed his hands in front of his face, as if defending against an attack.

Khajee told me, "Trust me when I say my uncle's not to be trusted."

The old man smiled, apparently understanding her English just fine.

"He's got a neighborhood boy who sneaks him cigarettes." Than lifted his shoulders but didn't deny anything. Next to the old man was a walker with wheels on the back legs and tennis balls on the front. Khajee told me to help myself to whatever was in the fridge and went off to get her shower. I had toast and some microwaved eggs, watching a repeat of the *World Series of Poker* with Khajee's uncle, who flinched every now and then at somebody's decision. "Bad bad choice," he'd mutter. "Not so good."

As I watched, I slowly became aware of a sound I couldn't quite place at first. It came from the background, this soft voice beneath the hush of the shower water, which we could hear easily from the living room. Khajee was singing. I couldn't make out the tune, but her voice was powerful — true and strong and somehow vulnerable. Than saw me listening. "Like angel," he said, nodding. I couldn't quite match that voice with the tough fighter I'd met.

As Khajee left for school, she reminded me to stick to myself at the gym and kissed the old man on the cheek. She said something to him in Thai and he grinned at me widely.

"What?" I asked. But without answering, Khajee left us on our own.

I took a while cleaning up in the bathroom and when I got

back to Than, the poker was over and *Family Feud* was on. The host prompted, "Name something a customer might do to annoy a waitress."

"Tip less than fifteen percent!" Than shouted. I was surprised, then impressed when it was the number one answer.

"Good job," I said, and he turned, looking like he'd forgotten I was around.

"Eddie. You do the fight, yes?"

I nodded. He tapped his own chest. "I do fight too." He coughed then, hard, and I asked if he was all right. He sipped at some tea from a TV tray next to his chair and pointed to a closet. "Get box now, okay? High up on shelf."

I did what he said and brought him a dusty cardboard box. Inside we found a couple dozen VHS tapes, things I hadn't seen in years. Each one had writing scrawled on it, but not from any alphabet I knew. Than lifted a couple and considered them, then finally seemed satisfied with his selection. He aimed a shaky finger at a VCR on top of the TV, and I inserted the tape. Moments later, a grainy image appeared. On the screen, two sinewy fighters faced off in a ring. They had colorful ribbons tied to their elbows — yellow and red — and the crowd, all Asian, were roaring in anticipation. The boxers were cobra quick, and just like Khajee under the bridge, they spun and flicked their fists and feet, spiked their knees into each other. "Muay Thai?" I asked.

Than straightened in his chair, beamed a bright smile, nodded deeply. "Muay Thai."

Together, with Rosie snoring on the carpet between us,

we watched a few fights without speaking. But then, Than began to make small comments on what we were seeing. He pointed out the way one guy telegraphed his spins and how another worked combinations. Fumbling with the remote control, he'd pause the tape and lean into the screen, tap at a guy's exposed face or belly and say, "Not so good." When he resumed the play, inevitably a punch or kick would land where he'd indicated. He used the same comment when a fighter tried a lame punch or half-assed spin kick. Other times, especially after a devastating knockout, he'd rewind the film and point to the fighter's stance or mimic how he held his fists. "Good," he'd tell me, nodding and pointing with a shaky finger. "Do you see?"

When that first tape finished, he picked another, and we ended up spending the rest of the morning viewing fights. I couldn't get over the speed of the slender fighters and their ferocity. Gradually I started perceiving the openings myself, before Than pointed them out. And I got good at predicting which fighter would win after just the opening exchanges. I'd tap the screen and give a thumbs-up. Sometimes Than would echo my sign and others he'd shake his head. Every now and then, our viewing would be interrupted by a coughing jag. Once he hacked something nasty into a handkerchief, but I acted like I didn't notice.

During one of the later matches, a somehow familiar boxer bounded into the ring. Than's eyes grew bright.

"Is that you?" I asked.

He hesitated for a second, like he was trying to decide

something. "Me," he said, patting his chest with a trembling hand. "So very long time ago."

On the screen, young Than's motions were slick and smooth. He was a deliberate fighter, not wasting any energy, only punching when he had a clean shot. His opponent bloodied his nose with a kick, and in the end the judges awarded the other guy the victory. I said, "Tough match. You fought well."

"Fight good," he said with a shrug. "Still make loss." Then he laughed. He slumped a bit, then nodded to himself. "But fight good."

After that tape ran out he pinched two fingers to his lips and inhaled, lifted his eyebrows my way.

"Sorry," I said. "I don't smoke."

He seemed disappointed, but not surprised. "Okay," he said, then dragged his walker around in front of his chair. He pulled the blanket off his lap and I was surprised to see his right leg end in just a stump, cut off at the knee. That pant leg was knotted. It took Than effort to rise up, and I recovered from my shock in time to set one hand on his back and anchor the walker with the other. "Yes thank you," he told me. Slowly, he ambled into the kitchen, planting the walker and hopping. For lunch, he made us some soup. I don't know if I expected some sort of Thai food, but when I tasted it and glanced his way, he shrugged and said, "Can't beat chicken noodle."

I cleaned the dishes and decided to violate the terms of Khajee's parole, walking Rosie down to the river a few blocks away. She liked the grass and the sun. When I got back, Than rubbed the dog's head and said, "Eddie, now I do nap. Okay?"

"Sure," I said. I pointed to the TV. "Thank you very much. I'll go work out." I made lifting motions with my hands, mimicking military press and curling exercises. He nodded and crept away on his walker. I couldn't help but wonder what happened to his leg, but it's not the kind of question you ask somebody. At his bedroom door, he paused and looked back. "Eddie," he said. "Do you know Peppermint Patty?"

I thought of the character from *Peanuts* and I'm sure I looked confused. Than brought pinched fingers to his mouth.

"Oh," I said. "The candy? Yeah sure."

"Maybe you buy a couple some for Than, okay?"

I could feel my cheeks bunch up as I smiled. "You bet," I said.

I dug my MP3 player out of my duffel and made my way back to the alley where Khajee showed me the gym. "Gym" was a bit of a stretch really. I've worked out in some beat-up places, but this was more like a scene from one of those stupid *Saw* movies Shrimp always wants to watch. When I opened the door, I had to step down three or four stairs to the concrete floor, and I planted my sneaker right in a standing puddle. This was explained by the dripping pipes crisscrossing the ceiling. There were no windows in the room, and the only light came from mismatched lamps hung overhead, along with flickering fluorescent bulbs. A half dozen guys were scattered across the space, which was the size of two basketball courts. They turned when I came in, but nobody asked for a membership card or anything. They just went back to what they were doing, and I got to work myself.

I stuffed in my earbuds and dialed up some Pink Floyd, comfortably numb sounding like a pretty good way to feel, then found an empty weight bench repaired with duct tape so many times I couldn't tell what color the original was. The weights were a random mix of different brands, and it took me a while to be sure I had the same amount on both sides. It was good to lose myself in music and sweat.

Between reps, I tried to take in the other guys. A black kid with cornrows braided across his scalp and long dreads draping down his back worked a heavy bag with punches and spin kicks, making it swing on its chains. His gut was ripped like a body builder's, and as he danced around the bag, his beaded hair swam. A chubby guy, pasty white, tried jumping rope, cursing with each missed effort. In another corner of the room, a thin Latino dude with a Jesus beard was practicing some sort of kata on a mat. I recognized the choreographed karate moves meant to simulate battle from my time at the Y. Older kids had to learn these to test for higher belts.

In a fighting stance, Jesus punched the open air, hollering "Keeya!" then circling his forearms, blocking imaginary blows. He unleashed a volley of elbow shots, punctuated with "Hu! Hu! Hu!" and then twirled and retreated, advanced again on his invisible opponent, crouched low to the ground and did a 360 leg sweep, and rose up once more. Apparently this dropped his foe, as he looked at the mat grinning with satisfaction. For the finale, he executed a forward flip with a rattling "Sai!" and pounded his front foot into a space I'm sure he pictured a face to be.

I had to admit there was something undeniably elegant about it all, like a violent ballet.

Every now and then the gym door would open, casting sunlight into our netherworld, and somebody else would enter. A couple guys gathered together here and there, and I saw their faces turn my way as I progressed from set to set. My presence hadn't gone unnoticed. Through my earbuds, Roger Waters and David Gilmour advised me to "run like hell," but I was pretty sure that was just a coincidence.

At one point I had to use the john, which made highway gas stations look like five-star hotels. There was a running toilet I knew I could take care of with the right tools. When I came out, I found myself looking up into the face of Maddox, the blond brawler who lost at the barn. His pimpled cheeks were puffy with swelling, and a blue-black bruise rimmed one eye. "Tough match last night," I said, waiting for him to get out of my way. "My name's Eddie but most call me Mac."

He stared at my hand, extended for a shake. "Nobody gives two turds what the hell your name is."

We stood there for a few seconds, and I was aware of eyes on us. The clanging of dumbbells behind us stopped, and over on the mat, young Jesus paused from his kata to openly stare. Maddox shoved past me, bumping shoulders as he said, "I got to take a leak."

I didn't take the bait. Instead of responding to the guy's big bad move, I walked back to my workout, and everyone watching turned away, tension diffused. Pecking orders get established every time you put a bunch of testosterone in the same room. I knew that. I figured I'd call the encounter a draw.

It was important to get right back to something, to show I didn't care about the diss, and I considered trying to work the speed bag. But it'd been a while, and I didn't want to look like an amateur. So instead, I made my way over to the squat rack, which faced a grimy mirror. My thick legs have always served me well on the mat, and a strong back is the key to not getting thrown. I was happy to see a weight belt hanging on a nail, and I slipped it around my waist for the support. Only a fool risks getting injured.

My first two sets went great — I could feel that healthy burn in my thighs — and I was considering how much weight to add for a third when Maddox stepped into the squat area. Just off his flank was the kid with the dreads. I figured they weren't here to give me friendly advice.

"One more set," I said, pulling out an earbud.

"Yo Dominic," Maddox said. "What's with new boy wearing my belt?"

Dominic shrugged. "Very disrespectful, you ask me."

In response to all this, I hefted a twenty-five-pound plate and slapped it on the right side, then screwed the collar tight. Then I got a second plate to balance the bar. But when I moved around to the left side, Maddox blocked my path.

"Look," I said. "The belt was hanging on a nail."

"I know," he told me. "That's where I keep it."

Still gripping the plate to my chest, I sidestepped him and walked right into Dominic. He grinned and asked, "You think you can come in here and just own the place? You think you're special?"

Again, all the other brawlers had stopped. The air felt tense. And here I had one of my prophetic visions, the first since my match with Dunkirk at the Giant Center. Even before what happened happened, I knew what was going to go down. I even felt the crunch of broken glass underfoot.

Dominic reached out and ran a hand along my cheek, like he was checking to see how close my shave was. Then he plucked free my other earbud.

"Look," I told Dominic. "If you meatheads want a fight, just ask next time." And with that, I heaved the plate into his gut.

As he caught it, I popped a right hook across his chin, sending him tumbling back over a rack of barbells. When I turned to Maddox, he was wide-eyed and backing away with both hands up. Guys with freshly tenderized faces shouldn't be starting something they aren't prepared to finish, which he was just realizing. I advanced on him, undoing the belt, and he said, "Hold on now." But we'd passed that point. I snapped the belt from my hip and whipped it overhead, walking steady as he scrambled backward. As he passed under a loose hanging light bulb, I twirled the buckle and bashed it, then felt the crisp crunch under my sneakers. "You want your freakin' belt?" I asked, with every intention of smashing it into the side of his thick head.

I felt the rush of blood, the thrill of seeing Maddox's wide-eyed fear, and knowing for sure that soon, any second, he'd be begging me to stop. I get that violence is wrong, sinful, etc. But there's nothing like that power, that safe sense of control.

"Yo Hothead!" a voice cried out, freezing the room. This wasn't part of my vision. I steadied my right hand, gripping the belt behind my head like a whip about to crack. Young Jesus walked toward us, bending to snag something off the ground.

Maddox said, "I got this Santana. You just —"

"Shut up," Santana said. Up close, I saw thin scars slicing across his forehead, one bisected an eyebrow. Looked like sloppy stitch work. "If Sunday hears about this, all your asses will be in a sling. You want to fight, spar on the mat." He tossed each of us a rubbery headgear. I looked down at what I was holding, and he brought his face closer to mine. "You boys can work out your differences all civilized, and I can offer you some pointers."

"Pointers?" I said.

"Advice don't come cheaper than free," Santana said. I noticed his fingernails were long and trimmed into points, almost like tiny claws.

"I'm game if Blondie is," I said.

Maddox worked his lower lip into his mouth and shifted his glance left and right. With his bruised face, he had no appetite for a fight, but he couldn't back down now. Mustering all the gusto he could, he said, "Let's get it on."

My chest swelled with what was to come.

At the sparring mat, Santana fit my headgear and slid on a version of boxing gloves that covered my knuckles but left my fingers free. I noticed an imperfection in his beard, a river of hairless skin along his jawline that could only mean another scar. My guess was those wounds weren't from a fight, not unless a blade was involved. When Dominic finished securing Maddox's chin strap, Santana said, "All set."

"Awesome," I said, pounding my fists together and crossing the space between us.

As we neared, Maddox rocked back on his feet, expecting me to box. But instead I dropped low and shot quick, scooping both his knees and dumping him hard enough to bounce his head off the mat. I briefly considered trying one of Khajee's chokeholds but instead just knelt across his belly and punched at his face. He covered with his forearms, and I tried some of those elbow strikes, even driving one straight down through his guard. Damn, I thought, if high school wrestling rules allowed this. I could've killed some kids.

I was just getting into it when I heard a door slam and Khajee's voice crying out, "Enough!"

I ignored her and whaled on Maddox's gut, which was totally exposed since he was busy protecting his face. An instant later, something painful broke my attention. Khajee had marched onto the mat and was twisting my ear. She pinched harder and pulled me off Maddox, then led me out of the sparring area. The gathered fighters had a good laugh.

Khajee let go of my ear and planted her hands on her hips. "What did I tell you about sparring? What were my exact words?"

"He started it," I said. "I was only —"

She cuffed me on the side of my head. "What are you, a kindergartner? 'He started it'? Come on, we're leaving."

"I'm not done working out."

"Hold up," Santana said, smiling strangely. "Your new boy was just getting started."

Khajee glared his way. "Forget it. No sneak peeks."

In the alleyway, after I'd shed my fighting gear and gathered my stuff, Khajee walked fast and ahead of me, just to show me how displeased she was. I asked her, "What are you so mad about? That Santana guy wanted to help me."

She stopped to face me. "He wanted to scout your moves."

I winced, realizing she was probably right. That double-leg opening was something I should've saved for a match. Khajee stepped in nearer to my chest. "This is Brawlers. You don't have any friends, got it?"

"What about you?" I asked.

She stepped back. "I'm not your friend. And I'm not teaching you cause I want to. I'm paid to be your trainer and that makes me the boss, and that means you do the damn things I say. So what exactly happened back there?"

As we continued walking, I gave her the short version and she shook her head. "At least you didn't try kicking. They don't know you can't kick."

"I can kick," I insisted.

Nearing her apartment, Khajee said, "I guess Blalock's right about you."

"Right how?"

She paused at the stoop of their apartment. "He called my cell just before I got to the gym. By the way, he wants to meet you for lunch tomorrow. He asked what I thought of you."

"What'd you say?"

"I told him you were a fast learner but raw around the edges and undisciplined, too green to fight so soon. But he said not to worry, that you have a secret weapon."

Tired of asking questions, I held my silence. Khajee obliged by leaning in and whispering, "Blalock says you're the perfect combination — stupid and crazy."

———

After getting a shower, I helped set the cramped table for dinner while Than cooked, leaning onto the countertops and hopping from fridge to stove. We had Mexican — tacos and refried beans. Later I did the dishes and then Than and I watched some more videos for a couple hours. Khajee bent over some textbooks she'd spread out at the table. After one of the tapes ended, I went in to get more water, thinking about calling it a night. Passing Khajee, I glanced down. She was studying a series of multiple choice questions — definitions to be matched with terms. "English?" I asked.

"SAT prep."

I winced. "That damn test gave me a monster headache. You got college plans?"

"No," she said. "For real. My dream is to train teenage boys intoxicated on their own testosterone."

"Ouch," I said, rearing back as if to avoid a blow.

"College for sure," she said with a smile. "Then I hope graduate school."

"For what?"

"Physical therapist?" She shrugged. "Physician's assistant? Something with the body where I can help people."

In the living room, Than hacked and spit something into a rag. I nodded at Khajee. "You'd be good at that. You're a natural. Sounds like a ton of school though."

"It all feels like a fantasy now," she told me. "A long way off. How about you?"

"Don't laugh," I asked. "But I'd like to be a cop. Maybe a state trooper."

Khajee considered my answer. "Guess I can see that."

The plans I'd had for a life — the criminal justice degree, making decent money, really being there for my mom — all that felt distant, impossible. And more so with each passing day.

Khajee leaned over her books. "I can't get over some of these words," she said. "Peripatetic? Obsequious? Mollify?"

"Sounds like Blalock."

She laughed, and I looked in to see where her pen was aimed. I read out loud, "Which word best describes a change in essential nature or form: a, immolate; b, objectify; c, eviscerate; d, transmute. Hell if I know."

"D!" came from the living room. I turned to see Than smiling, up on his feet and leaning into his walker. He continued, "Usually it refers to changing metals, sort of like what ancient alchemists were trying to do."

I couldn't believe what I was hearing. "What now?" I asked in amazement.

"Medieval scientists picked it up from the Arabs. In poetic

terms, it can mean any dramatic change." Than hobbled toward us, grinning.

Eyebrows scrunching and eager for an explanation, I looked back at Khajee. She said, "You'll have to forgive my uncle. He loves his little jokes."

In the kitchen now, Than shook his head. "You punks from the suburbs. You eat that Mr. Miyagi shit up."

"What the hell's going on?" I asked the room.

"It's a schtick he does," Khajee explained with a sigh. "Even with new doctors sometimes. He calls them all quacks. Than thinks his little voice thing is hysterical but it drives me nuts."

Beaming, Than waved at me from across the table, like we were meeting for the first time. "I was born in Thailand but moved to Atlantic City when I was four, Daniel-son. Later on, my parents brought us all back home when my kid brother was in his teens, in part so he could get serious about his boxing. I helped where I could, but he injured his shoulder and that ended his career, so we returned to America. But not without a wife for my brother. They started a family, had a fine daughter." He shucked a chin in Khajee's direction.

"This is crazy," I said, forcing a laugh so it seemed like I was part of this joke. "You people are sick."

Than cackled. "I'm a dying cripple. I won't apologize for my sense of humor."

"Don't blame me, Mac," Khajee said. "To be fair, you are pretty gullible."

I looked at the mischief shining in Than's eyes. "Hang on. Is that even you in those videos?"

He shook his head. "You catch on quick. That's my baby brother. He got the fighting talent in the family, along with the brains. That's where Khajee gets all that from. Me, I know enough about Muay Thai to be an expert in America, but in Bangkok, I'd be a hack at best."

"Unbelievable," I said. "My coach is a fraud." They both laughed.

Than said goodnight and made his way to the bedroom, and Khajee looked at the microwave clock. "It's late," she said, packing up her books. "We'll have another early morning."

"Sure thing," I said. "Sleep tight." I wanted to thank her for everything, but it felt wrong in the moment, like I'd be making a big deal out of it. So Khajee went to bed without hearing my gratitude. While I was feeling like a fool for being tricked so easily by Than, I also couldn't help but feel a little closer now that he'd come clean. I wondered if they'd kept the other fighters they trained in the dark. I also wondered just how these two got mixed up with Sunday in the first place.

Again I had a hard time falling asleep, tossing and turning. Once more, I snuck up and left the bathroom light on. I kept thinking of my mom, picturing her upset and Harrow consoling her. I was still pretty sure I'd done what was best but couldn't convince myself in the dark. And when I was finally able to push her out of my mind, my father came to me, images of when I was a kid. I thought of the beating I gave Maddox at the gym, and this made me feel less anxious. It was pretty screwed up, I knew. To drive all this from my brain, I tried listening to my MP3 — just a little Ozzy Osbourne — but the battery ran out, and I realized I forgot to pack my charger, so I just lay there awake and still.

At one point after midnight the bedroom door opened and Khajee crept past me in the shadows, followed by Rosie. I heard her open a cabinet in the kitchen and the faucet came on. From the back, Than coughed and groaned loudly. I wondered if he was in physical pain, or if he was tormented by nightmares. I would've asked Khajee as she snuck by me on her return, but it seemed too personal, so I just pretended to be asleep.

When she closed the door, I saw that Rosie was still with me. My hand was hanging out of the covers along the side of the couch, and the pit bull sniffed at it, then licked my knuckles. I patted her on the head and said, "Good girl," and she curled into a ball next to me. I could hear her breathing and it was good to not be alone.

06

*W*ednesday around noon, I met up with Blalock at a diner not far from the capital, where state representatives rubbed elbows with the workingman, a greasy spoon called Pancakes and Porkchops. Mrs. DJ, my former English teacher, would like the alliteration but personally I didn't think the image was worth it. When I showed up, Blalock was already in a high-seated booth in the back, talking on his phone. He saw me by the counter and waved me his way, flashing that phony smile. "My boy," he said, tucking his phone away. "I'm glad to see you appreciate punctuality."

He shoved me an open menu and recommended the cheese-steak, then signaled a waitress. "Unless you object, I propose we order posthaste, yes? I'm meeting some associates in York." Up close like this, his thick glasses magnified his eyes in a really freakish way. Combined with the tufts of wiry hair springing from his ears, it felt like I was having lunch with a human owl.

I wanted to ask him what business he had in York, how else he made his money besides being a promoter, if when he and my dad worked together this Sunday character was involved. But there's a long list of things you're better off not knowing.

I scanned the menu, then handed it to the waitress. "Grilled chicken salad and water."

Blalock lifted a single finger to hold the waitress. "Actually we'll just have two cheesesteaks, miss. All the way."

I didn't want to be heavy for my afternoon workout, but clearly Blalock liked the role of being the guy who calls the shots. After the waitress was gone, he said, "I heard there was an incident yesterday at the gym."

"Just making new friends," I said.

"Play nice," he told me. "I insist."

"Sure," I answered.

"You represent an investment of capital and time, Edward. Plus, at this point replacing you would present an insurmountable challenge."

"Point taken," I said.

Satisfied, Blalock grinned and asked what I thought of Khajee.

That morning, I'd had another early run and workout with her, focusing on striking combinations and a technique she called "hammer fisting," basically pounding the crap out of a guy once he's down.

"She's great," I told Blalock. "Knows her stuff." Again this morning, she sang in the shower.

"She has a nasty streak of irreverence and a tendency toward intransigence," Blalock said, "a lot like her uncle was before he got sick." His tone sounded hostile, but there was another emotion too, something between respect and fear. During my morning tape session with Than, he got wracked by a couple coughing fits that doubled him over. He seemed sort of out of it, weak, and I tried to get him to eat some heated leftovers. But he said, "It's okay. I'm just tired," so I carried him to the back room, laid his body in his bed.

The cheesesteaks arrived and, sure enough, were damn tasty — juicy and filling. When he was nearly finished, Blalock dabbed a napkin to his lips and leaned over his plate. "A new development in your situation," he said in a quiet voice. "You are officially a wanted man."

I swallowed what I'd been chewing and looked around, like somebody might hear.

Blalock plucked a handkerchief from his pocket and wiped his glasses clean. Without them, his face looked naked, babyish. A red mark arched across the bridge of his nose. He said, "An acquaintance inside the department tells me the warrant for your arrest was filed this morning." He replaced his glasses and lifted his water as if toasting me. "Congratulations. You are now a bona fide fugitive from the law."

I put my sandwich down and leaned back. Somewhere, my mom was dealing with this news. I pictured her running her hand through her hair like she does when she's getting anxious, tightly curling a strand around her finger. Meanwhile, Blalock looked gleeful. "Growing out your beard's not an entirely original disguise, but it seems prudent."

I rubbed my chin, felt three days of stubble. This wasn't something I'd done deliberately, just a combination of new routine and oversight.

Blalock went on. "Don't be overly concerned though. It's unlikely you're a top priority."

I started to slide from the booth and he said, "You haven't finished."

"Lost my appetite."

"Sit down," he said sternly.

I went back to where I'd been and he continued. "Ahead of your debut, Mr. Sunday has made some special arrangements. Tomorrow night. Consider it a tune-up. He's interested in an exhibition of your skills before the first broadcast fight. He wants to preserve the quality of his brand, totally understandable. I'll give Khajee the details."

I shrugged. The idea of a fight felt good to me. Better to know what you're dealing with on a mat or in a ring than have to figure out shifty schemes like the ones Blalock and Sunday were running. "So can I go now?" I asked.

He pulled out a wad of bills from his pocket, peeled off a couple, and dropped them on the table. His tip was almost as much as the meal itself. I thought back to the time I mowed lawns for a month to take Mom to Friendly's for her birthday. Blalock must've seen me eyeing up the money and said, "You require some petty cash? For incidentals?"

Before I could think better of it, I remembered a pharmacy I'd passed on the walk over and said, "I need a new charger for my MP3 player."

He set down five twenties.

"I don't need that much," I said.

"Consider it an advance," he offered.

Feeling just a little dirty, I slid the bills into my pocket, then asked, "I'll get paid for this tune-up thing?"

"Of course," Blalock told me. "This is a professional operation."

After lunch, I stopped by that CVS and spent fifteen

minutes scouring a rack of chargers that all looked the same before deciding I had the right one. In the checkout line, I grabbed a handful of Peppermint Patties.

When I opened the apartment door twenty minutes later, I was greeted by a sweet burning smell, and I thought of those special masses when the priest burned incense at St. Sebastian's. In the living room, wisps of white smoke slipped from a pair of skinny sticks spiked into a bowl of sand on that corner table, the one with the bronze figure. Than was on the couch, and his position matched that of the statue's as best he could — his half leg bent into the other, hands resting upturned on his thighs. Than's eyes were closed, and it looked like he might be asleep.

Clearly, I was disturbing something, and I turned back to the door, but then I heard Than say, "How was lunch?"

He was smiling pleasantly and looking at me. I said, "I ate too much." He nodded and I went on. "I'm sorry I interrupted you. Were you like praying or something?"

"It's not praying like you'd think of praying, but sort of."

"How can you sort of pray?"

"We call it samatha," he explained. "A meditation to clear your mind."

"Cool," I said. "That way you can break bricks with your glowing fist and stuff like that?"

He looked at me to see if I was serious and I said, "Just messing with you." I dropped the CVS bag at my side and sat in the armchair. "So like, how do you do it?"

Than inhaled sharply through his nose. "It takes a long time to get right."

"Okay," I said, not wanting to be a pain. But his face radiated this look of ease and contentment. It reminded me of Father Singh at St. Sebastian's when he was consecrating the Eucharist, an expression that suggested peace with one's place in the universe. It made me jealous. "Well, say sometime a guy wanted to try, how would he start?"

Than tilted his head, as if shaping some calculation. Then he said, "Take off your shoes. Sit up straight. Relax in your chair. Be comfortable but alert. Be present. With me so far?"

"Sure," I said, following his instructions. "I'm with you."

"Now close your eyes and focus on your breathing. Don't force anything, just let the air come in and go out. It's a natural thing. You do it all the time. Breathe and let your mind be still."

Curious, I did what he said and there was just the darkness, the incense smell, and his calm voice. "Don't think about what you should do or what you shouldn't do. Yesterday's gone and tomorrow isn't here yet. Just be here now with your body. Take ten good slow breaths and let that be everything." He counted them out for me — *one, two, three, four, five, six, seven, eight, nine, ten* — and with each number his voice grew distant. I felt a little woozy, almost like I was being hypnotized. The blackness surrounded me and it seemed I was floating. It was trippy. But after a few seconds, the darkness brought the mothball smell, and I snapped my eyes open for the light.

"No, no," Than said gently. "It's important to keep your eyes closed. It looked like you were getting somewhere."

I shook my head. "I'm good," I said. "I think you were right about it being too hard."

He could tell I was a little rattled, and he tapped my forearm gently with his crooked fingers. "It's hard not to think. Your mind is eager to be active, awake, excited. Instead of all that, just look into dark. Thoughts will come up, some happy, some sad. Just breathe with whatever comes and say, 'Okay, there's that thing but I can let it go,' and get back to your breathing. Stay in the moment."

I looked at one of the incense sticks turning to ash. "But it's impossible to not think. You can't turn your brain off."

"You're right. But trying has its benefits. In your mind, picture nothing but a summer sky, all blue. And when a thought emerges, some problem you're facing or a troubling memory, picture it like a puffy little cloud drifting by. Focus on it fading, disappearing until it's gone. Keep your sky blue."

I pondered this weird idea. The ash curled and tumbled into the sand. "What's the point though? I mean, if you still have all your problems when you come back?"

Than unfolded his good leg, setting his foot on the floor. "Struggling to find answers doesn't always provide them. Samatha helps me understand better."

"Understand what?"

He lifted his hands palm up and looked around the living room, even glancing out the split curtain of the window. "Everything."

I was baffled but sick of asking questions. So when a commotion at my side got my attention, I was glad for the distraction. Rosie had appeared and was burrowing her nose into the plastic bag from CVS. She had a Peppermint Pattie between her teeth. "Hey!" I shouted. "Little thief!"

She bolted back to the bedroom with her stolen treasure, and I snagged the bag, handed it over.

Than took it and glanced inside. What he saw made his eyes shine. He was quick to unwrap one of the patties and take a bite. "I love these things," he said. "You just bought yourself one more night at the inn."

I knew he probably wasn't supposed to have these, for some reason, and I wondered if the incense hadn't been cover for a snuck cigarette, at least in part.

I gathered some things and went into the bathroom to change into my workout clothes. When I came out, the incense had burned out, and Than was back in his easy chair. Some home-repair show was on the TV, and Rosie was curled up looking guilty at his feet.

I told him I was heading to the gym and he nodded. "Have a good sweat," he told me. At the door, I paused and looked back, feeling his stare. Sure enough, when I looked his eyes were on me. "Eddie, it's not easy, but if you can quiet your mind in that darkness, settle your heart, sometimes you can actually see things more clearly. Believe me."

"Sure," I said, clueless as ever. "I know what you mean." I wondered what Than knew of my troubles, what Blalock told Khajee and what she told her uncle. It was all a mess.

"One last thing," he said, raising a quivering hand and jabbing a finger my way. "That Sunday guy. He's not so good, you know?"

I appreciated what the old man was trying to tell me, but I didn't need samatha to tell me Sunday was out for himself. I nodded to show Than I appreciated the advice, then closed the door.

At the gym that Wednesday, everybody gave me space, and I burned my way through two albums by Metallica and Megadeth. I was just in that kind of metal mood. I worked my chest first (bench press and inclined barbells), then shoulders (seated military, shrugs) and arms (upright rows, curls with an old preacher bench that made me feel like I was in confession). On a rusty universal machine desperate for a can of WD-40, I did dips and lat pulldowns, working the creaky pulley and letting the weights crash at the end of each set. I jumped rope for twenty minutes at high speed, lost inside the buzz, not thinking about anything but the moment. I wondered if what I was feeling was something like what Than found in his meditation. There's a purity of purpose that comes on the mat too, even better than working out, in the middle of a match with a guy who really challenges you. You're not worried about all the things you've done wrong in your past, and you're not trying to figure out any big decisions about your future. You're just wrestling, and crazy as it sounds, it's peaceful.

Craving some version of that, I decided to go for a hard run. Between my hoodie tucked over my head and the stubbly beard that had sprung up over my chin, I hoped I wouldn't draw the attention of any police, but still, I jogged along the river with my head down. The flowing water didn't seem to care about my problems, and my music stopped without me noticing.

I got back to the apartment to find Khajee doing homework on the couch and Than hobbling around the kitchen, where the air was thick with amazing smells. I tried to lift the lid off a pan and he thwacked me with a spatula and ordered me to get cleaned up. After my shower, I came out to find dishes spread around the table, something I'd expect to see in a fancy restaurant. There were three plates, each heaped high with white rice, and big bowls in the center, filled with steaming, colorful food. My mouth watered and I asked, "What's all this?"

Khajee closed the book she was reading and came in from the living room. "Your last meal if you take tomorrow's fight lightly."

"Thanks for the vote of confidence."

We each settled into a chair and the old man rolled an open hand over the table. "Traditional Thai dinner," he announced. "Family style."

I couldn't be sure, but I felt like he put a little extra emphasis on the word *family*. Could be I was only hearing what part of me wanted. I covered my rice with what Than had prepared: pan fried pork, steamed veggies, and curry so spicy my eyes teared up. At this, Than mumbled something in Thai that got a good chuckle from Khajee. I gulped some water, then dug in for more.

Even though my belly felt full, I was reaching for seconds when Khajee said, "Enough. Help my uncle with the dishes while I walk Rosie and let this digest. Then we need to work on a couple things."

I slid my chair back. "Okay, Boss."

And so half an hour later, we were clearing a space on the living room floor and Khajee continued my education on the subtle art of the chokehold. Rosie watched from the couch, barking every now and then. From his chair, Than offered his advice in between coughing fits. Sometimes he'd say something to Khajee in Thai and they'd both have a laugh or nod together. But he also gave me some looks of approval, and even a thumbs-up at one point. When we finished the practice session, I asked him, "You think I'm ready for my big debut tomorrow?"

He shifted back to his broken English and said, "My belief, not so important. What Eddie think? Eh? This decide you, okay?"

I glanced at Khajee, then back at Than. "That's a little more Yoda than Miyagi, don't you think? What're you trying to say now?"

Than grinned. "It don't matter crap what I think. Nobody knows if you're ready but you. Either way, you'll have an answer tomorrow night."

*A*bout twenty-four hours after our impromptu living room training session, the three of us were waiting for Blalock to show up. Khajee boiled a plastic mouthpiece in a teapot and shoved it between my teeth still hot, telling me to bite down and suck hard to make a good mold. When we heard Blalock's horn beeping out front, I stood and Khajee grabbed a backpack. Than leaned into his walker to rise to his feet and shook my hand. His grip was weak but his eyes were bright. He said, "Be tough tonight, okay? Tough like the Tiger King."

Slightly confused, I figured he was messing with me again, so I just said I'd do my best.

I sat up front next to Blalock during the forty-five minute drive. As we headed up the highway, he asked Khajee how her uncle was getting along and, from the back seat, she said, "Fine."

"Diabetes is a vexing affliction," Blalock said.

Khajee answered, "Yeah. It's a bitch. Poor man's got a list of problems as long as my arm. He's dealing with them his own way."

Something struck me. "I saw him meditating yesterday," I said.

Khajee said, "It helps with the phantom pain."

Blalock changed lanes and passed a minivan, then glanced in the rearview mirror. "Phantom pain?"

"From the amputation," Khajee explained behind us. "That

leg's been gone for nearly two years, but that foot still bothers him. Sometimes it's an itching sensation. Others it's more of a burn. Damaged nerve endings."

"That sound intolerable," Blalock said, naming what I was feeling.

Blalock and I traded glances, uncertain how to follow up. This notion of feeling pain from something no longer there, something literally cut away, seemed familiar, almost like déjà vu. I couldn't place it. The SUV was quiet for a while, and we eased past a cop parked on the side hiding in wait for speeders. I turned to Khajee and asked, "What did Than mean before, about the Tiger King? He was just yanking my chain, yeah?"

Khajee glanced at Blalock, like she wished I'd asked when we were alone. But still she said, "That's King Sri Saan Petch, an ancient ruler of Thailand. He was a great Muay Thai fighter, so fierce he could not be defeated. At a certain point, he couldn't even find opponents because none of his loyal subjects would fight him if they recognized that he was the king. So he cut off the head of a tiger and wore it as a mask to hide his identity."

Blalock said, "Charming ancestral mythology."

Khajee didn't say anything more and I realized I was glad. For some reason, I didn't like picturing a man with a tiger's head.

I was surprised when we pulled off 78 and seemed to be following signs for the Taj Mahal Resort, one of Pennsylvania's first casinos. The electric billboard out front blinked "Tonight Only, Men at Work."

"Guess I'm not the headliner," I said.

Blalock parked and told me, "The evening's exhibition is an atypical affair."

I stared at him, and he said, "Out of the ordinary. Unusual."

"I know what you meant. I just can't tell why you talk like that."

"Your opinions aren't especially material. But know this too: Hold that loose tongue in Mr. Sunday's presence. He isn't a man who brooks foolishness. Is the meaning of these words also clear?"

I heard Khajee's breath shift behind me and wondered what was up. But I said only, "You bet."

Blalock led us inside, through the throngs of would-be winners crowded around roulette tables and hunched over clanging slot machines. One old lady wore a single white glove, and its tips were black with ink from the coins she was losing one at a time.

We made our way to an elevator marked, "Employees Only — Service" and stepped in. Because I was behind Blalock, I didn't see what button he hit, but I could feel us descending, down into the lower levels. When the doors split open, Grunt was standing there like a brick wall, arms crossed and blank-eyed. He didn't grin or welcome us in any way, which seemed to be his MO, and this second time around really hit home how the guy had no discernible neck. His eyes were set deep in his face, two black marbles that didn't even register recognition. He just turned and started walking.

The three of us followed Grunt down a dim concrete

corridor to a door with "Banquet Storage" written on it, and when he opened it, I could see tables and chairs stacked against the walls. But the center of the large room was cleared, and the fluorescent lights on the low ceiling overhead illuminated just four figures. In his white suit, Mr. Sunday stood next to a gentleman seated in an electric wheelchair. The light cast a shine off Sunday's bald head. Behind them both, on the fringes of the shadow, was a young woman — a nurse, or a young bride, or both. The old man's arms twitched involuntarily, some sort of spasm, and his hand trembled as he lifted a cigarette to his thin lips. He blew smoke into the air and clapped as we approached.

The fourth figure, clearly my opponent, was off to the side, shadowboxing against a cinderblock column. He turned at the sound of the thin applause, and I sized him up: about 220, a bit shorter than me. He wore a black tank top, gym shorts, and sneakers.

Sunday said, "Mr. Kaminski, your date has arrived." He met us in the center of the cleared square of concrete and continued, "Mr. Blalock, would you handle the introductions, please?"

Blalock frowned and said, "Mr. Sunday, Edward MacIntyre. Edward, Mr. Sunday."

Sunday offered his hand and we shook. His palm was sweaty but his grip was strong, especially for a geezer. He fixed his blue eyes on me and said, "Ed MacIntyre Jr., isn't it? It's true what they say. You're a dead ringer for your old man, Kid."

As usual at the comparison, I flinched on the inside. He went on, "I've also heard you're a scrapper like him."

"I can handle myself okay," I said.

He released my hand. "That's what we're here to find out, isn't it?" He reached inside his jacket pocket and pulled out an envelope. "Two thousand to the winner. Loser gets an ice pack and a coupon for a free buffet upstairs."

Blalock and I hadn't discussed specifics, so I saw no chance to negotiate these terms. With his cut, I'd make just over $1500.

In the far corner I shrugged off my hoodie and unlaced my sneakers. Something buzzed in Khajee's backpack and she pulled out her phone, checked a message with a regretful look.

"What's up?" I asked.

She shook away my question but answered. "Just some friends from school. I was afraid it might be Than." With this, she returned the phone and pulled a bottled water from her backpack. I took a shot but my mind snagged on this notion that she had friends at school, of course. Outside this fighting world, she had a whole other life. But for now, she was laser-focused. "Get warmed up," she said sternly. "Don't let them rush you." Khajee wrapped some tape around my knuckles and wrists and then eased my mouth guard into place, something I wasn't used to but knew I'd need if I wanted to keep my teeth. "Stick to what you know with this guy. Ground and pound. Don't box him or try to finesse anything."

"I don't do finesse," I mumbled out.

"All right," she said. "Lose the sneakers."

It felt weird to be barefoot, the concrete floor cool on my

toes and the balls of my heels. I bounced on my chilly feet, cranked my head left and right, then slapped my cheeks a few times to get the blood going. I heard Couch Gallaher saying, "Your moves. Your moves." My opponent watched from fifteen feet away, eyeing me up. He looked like he was in his later thirties, maybe even forty. His mouth guard was black, and he was sporting two enormous cauliflower ears, bulbous and thick. I nodded to Khajee and said, "All set." She signaled Sunday.

Blalock had unfolded a seat and settled in by the wheelchair. Sunday bent to whisper in the old man's ear, who pulled the cigarette from his lips, kissed out a cloud of smoke, and croaked, "No mercy! Prepare! Brawl!"

I guess I wasn't worthy of cameras or gongs just yet.

I trotted to the center and, purely from habit, extended a loose hand to shake. Kaminski swung a left hook over the opening and connected square on my cheek, hard enough to crank my head. I backed up, blinking away the stars, and saw him advance through blurry vision. He landed a couple shots to my ribs, and I finally woke up. Hunched like a wrestler, I grabbed one of his wrists but he yanked back, staying in a boxer's stance. I lurched forward and grabbed his other wrist, but that one too he snapped free.

We circled each other, then his fists flew in rapid combination. I lifted my forearms to protect my face, but he just pummeled my gut, bending me over into a crouch. With no real target, I poked out a few punches but only found empty air.

His assault paused for a moment, and when I looked up, between my raised fists, I saw Kaminski easing back, sucking air hard. His tank was emptying fast. I charged in blindly, only to eat his knee as he plowed it up into my face. Dropped to all fours, I saw my mouth guard on the concrete. When I reached for it, Kaminski booted me in ribs. I collapsed on my side, right by the shiny black wingtips worn by the man in the wheelchair. He leaned over and I looked up at his face. Behind him, his nurse/wife/girlfriend looked down on me with pity. The old man turned to Sunday and said, "Singularly unimpressive."

Sunday glanced at Blalock. Next to him, Khajee said, "Get up, Mac!"

But that didn't happen because Kaminski made the mistake of his life — or at least of the night. Instead of attacking right away or waiting for me to get up and go back to boxing, he circled with his arms on his hips. His gut was sucking in and out, and I knew he was just catching his breath. So sure, I sort of played possum, rolling to my back and going limp. Lured in, Kaminski stood over me and stretched down for my right wrist, extended my arm, and pinched my elbow between his knees. Most guys would panic, getting locked in an arm bar, but not me — I saw what was coming next, as clear in my mind as a movie on a screen. Standing with my arm, Kaminski planted one foot under my neck and one under my armpit, and when he sat to his butt, he expected to stretch out that arm until I screamed in pain and gave up. Instead, as he dropped down, I snapped to life, rolled into his momentum, jabbing my elbow into his belly, freeing that arm, and ending up on top of him, chest planted on chest. I righted myself, kneeling over his body, and my hammer fists rained down on his face like bombs. I even sprinkled in a few elbows just to show Khajee I'd been paying attention. Exhausted as he was — and shocked by my resurrection — Kaminski put up a crappy defense, barely deflecting any of my strikes. When he realized he couldn't protect his face, he managed to slide onto his belly and tuck his forearms along his head, a turtle retreating to its shell. So I whaled on his arms for a minute, and Blalock cheered. I glanced up and saw them smiling, Sunday and the old man and his nurse/wife/girlfriend. Khajee simply nodded, satisfied by the turn the fight had taken.

Beneath me, Kaminski had gone still except for his breathing. I could hear him wheezing, and when I stopped my attack he turned his face a bit to look up at me. I lifted a fist and said, "We all done?" But he didn't try to escape or tap the ground. Instead he just curled up again in a guard position.

Blalock said, "There's no bell here Edward. You're compelled to make him submit."

Khajee shouted, "Make him tap!"

No problem, I thought, and without much trouble I slid in a half nelson, sneaking my right hand under his armpit and latching it behind his head. Usually this is a move we use to turn a wrestler to his back, show him the lights, but I realized here that without a ref to call him pinned, that was no good. I also realized something else: No ref was going to call me for a full nelson.

Seconds later, I had my left arm in the same position, with both hands on the back of his head, his arms splayed, and his face fully exposed to the concrete floor. Without my mouth guard in, I could clearly say, "Dude, you know where this is going, right?"

He didn't make any sign that he'd heard me, so I decided to get his attention. Lying flat on his back, my chest on his shoulder blades, I curved his spine up and then drove us both forward, smashing his forehead into the concrete. He turned his face to the side so his cheek took the brunt of the impact, but it still made a sickening thunk. Blalock said, "Brutal!" and I heard the old man in the wheelchair chuckle. I realized that since I had Kaminski's arms locked out like that, he had no way to tap out. So I asked him good and loud, "You had enough?"

His only response was a weak thrashing, but he couldn't shake me. His breath was heavy, and I knew he'd take some more convincing. So I banged his head again, then a third time. I was totally jacked on the adrenaline now, certain of my victory, totally in control, and I wonder how many times I'd have smashed his face if not for Khajee. She muttered something in Thai and I looked over at her. Her green eyes blinked as she tried to process just what she was seeing. But I could tell she wasn't entirely pleased. Beneath me, Kaminski was limp, a 220-pound rag doll, and when I released the full nelson he slumped onto the ground. I got to one knee and glanced Sunday's way. "Guess I'm tuned up now."

Sunday clearly wasn't a fan of my tone. He stepped forward and commanded, "Turn him over."

When I did, we all saw Kaminski's face, which resembled raw hamburger. His eyes rolled in their sockets but he managed to give us both a nasty look. Blalock appeared next to me and patted a hand on my shoulder. "Imposing display, Edward." The old man had the woman push him over and he leaned forward to stare down at the defeated man. Then he craned his face to Sunday. "I was promised blood."

"So you were," Sunday said. "Kid, please oblige our good patron."

"What now?" I asked.

"Hit him again," Sunday explained. Behind him, Khajee sucked in her breath.

"This guy's had enough," I said. "Fight's over."

Sunday's eyes tightened in anger. "Your opponent hasn't submitted and is still conscious. The fight is over when I say it's over. And I say, hit him."

I looked down at Kaminski. "It's not your night," I told him. "You're done. Tap out."

Instead though, he turned his face to the side, spit onto the concrete, and said, "Kiss my ass."

That was all the motivation I needed. Genuflecting over his chest, I dropped a right straight down on his nose, and the crunch sounded like the break on a pool table. Kaminski smiled, so I popped a left into his mouth. Since he couldn't seem to stop grinning, I capped things off by lifting my right elbow above my shoulder and pumped it like a piston, jackhammering his face. I heard myself saying something. Maybe it was "You still smiling now?"

The dream got popped when someone's hand settled on the back of my neck, and I turned to see Khajee, horrified. Sunday didn't seem annoyed, as his lips smirked in satisfaction.

Also, as I came back to the world, I heard the old man clapping in his wheelchair. When I looked down at Kaminski, his lower lip had ballooned. Worms of blood slithered from each nostril, and the bruise under his eye had split open, oozing.

I got to my feet, unsteady until Khajee draped my one arm across her shoulder. She lifted a bottle of water to my lips, and I drank and spit as we started for the elevator. Blalock got ahead of us and pushed the button. Behind us, the old man applauded and crowed. "Worth every penny," he told Sunday as the doors opened and we got in. "That boy's a natural."

On the ride home, Khajee didn't say much. There were no congratulations from the back seat, no commentary on how I fought or what I could improve. Even when we were alone in the apartment, with Than sleeping in the back, she was quiet and only spoke to excuse herself to the bathroom. The medicine cabinet creaked. The water shushed in the sink. When she came out, she looked at the carpet and told me, "You should wash up." Our eyes never met. That's when I realized just how much blood was on my hands, staining my knuckles red. Under the shower's hot blast, I scrubbed away the evidence.

Even though I was exhausted from the fight, my adrenaline rush kept me wide-awake on the couch, thinking. It's not like I haven't made guys bleed before. Our school's 185 pounder, LeQuan Thompson, used to have a bloody nose every practice. Got so bad he took to wearing a foam face mask attached to his headgear. But what happened with Kaminski felt different. That blood wasn't incidental. That blood was the point. I knew Coach Gallaher wouldn't be proud of my sportsmanship. And it wasn't hard to imagine the way my mom would have looked at me if she'd been there to witness. But none of these people were there in the darkness, just their shadows.

Those spirits haunted me enough so that I couldn't really sleep, which was getting to be a nightly routine. I thought about Than's blue sky meditation thing but it just felt too far out. For a while I turned on the TV and watched a basketball game with no volume, but I never could generate a lot of interest in that sport. Too many rules and not enough contact. Finally, I surrendered to my MP3 and listened to Van Halen's *1984*. Midway through "I'll Wait" (probably my favorite song and way better than "Jump"), Roosevelt came trotting past me from the bedroom. She sniffed my hand, then padded silently to the door. She growled low, then barked twice.

The knocking came loud and hard, insistent. According to the microwave's green display, it was 4:15 a.m.

I sprang up and pulled on some gym shorts quick, but somehow Khajee beat me to the door. She took hold of Rosie's collar and told me, "Open it."

Grunt filled the doorframe, a perfect rectangle shape himself. When he took a half step back, I could see Sunday's white limo, both passenger doors open. Grunt aimed a finger at me, then Khajee, then stiffly headed down the stairs. Rosie was snarling, angrier than I'd ever seen her, straining to break free. But Khajee calmed her enough to quickly drag her into the bedroom. A moment later she came out, dressed in street clothes, and I asked her, "What's this about?"

As she brushed past me, she said, "Just come on. Lock the door."

I ended up in the back seat with Sunday, who seemed wide-awake and alert despite the hour. He didn't talk until we'd reached the highway, which was nearly empty except for a few tractor trailers hauling freight. Then he reached inside his jacket pocket and pulled out an envelope, which he tossed on my lap. "Typically I pay Ray and he pays you. But this first time, I wanted to do it this way, just so you're clear on the source of the money. He's already got his cut."

I split the envelope's top and peered in. The highway lights flashed down into a thick stack of crisp twenties.

Sunday leaned across the big back seat, bringing his face close to mine. "Eddie," he said, "some men have a propensity for violence. It's a talent, a gift even. Certainly your father had it, and from what I've seen and heard, I think it's a good bet you inherited it."

"My father?" I said.

Casually he leaned back. "This talent makes you valuable to a man like me. You're an asset. But I have to trust you and your loyalty. Can I count on you, Eddie?"

"What do you think you know about my father?"

"Quite a bit actually. I know that he could be counted on. I know that he, like you, was an inflictor of pain."

"So my father used to work for you?"

"Not so much *for* me as *with* me. We were partners of a

sort. When we started most of our loans went to the less fortu-
nate. I supplied the bankroll and handled the numbers. Your
father —"

I held up a hand. "I can guess what he was in charge of."
My eyes fell on the back of Grunt's boxy head.

We passed over the Susquehanna on 81 South and took the
first exit, down into Enola. I could tell Khajee was listening
closely in the front seat, though she remained silent. We drove
along the houses lining the west shore. All their lights were out.
Grunt turned into the rail yard.

Sunday said, "Your father was passionate but impulsive. He
let emotions cloud his judgment and got sloppy, careless. I've
made a career by being a cautious man. That means I exercise
a lot of control over my interests, especially my employees. Can
you understand this?"

Grunt bumped us over some tracks. I nodded to Sunday.
He pinched at the end of his white beard, curling it down into
a peak. "So you'll understand my concern when, earlier tonight,
you questioned my instructions?"

"The guy was practically out cold," I said. "Anybody could
see he was through."

Sunday bristled. We approached a handful of cars parked
right along the rail line, in the shadows of a boxcar. Grunt pulled
in and turned off the ignition, but didn't open the door.

Sunday patted my leg. "Here's the thing, Kid. I have an
expanding organization and it's easy to see a place for you in it.
I see potential. But you've got to understand that this is my world,
so we go by my rules."

I nodded.

"Say it," he ordered, squeezing my leg till it hurt.

"Your world," I said with a shrug. "Your rules."

This brought a smile to his face. "Wonderful. I'm glad we could come to an agreement. Let's seal our new deal."

At this, Grunt got out and opened Sunday's door. I guessed that meant I should go too, so I got out and followed him to the boxcar, where the door was slid back and a short ladder was propped up. I felt Khajee right behind me.

Inside the boxcar a half dozen figures stood waiting. A few were holding flashlights, and in the bubbling light, I could see Santana, Maddox, Dominic, and a couple others I didn't recognize. One of them held up a phone with a tiny white light shining, and I realized he was recording.

Bahadur stepped to the edge of the shadows but not into the light enough that I could see his face. I only knew it was him by his bulky shape. I heard him make an exaggerated sniff of the air and he said, "Hey Baby Blue. I told you guys I smelled fresh meat."

So this was the deal, I thought, an initiation where I take a beating. I was okay with some hazing, knowing they wouldn't go too hard with me having a fight on the schedule, but I was worried about Khajee. Surely they wouldn't hurt her?

Then I heard a groan from the far corner, which was pitch black. The others aimed their flashlights, and I was surprised to find some guy huddled on the floor. He was middle-aged and balding, just a crown of hair around his head. In boxers and a white tank top, he cowered. His face was streaked with sweat and tears and boxcar dirt. "Mr. Sunday," he said, sniffling. "Let me explain."

Sunday folded his hands calmly. "The time for explanations has passed, Leonard. Best now if you just shut the hell up."

"Who is he?" I asked.

"A man who thought he could live by his rules in my world. He's about to learn an important life lesson. Bahadur, the bat please."

Badder extended an arm to offer me a wooden bat with the handle wrapped in gray duct tape. He didn't let go of it right away, forcing me to tug it from his thick hands. The wood felt heavy, and the head rested on the floor. Leonard shoved with his heels, pressing into his corner. He tightened into a fetal tuck.

"Not his face," Sunday told me. "He's in sales, and we wouldn't want him to miss work. At least, not too much." Behind me, the others laughed. I glanced back and saw Khajee, in the tip of a triangle of moonlight angling through the open door. At her side, Grunt gripped her bicep.

I looked at Leonard and asked, "What did he do?"

Sunday said, "It's a mistake to burden yourself with too much information. All you need to know is that I desire for this to happen. I need you to do it. And if you don't, Grunt here will shoot him in the left kneecap. So don't think you'd be doing the guy any favors."

I tightened my grip and raised the bat, resting it on my shoulder as I entered the darkened corner. I was thinking that maybe I could pound the floor, or try to hit the wall and Leonard's body at the same time, to take some of the edge off the blows. But then as I neared him, I inhaled and caught a pungent odor. Badder said, "Oh damn. That's just disgraceful. Miserable puke's gone and pissed himself."

I remembered Harrow's first words to me. *You poor baby. Let's get you cleaned up.*

"Quit crying," I growled at Leonard. "Take it like a man."

Even as I said that line, I recognized where I'd first heard it, and my mind flashed red and the bat didn't feel heavy at all. It went weightless in my fists as I brought it down on Leonard, again and again and again.

08

*T*he morning after the boxcar, I slept late. I never even heard Khajee get up for school, but she was gone when I woke, so I jogged alone, troubled and slow, just me and my heavy thoughts. Later, at the gym, the other brawlers gave me a little more space. In the afternoon, I took Rosie for a long walk and watched fighting tapes while Than stayed in bed, too sick to rise. I warmed up some soup for him but he brushed it away, hacking up something green and nasty into a handkerchief. His face looked pale and his eyes had no brightness when he looked at me, though this could've just been from his illness. I wasn't sure what Khajee had told him, but I had the feeling that he knew what I'd done.

As soon as Khajee got home, I said, "He's having a bad day," and she dropped her backpack and went to him. When she came out, she told me he was resting.

"What's wrong with him?" I asked.

She turned to hide her face. "It's a long list. Short version: He's old and he's sick. According to him, he should've died ten years ago."

"I tried to give him soup," I told her.

Khajee was clearly uncomfortable. She kept shifting her feet and not looking at me. Or maybe she was upset by what she'd seen the night before. I wondered for a second where Leonard was, if he could even stand today on those battered legs.

"Let's run," Khajee said.

"I ran this morning."

She got on her knees and dug her arm under the couch. "Then this will be your second time. Get your sneakers on."

When she pulled her hand out, she was holding a ratty tennis ball. Rosie perked up and trotted over, but Khajee said, "No girl. We're not playing now." She turned to me. "Your grip strength needs work. That guy last night in the casino nearly cleaned your clock because you couldn't control him. You don't have the experience to box with these guys, so you've got to make them fight your match. If you've got hold of some-body's wrist, they can't punch you."

All this made good sense, but still I said, "My grip strength needs work?"

She cocked an eyebrow and tossed the ball into the kitchen. Rosie gleefully bounded after it, and Khajee squared up on me. She held up her arms. "Try to hold me."

I grabbed her tiny wrists, encircling the thin bones in my hands. Swiftly, she took a step back, extending my elbows, and rotated her wrists inward, instantly twisting free. "Always turn toward the thumb," she said, "away from the fingers. Even with that trick though, you should be strong enough to hold me. If you can't do that, how can you expect to hold some brawler?"

Satisfied and a little shamed, I nodded. Rosie trotted to our side and Khajee looked down at the ball, now covered in slobber. "That's for you. While we run, squeeze it as hard as you can. Right hand on our way out, left on the way back. Wax on, wax off. Got it?"

"Sure thing, Boss," I said. All day long, I'd been expecting we would talk about what happened last night, review the fight more, maybe get into it about the boxcar. I had the strange urge to confess to what she'd already witnessed. But from what I could tell, Khajee didn't seem interested.

Instead of following our usual route to Wildwood again, we jogged across the Harvey Taylor Bridge, in the direction of my home in Camp Hill. I got nervous when a cop car passed us and casually tugged my hoodie a bit tighter, but in truth, I wondered what sort of real manhunt could be generated by a suburban police force. It's not like there were wanted posters out or anything. We jogged up a hill and came within a half mile of the Perkins where my mom would be working the night shift later. I thought about how she got meals at half price during her shift, and the way I'd often find chicken tenders in the fridge, wrapped in napkins. Was she still bringing food home for me out of habit? I had no doubt my mom was worried sick about me, and I felt the strong urge to see her, tell her I was doing just fine. That this wasn't entirely truthful didn't matter.

We weaved through a neighborhood to get to Seibert Park, where there's a city pool and a playground and even the stadium where the high school plays football. We jogged down the steep hill my dad brought me to when I was in second grade to go sledding, and past the ruins of the old stone cabin where we took a break. He pulled chocolate granola bars from the pocket of his thick winter coat, and this seemed like magic.

Khajee ran us deeper into the isolated forest and we crossed over a creek. Like every kid in Camp Hill, I knew the trail well.

It followed the wandering path of trickling water down to the Conodoguinet, nestled between two slopes covered in trees. Something about this place, the way the branches overhead interlaced to form a canopy maybe, helped make the woods feel like an empty cathedral, serene and sacred. I don't know why, but I've always felt the presence of God more when I'm alone than in any crowd. Khajee jogged down the center aisle. Finally she stopped by a park bench somebody had put up in honor of "Cecelia, who loved walks in the woods," or so the plaque announced.

"We heading down to the water?" I joked. "Gonna hunt crayfish?"

Her face shifted, softened somehow. Wistfully she said, "My mother and me, we went tubing on the Conodoguinet a few times, just floating along under the sun. Once, we even saw a bald eagle."

"That sounds like a nice time," I said, weighing each word.

The muscles in Khajee's face tightened. Something was being balanced carefully. Then she shook her face, and her expression went back to normal. "How's your hand?" Khajee asked.

Rather than ask about the place she just mentally visited, I looked down at the tennis ball I'd been gripping. Had I squeezed it constantly? For the most part. "Good," I told her. I smacked that forearm muscle. "I got a decent burn."

"It's about to get worse," she said, and then she bushwhacked into the woods, making her own winding trail in the thick brush. I followed her for about a hundred feet, and we came to a sheer rock wall that stretched straight up, tall as a three-story building. Above, I knew there was a ritzy neighborhood where I used to trick or treat when I was a kid. The rich families there gave out whole candy bars, not just the mini ones.

Without saying anything, Khajee approached the wall, reached up with one arm and found a handhold, then hoisted herself off the forest floor. I watched her scale the stone face, pausing here and there to look at her options, digging her bent sneakers into cracks, searching for purchase with her fingertips. At first I got beneath her and readied my arms to catch a tumbling body. But Khajee didn't need my help. In fact, when I finally stepped back to just watch her, she looked like some female version of Spider-Man, zigzagging up a skyscraper.

In less than ten minutes she reached the top, turned, and looked down at me from the edge. "Now you," she said.

"You're out of your mind," I yelled up.

"That may be," she replied. "But you're still going to come up this wall. Try."

I flashed back to the rope climb in the high school gym, Coach Gallaher telling me not to use my legs as I struggled to get to the bell at the top. Climbing's never been my thing. But Khajee's green eyes burned down on me, and I made my way to the base. From the bottom, the wall seemed ever taller, and I stretched one arm up high for my first grip. With a heave, I began my ascent.

At first the climbing wasn't nearly as bad as I'd thought it would be. The rock was cool against my face. Sure the skin on my fingers got rubbed raw by the sharp edges, and I scraped my bare knees against the stone till they stung. But my shoulders and arms felt strong, and I found I could shift my weight to whichever hand or foot had the best hold. My body learned pretty quick that this was the only way up, to take the weight off whatever arm or leg you wanted to move — and move it quickly. The tension in my body increased, tightening my muscles until I felt like all of them were connected, like everything from my delts and lats all the way down to my quads had fused into one single tendon.

Sweat slid down my forehead, biting my eyes. But I could only blink away the burn, unable to waste a hand to wipe. Every time I boosted my body up farther, I found it a bit harder to find a good anchor. I started to feel less confident stretching my arm out far and reached just a little ways. My progress slowed and I saw Khajee to the side, sliding down the leaves of a steep bank next to the wall. From beneath me now, she said, "You're doing great. That's almost a third of the way. Don't stop."

This shocked me. I'd thought I was much nearer to the top. But when I glanced down, the leafy carpet of the forest was only ten feet below me. Clinging by my fingertips and toe-holds, I cursed silently and said, "I'll never make it."

"I did," she reminded me.

"You're smaller than I am."

"Yes," she conceded. "And so are all my muscles." Something jabbed me in my rear and I craned my neck. She'd found a long branch and was poking at me. "Up," she said. "Break time's over. Don't think about getting to the top. Just focus on the next thing you have to do. No matter how mighty the task we face, we do so one choice followed by another."

"That from some lame self-help book?"

"My uncle." She thwacked me with the stick, nearly dislodging my left leg. "If he were here, he'd be throwing rocks at you by now. Seriously though, it's no different than a match. Take it one move at a time."

I took a few short breaths, then spied a slim ledge a foot up from my left hand, diagonally. That seemed like a good next step. I strained for it, secured my grip, then shimmied my left sneaker along until the sole latched on to some tiny outcropping. Next I scanned for another ridge. Moving like this, I scaled higher, paying for every inch with pain. The burn in my muscles began to glow brighter, sharper. It was good to be focused on a physical task, absorbed by something uncomplicated and pure. Again, I wondered about what Than found in the darkness when he meditated.

All the constant gripping took a toll, especially on my hands. It got harder and harder for me to take hold with any confidence. I relied more and more on my legs to take my body's weight, and that wasn't without consequence. My right calf began to twitch and tremble, the way muscles do before they cramp up. I lifted it and tried to shake it out, but the extra strain on my hands was too much. "I'm going to fall," I said.

"That's one possibility," Khajee said calmly.

"What should I do?" I asked, fifteen feet up and losing my grip.

I heard her shuffling back, away from where I might come to earth. "I'd recommend avoiding the large boulders."

As best I could before my arms surrendered, I gave a heave to propel myself away from the rock wall. But really, gravity just took me, and I dropped. With my right leg out of commission, I collapsed when I hit the ground, crashing to the earth amidst the sticks and leaves and mossy stones.

When Khajee appeared over me, the wall loomed above her and the sky beyond. She said, "You fall pretty good."

I rolled off a grapefruit-sized rock lodged at the base of my spine and sat up. "I've had practice."

Khajee said, "You need more," then took one of my hands in both of hers and tugged me to my feet. She high-stepped back through the vegetation, over a decaying tree on its side, and led us back to the trail. At Cecelia's bench, we took a seat. Above us, birds fluttered from branch to branch. And the thin stream rippled along, burbling over rocks, swirling in small eddies. I said, "Water always makes me feel peaceful."

Khajee stood unexpectedly. "Not everybody feels that way."

I couldn't tell what landmine I'd just stepped on again, and Khajee was clearly tense that she snapped like she did, so I deliberately moved us to safer territory. "We should work on my kicking."

"You don't need to kick. That long-range stuff, it takes years to get right. We've got two more days till your match. You're better off staying up close and personal."

This made sense, but I still wanted to learn something new.

"I know, I know. Ground and pound. C'mon though. When do we get to the scene where you reveal some secret ancient kick-ass move that makes me invincible?"

She turned her head with a face that had gone deadly serious. She returned to the bench, sat next to me, and placed a hand solemnly on my leg. "Climbing the wall will show me you are worthy. Only then can I reveal to you the secret Tiger Claw Strike." Here she crooked all five fingers and scratched at the air. "The truth is that it has been passed down from King Sri Saan Petch, through the bloodline for thirteen generations, but my uncle has no male heirs. He and I dreamed the same dream. You are the chosen one."

I stared at her and she didn't blink for half a minute. Then a wide smile bloomed across her face and she said, "You watch too many Hollywood movies." Her laughter sounded sweet in the forest.

"Well," I told her, "it didn't hurt to ask."

"Hit them harder than they hit you. That's the secret."

"I'll keep that in mind."

"Good," she said. "And next time you're watching one of those stupid movies, ask yourself why the chosen one is always some lily-white kid."

This caught me off guard, and Khajee pressed her opening. "Seriously, you ever wonder how come it's not someone like me who gets to save the world?"

I thought for a minute before offering, "Could be Hollywood likes formulas and what's familiar? They're afraid to take chances?"

"I know," she said. "I get it. That's just the way the world is. Over and over. Doesn't make it right. Last spring at school —" Khajee caught herself, drew her lower lip in between her teeth.

It was a weird silence, one that made me feel awkward. I shrugged and said, "I guess I don't think it's right either. It's not something I've thought about a lot."

"No," she said, looking at the ground. "Why would someone like you have to?"

I inhaled and folded my hands. "So what, you think I need to apologize for being the lily-white kid?"

She faced me and grew sober. Too quick for me to react, she drove her right palm up into my nose, snapping my head back. As I brought it down again, she shot to her feet and slapped my cheek with a darting left. "No," she said. "I think you need to apologize for being slow and not being able to kick worth a damn."

We laughed together, pretty hard. I sneezed from her blow and rubbed at my stinging face. In a quiet voice she said, "I don't expect you to fully understand, but it's nice Mac, nice that you're at least listening. It's more than most guys like you. Maybe there's hope for you yet."

What Khajee was saying made sense, but I could tell from her tone that she didn't have specific suggestions on how that hope may translate into action. In the silence, I found myself wanting to ask her what happened at school. But Khajee reminded me of a wrestler protecting a lead in the third period — she was content to keep her distance, not interested in offering any easy openings. Just then, two joggers appeared at the head of the trail. They padded toward us then passed between Khajee and me, heading for the Conodoguinet down below. I sensed something building up in Khajee, and I thought it was about what we'd been talking about, but instead, she went in a different direction. "Mac, about last night —"

"I'm not proud of that," I said. I wanted to forget about Leonard.

"I didn't say you were."

"But?"

"But it worries me. All day long at school today, I kept thinking about it, the way that you —"

"I was there," I said, interrupting her again. "You don't need to describe it to me."

Khajee dragged a heel along the trail. "It's just . . ." She hesitated, then started again. "To fight well, you need passion. And sure, a bit of anger can fuel a fighter. But hate, rage, whatever animal instincts settled over you in the boxcar, those things can blind you. When you're not seeing clearly —"

I stood up and took two steps toward the creek. "That rage helped me win over a hundred wrestling matches in four years."

"Fine then. Think of it as a fighter you're facing. You control him or he controls you, right? I'm only wondering where this rage comes from, and worried about where it might lead you."

With this, she moved to my side, and when she put a gentle hand on my forearm, I jerked away. Then I turned back to her and said, "What do you want to hear? That my old man lost his cool and things got out of hand? That finally the cops had to lock him up? It's not a complicated story."

She nodded thoughtfully. "I'm sorry about your dad. Really. How long since you've seen him?"

Was she apologizing that he was in prison or for what he'd done?

"Eight years," I told her. "Eight birthdays. Eight Christmases. Not like I'm counting."

She was quiet, then asked me, "So have you ever like, visited him there?"

I shot her sidewise eyes that had the same effect as a slap. But before I could apologize, voices turned our heads up the trail. Three kids, grade school boys, were coming our way. Two had walking sticks and the third was looking at his phone. They passed without comment and disappeared below.

Khajee let them get out of hearing range. "I'm not asking you to tell me your life story. It's just . . . look, this sounds damn cheesy, but the guidance counselor at my school has this sign up in her office. It says 'Life is like monkey bars. You can't go on unless you let go.'"

The muscles in my forearms were still knotted up from the wall. I took turns rubbing at each and said, "I can't believe you had me try to climb that freakin' wall."

She stepped in and massaged the tightened flesh, easing it till it relaxed like an unclenching fist. "Good news," she told me. "It'll be here tomorrow and we can try again. That's the thing about walls like that."

"What?"

"They always give you another try." With that she started jogging back up the path at an easy pace, knowing I would follow. We wound back through the park and I realized I was unnerved by our conversation. I didn't like that I'd let her see me so upset about my father. Usually when I run my mind sort of goes blank, but thanks to Khajee, I couldn't unhook from just how screwed up my life was. How I'd failed my mother, screwed up all through school, what I did to that ref at states, this massive mess with Sunday. It all felt like a wall a mile high, one I could never get to the top of. My life was the one broken thing I couldn't seem to fix.

We cut through the hospital complex, took a shortcut back toward the bridge, and over the rise I saw the tip of the huge American flag they fly outside Perkins. I thought of my mom, just what her life must've been like the last few days. And even though I had no idea how I'd climb the whole wall, I had a pretty good idea of the next step. "Hey," I shouted ahead of me. "I might need a favor tonight."

09

When we got home, Than was in the living room but asleep in his chair. Judge Judy was on the TV. Khajee slipped into the shower, and while it made me feel like a stalker, I found myself lingering, listening. Sure enough, not long after the water started blasting, there was a soft humming. The humming rose into a song, something soulful and sweet I'd never heard before. There was pain in Khajee's voice, pain and sadness. But above that, this ferocious determination.

The shower shut off and, nervous that I'd be caught, I took Rosie for a walk. When I got back I cleaned up while Khajee microwaved a frozen bag of beef and broccoli. The food seemed to revive Than some. I wanted to find a way to compliment her singing without sounding creepy, but Than and Khajee kept chatting in Thai. Now and then, they would look at me together. Than would nod and purse his lips, looking concerned.

As we were finishing, he turned to me and said, "So Eddie, my niece thinks you could use some anger management classes. What's the deal with that?"

I didn't like holding back on the old man, but I wasn't sure how to explain the long story of my mom's lazy eye and how my childhood was more nightmare than fairy tale. "Maybe I just got a rotten heart."

He drew a fork from his mouth, shook his head. "You have a heart like Rosie." At her name, the dog unfurled from her spot on the floor and rested her face on the old man's lap. Than went on. "Fierce, but also loyal and soft."

I banged my water glass. "Don't call me soft."

"Easy," Khajee said, setting a hand on mine. "He meant it as a compliment. Like gentle."

Than was unrattled by my outburst. He patted Rosie's head and said, "Anger's like fire. A little fire can cook your food or warm you up. But a fire out of control can burn down a house, a neighborhood, you know? A fire can scorch a mountainside."

I stood up and grabbed my bowl. "No offense, Father Than, but I already got this sermon back in the woods. Can somebody just give me my penance already?"

I stomped to the sink, and behind me Khajee said, "If somebody's preaching at you, maybe there's something you need to hear, Mac. And just for the record, we're Buddhists."

I had no response to that.

After dinner, Khajee flipped through a book she got from the school library — 50 *Great Careers in Medicine*. Then she dug into more SAT prep (did I know the difference between corollary and ancillary?). Meanwhile, me and Than watched some fights. The color in his face started to look better, definitely improved over the day before, and he really got into a couple, shouting at the TV in Thai. I tried to find an opening to apologize for losing my cool at dinner, not that Than seemed bothered in the least.

At one point between bouts, he said, "My brother always said a good fighter is like a warrior." He smacked his one shin and both forearms. "Shields, to defend." He extended a bony arm.

"Sword, to attack." He bent the arm and swung the elbow, then tapped it. "Knife, for up close." Then he unfolded his one remaining leg, angling his socked foot to a point. "Spear."

"No kicks!" Khajee hollered from the kitchen table.

Than smiled and shrugged, then ran a hand along his left leg, the one that ended in a stump at the knee. "No use anyway, I've got a broken spear," he said, laughing at his own joke.

———

A couple hours later, after Khajee helped her uncle get settled in bed, the two of us headed over to the river again, back into Camp Hill. The night air was cool and we took the jog slowly. Midway across the bridge, I asked her what happened to Than's leg.

"Diabetes," she said at my side. "His foot went bad and the doctors had to amputate."

"So all that coughing — that's diabetes?"

"No," Khajee said. "Just this cold that won't go away. Plus, he keeps getting cigarettes somehow. I ever find the neighborhood brat who's sneaking them to him, and I'll show you a chokehold you won't believe." She eyed me up here, and I felt the urge to confess about the Peppermint Patties.

"I love that man. But his health isn't the only thing he's handled badly. Trust me when I say that for a guy who talks about right action, he's made a lot of wrong choices. They haven't made his life any easier."

Or yours, I wanted to say. But it seemed understood. Khajee was stewing a bit.

When we reached the west shore, we began to walk along the shoulder up the incline that leads to Camp Hill. We passed under a bridge with a rumbling train. Traffic whizzed by, close enough that we could feel the breeze. I backed into the shadows and rubbed a hand over my beard, which was thick enough now to change how I looked a little. Combined with my hoodie, it wasn't a world-class disguise, but I wasn't about to color my hair or anything stupid like that. The silence was bugging me, and I wanted to be distracted from our destination, so I asked Khajee, "That thing you said before, about being a Buddhist, was that like a joke or something?"

She tossed me a nasty look and stopped. "There you go again, Mac, with that awesome impersonation of a sheltered white kid."

"Sorry," I said. "I'm just curious."

She shook her head and resumed walking. "Just don't say 'I never met a Buddhist before.'"

"How'd you know I was going to say that? Can you read minds with your mystical powers?"

This crack got her to lighten up and she tried to hide her smile as we moved on. After twenty feet I said, "Really. I want to know. What's up with that? Is that bronze statue in the living room this Buddha dude?"

Maybe she was tired of me asking, or maybe she figured out I was serious. "Cliff notes version? Buddha lived in the sixth century BC. He was heir to a throne, legit, but he walked away from wealth in search of truth. What he discovered was the biggest cause of all suffering is desire — wanting things. So the way to end suffering is to stop wanting."

"That's impossible," I said.

She dropped a cold stare on me. "From what I heard, your guy wants you to stop sinning."

"Point taken."

As we finished the hike up the hill, I thought of St. Francis and how he, like Buddha, had rejected a life of riches to get closer to peace.

"I'll tell you something else," Khajee said behind me. "Buddha teaches that the mind is the source of everything — happiness, sorrow, anger."

I stopped and faced her. "I'll bet you a dollar Buddha's dad never smacked him around."

Khajee looked into the trees. My pissy comment brought our world religion class to an abrupt and awkward close.

The Perkins sign read "Tr your newd ishes" which didn't make any sense until I realized somebody had messed with the letters. The restaurant sits in this huge parking lot outside a Radisson hotel and an industrial office park. Right next door, down a little grassy slope, is a gas station, and Khajee and I snuck behind it to finalize the plan. I handed her a folded-up five-dollar bill that I'd tucked a note inside of and said, "Okay, at this hour it won't be real busy. Just go in and give this to whoever is up front. Tell them Janice was your waitress before and you forgot to leave a tip."

Khajee took the note and the money, nodding.

"If you see any cops or somebody giving you a hard stare, bolt. Otherwise, head for the train underpass. I should be there in like fifteen or twenty minutes, depending on when my mom can take a break."

Khajee said, "Be careful," and just stood there. Behind the gas station, the light was dim, and in the shadows I couldn't see her face all that clearly. But part of me had the sense that she might give me a kiss, just for good luck. The idea warmed me and I leaned down, bringing my face closer to hers. We froze then, our lips only a few inches apart, till Khajee took a full step back. "See you under the train bridge," she said, turning then to scamper up the hill.

Alone behind the gas station, even though it was dark, I felt exposed and anxious. The back of my neck warmed with sweat. I had no good reason for being where I was if anyone asked, and I considered going inside to buy something, a can of soda even, just to have an excuse. But then I pictured the cameras that always hang from the ceilings in places like that, how they record everything. I had no idea how much the cops were really searching for me. On one hand, I hadn't committed a murder or robbed a bank, so it's not like a manhunt was going on with bloodhounds and helicopters. On the other hand, Camp Hill's pretty small and my dustup with the ref had made a lot of noise, even in the Harrisburg paper. So the notion that somebody like Harrow could be keeping an eye on my mom didn't seem all that crazy.

That's why my note to her just said, "It's me. If the coast is clear, come down to the gas station on your next break. I'm by the dumpster."

I knew that if she could, she'd take a break right away, and that's just what happened. Khajee was only gone a few minutes before my mom appeared at the top of the rise, rushing down in her waitress uniform. She nearly stumbled in the shadows, and she was running so fast that she'd have fallen if I hadn't caught her at the bottom. She collapsed in my arms, weeping, and I held her close, careful not to squeeze too hard. The hug felt warm and good, and I didn't want to break our embrace, but I also knew she didn't have long, and we could be spotted at any moment. When I pulled back, she wiped her eyes and ran a hand over my face. "You haven't shaved."

I chuckled and then she hit me with a flurry of questions. "Where have you been? Why did you leave? What are you eating? Where are you sleeping at night? Who was that girl?"

I held up both my hands and spoke quietly. "Hold it. All that matters is that I'm okay. I'm safe and taking care of myself. I feel bad I didn't have a chance to say goodbye."

"Is that what this is?" she asked. "You came back just to go again? You have to come with me. Right now. We'll call Detective Harrow. She's worried about you. She says that public defender Mr. Quinlan still thinks —"

"Mom," I said. "We're not calling the police. I'm not turning myself in. No way I'm going to jail, not for a day."

She sniffled back tears and looked confused, a little angry. "Then what are you going to do? Hide your whole life? Run?"

I crossed my arms. "I'm trying to fix things," I said, with some heat in my voice. "To make them right."

She fell quiet. A skinny gas station clerk emerged from a side door, spilling weak light into our scene. She dragged a bag of trash to the dumpster about ten feet away, lifted the lid, tossed the bag inside. When she dropped the metal top, it boomed, and she strolled away from us, into the parking lot. Far as I could tell, she never saw us. Soon as she was gone, my mom whispered, "You're scaring me, Eddie. You're sounding like your father used to."

Mom knew this would hurt, and her words hit me as strong as any gut punch. I wanted to get away, but first I had to do what I came to. I reached into my back pocket and pulled out the envelope Sunday had given me. Inside were eighty twenty-dollar bills. I handed it to her and she took it, asking, "What's this?"

"It's for you," I said. "Later, there'll be more. Maybe a whole lot more."

She peeled back the flap and reached inside. Her fingers pulled out a few of the twenties from the stack, and even in the shadows I could see her eyes get big. She shook her head. "Eddie! Where'd you get this?"

"Doesn't matter."

She dropped the envelope on the ground and buried her face in her hands. Her hair formed a gray-black veil around her cheeks. "Please please just come home with me now."

I picked up the envelope and held it out. "That's not going to happen. You have to take this."

"That!" she cried out, tears running down her face again.

"I want nothing to do with that! I don't know what's happened to you."

"Some sort of problem back here?" a voice asked. The skinny clerk stood over by the dumpster. She was holding a box.

Mom turned to the Perkins above us and said, "I need to get back. Kevin will be asking why I was gone so long."

As she started up the hill, my hand reached out for her, caught her one wrist and anchored her. She looked down at me and I shook the envelope at her. "I worked hard for this. You could use it. You should take it."

She tugged a little, but, without even thinking, I held firm. I could feel her thin bones in my grip. "Let go, Eddie." My mom leaned away from me, struggling to free her arm. "You're hurting me," she said, and I saw it in her eyes, heard it in her voice — something you might call fear.

Terrified, I released my grip and whipped back my hand, like I'd touched a hot stove. Mom had been tugging away so hard that now she stumbled up the hill, collapsing. The bills scattered on the grass.

"Hey!" the clerk hollered, dropping the box.

From her knees, Mom looked up at me, her eyes wet with tears. The lazy one aimed up the hill, again suggesting an escape route. She tucked her arm in close to her chest like a broken wing and covered it with her other hand.

"Mom!" I said. "Oh shit. Wait. I never meant to —"

She cleared her throat and said, "Just go away. Go!"

I couldn't be sure if she was talking to me or the clerk, but the skinny lady was quick to answer, "Like hell I'll go away." She started toward us, pulling a cell phone from her back pocket, and something in me just snapped. I sprang like a spooked rabbit, hauled ass away from the clerk and my mom and what I'd done to her, charging through the gas pumps and straight into flowing traffic. A car locked up its brakes and another laid on its horn, but I didn't slow down or turn. I just ran, a flat-out sprint across the private school yard soccer field and then down into the brush along the road. A minute later, sirens split the night air behind me, and I wondered if they belonged to a police cruiser prowling for me or an ambulance from Holy Spirit, sent to tend to my mom. I wondered if I'd really hurt her wrist, and I ran. Even when I got to Khajee I didn't stop. I charged by her and she fell in behind me, and we sprinted across the bridge, back into Harrisburg, crossing the water. Khajee asked me some questions I think, but I said nothing, only running, running, running from what I'd done, running from what I was becoming.

*R*ight on schedule, my first official brawl went down a couple days later, Sunday night. Blalock drove me and Khajee south, along Route 83 almost to York. Again there was a winding road off a random country exit, this one leading ultimately to "Vic's Auto Salvage Yard," according to the faded sign out front. Just like back at the barn, Grunt guarded the front gate. Blalock steered through a maze of abandoned cars with crushed front ends or missing tires or shattered windshields.

We came to a clearing by the main office, where a dozen expensive cars, including Sunday's limo, sat in gleaming contrast to the graveyard of wrecked vehicles. A crowd of maybe fifty spectators gathered around something burning. Blalock slow-rolled past and said, "Showtime." In my chest, my heart began to thunder.

He parked by a compactor surrounded by squares of crushed metal. Walking past the office, a sad-looking trailer waiting to collapse, we were startled by Dobermans. Black as midnight, the dogs charged at us, lunging as they neared, jaws snapping the air. I stepped between them and Khajee, but the dogs were caught short by their chains, staked to the ground ten feet back. They strained against them, drawing the links taut, and barked ferociously. Khajee stepped around me and extended a hand as she bent. "Easy," she said. The Dobermans stilled and dipped their heads. They looked baffled, clearly unaccustomed to tenderness. But then one snarled and the other showed its teeth, and in moments they were each growling, up again on their hind legs, choking themselves against their collars.

"Come along," Blalock said, ushering us away. "You can take the dog out of the fight, but you can't get the fight out of the dog."

I couldn't tell what this meant but didn't care. It sounded like he was quoting something.

As we approached the crowd, everyone turned. Some stepped aside to clear a path for us, applauding weakly and eyeing me up like a piece of meat.

In the middle of them, four barrels formed a rough square, each with a fire crackling from its mouth. The flames sent orange and red ambers drifting into the cloudless night sky, where the Big Dipper and Orion's belt watched from premium seats.

On the far side of the ring, Dominic stood between two of the barrels, not far from a man with a shoulder-mounted camera. A thin woman fiddled with a second camera, this one set up on a tripod. Behind Dominic was Maddox, eager to coach his protégé I guess. Dominic shook his arms out and started hopping on his feet. His dreadlocks whipped and snapped in the air like things alive, and I remembered my mom reading myths to me, the one about Medusa. But when my eyes met with Dom's, I didn't turn to stone. I sneered, and he stepped forward into the firelight to execute a series of spinning kicks, jabbing his feet high into the air. The crowd clapped wildly.

Blalock said, "I'd consider it highly advisable to avoid

Dominic's feet," then slid off, to locate Sunday I guessed. He walked past Badder on the fringe of the crowd, standing behind one of the fire drums. The flames played across his tattooed face, and his eyes were steely. I knew he was there to take notes, in case we ever fought.

I ducked out of my T-shirt and kicked off my sneakers. Khajee massaged my shoulders, kneading the flesh. "Fight your fight," she said under her breath. "Ground and pound." I squeezed my fists. Despite several more attempts at the wall in the days since my first try, I hadn't made it to the top, but my grip felt stronger.

Sunday, decked out in white as always, emerged from the trailer and climbed onto a box of some sort, elevating himself a few feet above the crowd. The firelight shined off his head's bald dome. Those assembled began to cheer, but he raised his hands to silence them. "Gathered friends, the offering this evening is a special one indeed. While you're all familiar with the high-flying assassin known as Dragon, tonight a new brawler enters the arena." With a sweeping flourish, he brought all faces to me and cried out, "Please welcome Wild Child!"

I wasn't a big fan of my new nickname, any more than I was of the sports reporter's "Brute Boy," but the rush of applause told me the audience liked it. Khajee helped me fit my gloves and settled my mouthpiece into place, then slapped me twice, hard, across the cheeks. She balled up her fists and banged my chest. All around me, I couldn't help but feel it, the energy of the crowd's lusty need. I knew what they wanted, to witness violence up close, to see me and Dragon batter each other bloody. Just like in all those high school auditoriums, their fever became my own.

Sunday lifted his tiny gong. At the first strike, the congregation yelled, "No mercy!" and with the second, "Prepare!" He paused for dramatic effect, drummed the golden disk a final time, and the air shook with, "Brawl!"

I started forward, hunched in my stance with raised fists. Dominic, strangely, stopped bouncing and went flatfooted, as if the fight had ended and not just begun. Maybe he thought this unexpected act would catch me off guard, but I've seen all sorts of stunts, so I just stayed on my game, plodding forward. I was about six feet away when he launched himself at me, left leg tucked up tight, right extended like a spear, just like Than said. The bottom of Dominic's foot landed flush in my chest and drove me back three steps. The instant his toes touched dirt, he sprang and spun left, swinging 360 degrees and driving a heel toward the side of my head. I blocked this with a forearm, but the force was still enough to make me stumble. The fans roared.

Blindly, I charged forward, hoping to tackle him to the ground, but he danced away, elusive and airy. He feigned another spin kick, locking me in position, then poked a jab through my raised fists, catching me flush on the nose. Shots like that don't hurt so much as sting, more distraction than pain, but it left him an opening to drive his right knee into my stomach, hard enough to fold me in half.

Coach Gallaher always told me that you don't really win a match on the mat, but in the practice room, that you've got to reach a point where you put your faith in your instincts and your training. This notion flashed through my mind when I realized that both my arms had locked on to Dominic's right leg when he kneed me. Realizing he was in a vulnerable position, he unleashed a series of blows onto the back of my skull, battering me with fists and elbows, but my head was tucked in tight to his thigh and I wasn't about to release my prize.

I swept a foot at his left leg, and he skipped over it deftly. Then I barged forward, and he hopped backward with a gymnast's balance. We ran right up to one of the fire barrels and I stopped and straightened. He grinned at me and tugged away, hoping to free his leg, but I yanked back with all my might, too late realizing he'd anticipated this.

Dominic used my energy and jumped into me, lifting his chest onto my shoulder and coiling his left arm around my neck. He quick slipped his other arm between us and locked hands, and when he arched his back my breath was gone. It felt like he was trying to pop my head clean off, which may indeed have been his intention.

In regular wrestling, choking is strictly illegal, so I wasn't used to the dizzying sensation that comes with having no oxygen. But I'd been in plenty of rough spots on the mat over the years, and the rush of panic faded fast. I still had his one leg wrapped up, and his other hung in the air; neither of his feet were on the ground. Shifting my grip, I scooped the free leg, and he cranked all the harder on my neck, knowing he was in trouble.

On a high school mat, the ref would stop the action at this

point, calling "potentially dangerous" because, since I now controlled Dom's body, he was essentially defenseless. But this wasn't high school, and no official was coming to Dragon's rescue.

I hoisted him up high as I could, tilted us both toward the earth, and drove down hard. My shoulder transferred my weight into his gut, knocking the wind out of him. But I've got to give Dominic some credit, because at the last second he wrenched my head so my face caught some of the impact. It wasn't enough to make me black out, but it did cause me to release my hold. I got to all fours, a bit shaky, seeing stars. Next to me, Dominic was retreating in an unsteady crabwalk. I crawled after him, certain I didn't want him to get to his feet again, and he planted a heel across my jaw, torqueing my face to the side.

"Get up Dragon!" Maddox hollered.

"Take Baby Blue's head off!" another — maybe Badder — added.

But in the cacophony of voices, I also heard Khajee, quiet and calm. "Mac, you're doing great."

Dominic rose to his feet, a dark silhouette right in front of one of the fire barrels.

I circled left and we again took up our dance. I sidestepped a few tentative kicks and countered with a couple jabs, nothing to hurt him but enough to slow down his assault. I took a shot on his right leg but he saw it coming and easily spun out of the way, tagging me in the back of the head with a fist along the way. He was fast, I'll give him that.

"Come on Dragon," a woman in the crowd shouted, "quit playing with this newbie!" Then she started a chant, "Dra-gon!

Dra-gon!" and others picked it up, until it became a wall of sound around us. Dragon grinned, his teeth flashing in the firelight. I'd been cheered against plenty of tournaments, and rather than distract me, it gave me fuel. I smiled back and waved him forward. He pounded his fists together and advanced on springy legs, loose and light. I knew an attack was coming and I backed up, arms raised, until I felt heat on my bare back. Dragon stopped bouncing right in front of me, daring me to charge. When I didn't take the bait, his back foot shifted and he twisted at the waist — telegraphing his strike — then unfurled in the opposite direction, corkscrewing on his base foot and swinging the other leg fast and hard. Already crouched, I dropped beneath it, and it passed over my head and connected with the fire barrel. So powerful was Dominic's kick that the can tumbled sideways, dumping burning wood and embers onto the ground. The audience erupted.

Pleased with himself and confident he'd regained the momentum, Dominic floated backward, to the center of the fighting area, and said, "Come get some!"

To stoke the crowd, he executed a couple of those high spinning kicks, wasting energy and broadcasting his intentions. Sometimes a guy's got a signature move and it's a good one, but you can go to the well once too often. With this thought one of my visions came to me, clear as a dream that wakes you. The future felt set in stone. I knew the fight was over and exactly how I would end it.

With a mouth guard in, your voice is a bit muffled, but you can still make yourself known. So Dominic heard me fine when

I said, "You kicked that barrel's butt. Any good at a moving target?"

My taunt stung him, and it got the desired result. He stormed across the open space between us. He settled into a fighting stance before me, and I waited for my prophecy to unfold. We traded some lazy punches, each easily blocked by the other, but it was obvious that he was probing for an opening. So I gave him one.

I'd been peeking between my raised fists, like Khajee taught me, but now I let them drop a bit and drift apart. As expected, Dominic seized on the opportunity and popped me in the chin, a quick jab meant to stun and distract. It did neither, but I stepped back as if that were the case.

And poor Dominic settled his feet and twisted at the waist, exactly like he had before. Anybody who'd been watching knew what he was about to do, and me, I'd been watching pretty close. So when he spun around and leapt into the air, leading with that leg again, I rushed into the strike — not blocking, not retreating. With my arms outstretched, I caught him three-quarters through his spin. My right arm hooked under his extended leg and my left latched around his head. I locked my hands together into a standing cradle, smashing Dominic's face into his own knee. Then I hoisted his limp body into the air, held it there and turned so everybody knew I had power to spare. I genuflected, making my right knee an anvil, and drove his spine down onto it. Dominic cried out as his backbone cracked, but I didn't release him. Instead I stood, lifting him again, ignoring his moans.

The fire that'd spilled from the barrel was only a few feet away, and I carried him easy since he was no longer struggling. Standing over the burning scrap wood, I could feel the heat radiating on my bare shins, and I guess Dom realized he was about to get cooked. He squirmed weakly and said, "What the hell, man? Put me down! I give! I give!"

The acrid smoke swirled up, filling the air with its rich scent. Through it, I could see the faces in the crowd clear enough, the wide eyes and open mouths. Even Blalock and Badder looked shocked, and at their side Sunday locked his gaze on mine. He nodded once, and I thrust my emptied arms overhead in victory.

Dominic's body collapsed onto the fire.

Of course he sprang out of there instantly, scrambling so fast his flesh barely felt the heat, like those folks who sprint across hot coals. Now it's true that his shorts got singed a bit, and an unexpected bonus was that some of those long dreads of his did indeed catch fire, but only briefly. He screamed and ran, feeding the flames and freaking out the fans. They scattered. After he did a high-speed lap or two around the ring, Maddox tackled him and smothered the flames with somebody's coat. For good measure he emptied a water bottle on the smoldering hair, which was a little shorter. But while he was rattled good, he was fine, and everybody seemed relieved.

Now their attention came back to me. I was still in the center of the makeshift arena, and again I punched my hands up in triumph. Now they could applaud, clap wildly and whoop their excitement. I turned slowly, letting everyone get a look — all the high rollers and the other brawlers and Sunday too. As I passed in front of the tripod camera, I snatched it with two hands and hoisted it, so the lens was right up to my face. Rather than roar or shout or scream, I stared hard in the eyes of everyone watching online, and I asked, "Who's next?" Then I whirled around, keeping my face in the frame, spinning everything behind me and probably making the home audience dizzy. Suddenly "Wild Child" suited me just fine.

Dominic limped off with one arm draped up over Maddox's shoulder. It felt weird, not shaking hands after a match, but it seemed these brawlers didn't exactly value good sportsmanship. I joined Khajee behind one of the remaining barrel fires, and she handed me a full bottle of water, which I downed in a few thirsty gulps. I toweled off and slid into a T-shirt and soaked up the gawking stares of the people who couldn't stop looking. After a win like that, you don't just feel strong. You feel invincible.

A few guys cleaned up the mess from the spilled fire, righted the barrels, I guess getting ready for the following match.

A handful of the high rollers gathered around Sunday and Blalock. They glanced at me, nodded, and smiled. And a few in the crowd made their way to my side. They slapped my back and squeezed my shoulder, or shook my hand and said things like, "Good match." "Nice job." "A pleasure to watch you work."

When we were left alone, Khajee finally spoke up. "Looks like you're a hit."

"I could've done worse," I said.

"Dragon lost his cool," she told me. "You got lucky."

I shrugged. "Rather be lucky than good. Didn't you ever hear that expression?"

"That's a new one on me," she answered. "And I can't say I agree. We need to work on your striking, elbows in particular."

"Whatever you say, Boss."

Blalock stepped in to congratulate me. "Exemplary debut," he said, nodding his approval.

The second match was between two fighters Khajee and Blalock had never seen before, out-of-staters who waltzed around each other like last place contestants on *Dancing with the Stars*. Mercifully, after about ten minutes, one tried a lame double leg and they collapsed into an exhausted heap on the ground. The other slipped in the rear naked chokehold Khajee had shown me. She saw the same thing I did and whispered, "Too loose." Despite this, it was a quick submission.

Sunday didn't hide his disappointment, turning his back on the brawlers as they left the arena.

The headline fight involved Badder versus a dude from Paterson, supposedly the Jersey champ. Could be he had an off night, or maybe Badder's theatrics got to him. But he was sloppy off the whistle, letting Badder arm drag him, yanking him by the elbow and slipping behind him. Badder was quick to lock his hands and bring the two of them down. The guy's cover was pretty good — flattening out, tucking his forearms up around his neck — something Khajee pointed out. Doing his turtle shell routine, he managed to fend off Badder's attempts at a choke-hold or arm bar. But this also frustrated Badder, and he angrily hammer-fisted the back of the guy's buried head.

After a minute of this, Jersey made a supremely stupid mistake. He drew his knees up, letting Badder snake his left leg around and inside his opponent's, hooking his foot on that heel. Turning sideways, Badder wrapped both hands around Jersey's right knee, and I didn't need my prophetic gift to know what was coming next. Khajee said, "This is about to get ugly."

Craning his head back and arching his spine, Badder flipped his opponent to his back. Then he straightened the leg he had entwined around his opponent's and tugged his other leg in the opposite direction.

Jersey's legs wishboned out away from each other and he screamed, slapping at the dirt to signal his surrender. Badder cranked it for another ten seconds, just to implant the memory, then released him and leapt to his feet. He whooped and yelled and did his warrior thing, which the crowd of course just ate up. He stomped over to the tripod camera and when the guy with the shoulder-mounted one chased after him, he extended his tongue and screamed bloody murder.

Meanwhile, there was something weird about the way Jersey looked as he left the ring, a sour glance he flashed at Badder. Some understanding I wasn't privy to passed between them.

With the fights concluded, the cameramen packed up their gear and the crowd began to disperse.

I was about to ask Khajee if she saw anything in Jersey's face like I did, but just then Blalock stepped up behind her. "Mr. Sunday requests the honor of your company," he told me. "Just you." He glanced toward the trailer, where the door was closing. There was no one else around now. All the other cars were gone.

"What's up?" I asked. "He want to do a postgame interview?"

"You don't ask what Mr. Sunday wants," Blalock told me. "He tells you."

I stared at Khajee. The dying fire danced across her green eyes, which looked a little nervous.

Blalock chucked his chin toward the trailer. "It's inadvisable to keep your employer waiting."

"Sure thing," I said, and I crossed the emptied ring. From inside the trailer, Grunt opened the door and made a mumbled sound in his throat. The small office was illuminated by a light bulb that was either dirty or yellow in the first place. Sunday sat at a metal desk, something you'd expect was military issue. His chair had a high back and armrests. Other than that, there were no seats, so I walked over and stood before him, glanced upside down at a desk calendar from August two years ago.

Sunday smiled at me. "Quite a display you put on tonight," he said. "It's hard to impress me, but you did that Kid."

I thought of how to respond and finally said, "Okay."

"I especially liked the way you looked for me before delivering the final blow. It reminded me of the way the gladiators would turn to Caesar and let him determine their opponent's fate."

"I wasn't asking your permission," I said. "Just being sure you were watching."

He ran a hand over his smooth scalp and smirked. "You're a willful boy, aren't you?"

It's true, I was riding the high of the fight, and the adrenaline rush was making me extra cocky. "You're the commander in chief," I told him. "If you say it, it must be true."

Now Sunday stood. Casually, he circled the desk. "Quite the piece of work this one is, eh Grunt?"

Grunt grunted.

Sunday eased back onto a corner of the desk right in front of me. "But that attitude is exactly what makes you special. You've got a mean streak a mile wide, don't you? Can't wait to take on the world, show what a tough guy you are? It radiates off you and scares some people. You're like a dog that can't wait to bite something."

I wanted to tell him I was nobody's dog, but I was tired of the verbal sparring. "Why'd you call for me?"

Sunday was struck by my unexpected directness. But not answering would make him look weak. He had to respond. "Fine then," he said. "To the heart of the matter. I like what I saw in that boxcar the other night, and this evening's entertainment only served to validate my initial assessment. You can be of use to me."

"I'm glad you like my fighting."

"I more than like it. In fact, I have plans to accelerate your advancement. I'm setting your next match in four days. You'll square off against Santana."

"Four days?" I repeated. I was used to wrestling twice a week, even a few times a weekend for a tournament, but this sort of fighting seemed to demand more recovery.

I could tell Sunday didn't like being questioned. He said, "You want to take a few months off between bouts, try joining the UFC."

"I didn't say that," I told him. "I can keep up." Still, it was no mystery why there weren't a lot of old brawlers.

His expression shifted, and he pinched at the triangular white beard capping his chin. "Ray seems convinced you can redeem his last fighter's regrettable efforts. I would tend to agree, given your lineage and record. Indeed, I might find even more use for you."

I wondered, of course, what all that meant, but I stayed quiet. Guys like Sunday love to hear themselves talk, and that's just what he did. "What I'm referring to is an additional role in my organization. From time to time, Grunt pays visits to individuals who owe me money or who need to be convinced to adopt a more enlightened view of one kind or another. On such occasions, it's not bad if he has someone to watch his back. I would, of course, compensate you for your contributions."

I stayed quiet. Sunday eyeballed me, and I could hear Grunt breathing. It came to me that this was the sort of work my father used to do back when he and Sunday were partners. "I'm not really interested in more baseball bats, if that's what we're talking about."

"Oh things seldom get that dramatic. But situations can get

complicated, and it's good to have friends we can rely on. Grunt would be eager to show you the ropes."

The big man looked on, his face devoid of anything eager.

I asked, "Are you asking me this or telling me this is how it's going to be?"

Sunday pushed off the desk and placed a hand on my shoulder. "I don't need an answer right now. I'm offering you an opportunity to apply your talents and make some additional money. Call it side work. But in the same breath, there may come a time when I'm not asking."

"And then I'll have to say yes?"

He tightened his grip. "I don't think you realize just how profitable this venture could become. I have many friends, and they have friends. Even as far away as Fort Indiantown Gap. If you refused me, I could make things unpleasant for your father."

At this, I jerked away from his arm and backed into Grunt, who took hold of my biceps from behind. He was as strong as he looked. "Let's be clear about one thing, okay?" I said. "If you think threatening my father is a way to get me to do anything, you don't know jack squat. You drive your fancy car, wear your fancy things, figure you know everything about everybody. You want to give that son of a bitch a beatdown? Be my freakin' guest."

Sunday stayed stoic throughout my rant, then he blinked a few times as if recalculating. "Clearly I misread this situation." He paused for a few seconds, considering me. "Tell me though, how would you feel about being the one who administers the beatdown in question?"

Behind me, Grunt snickered and relaxed his grip.

I leaned forward. "Say that again."

Sunday looped behind the desk, returned to his big seat like it was a throne. "I'm not promising a boxcar and a Louisville Slugger, but it's not outside the spectrum of possibilities that I could arrange a reunion. A very private one. You'd like that, wouldn't you?" Here his gaze snapped to mine and his eyebrows rose like the offer's temptation.

The answer to his question must have shown in my expression. I'd dreamt of smashing my father's face to pulp a thousand times. I'd do anything for the chance. But I played it cool. "Whatever," I finally said. "You're probably just talk. I should get back, unless there's something else?"

He leaned back in his chair. "I've said all I needed to say. But I'll leave you with something I read in a book once: *The world is naught but sheep and wolves.* We both know which one you are."

The morning after my first official victory as a brawler, I woke sore as hell, muscles aching and back on fire. But I was jacked up and ready to train hard, see what Khajee had to show me next. Only the bedroom door stayed frustratingly closed, even as I paced back and forth in the living room fully dressed in the predawn light. Than's coughing fits had woken me a few times overnight, and now he was wracked by them at regular intervals. Every so often I heard Khajee speaking to him, low and urgent. If he answered, I didn't hear. Finally, I knocked and said, "Anything I can do?"

Khajee cracked the door and the antiseptic hospital smell emerged. "You're on your own this morning." After a pause, she went on, "It was a bad night. I need to tend to him."

The care in her voice, the no-nonsense *this is what has to happen*, it made it easy to picture her as a nurse or a doctor, someone to count on in a crisis. "I can help," I said.

But she just shook her head. "I'll get him settled and go to school. I won't leave unless he's all right. You jog, give the wall a shot, and hit the gym. Check on him around lunch, okay? And don't let him smoke."

"Sure thing," I told her. I rubbed hard at my neck, where my muscles formed a knot that felt like a stone.

She vanished for a second and returned with the tennis ball, which she deposited in my upturned hand. It was wet with slobber, and I was certain Rosie had slept with it. Behind her, Than's voice was thin, weak. "Kà-nŏm bpang mâi dtông. Ao kâe nám sôm gôr por."

Khajee closed the door, and there was nothing else I could do. I knew the old man was sick, but I'd wanted to describe the fight to him myself. This was a silly and selfish thought, one I pushed from my mind as I readied for my run. Than was Khajee's uncle, not mine. I shouldn't be so desperate for his approval — or anyone's.

The day passed easily enough. I made three attempts at the stone wall over in Seibert, each time getting a bit closer but never reaching the summit. At the gym, my win seemed to earn me some small additional measure of street cred. There was no sign of Badder, Maddox, or Dominic, but the few other brawlers didn't crowd me. In fact, Santana shook my hand and said he was looking forward to our fight. The smile on his scarred face looked sincere. I wondered again if someone had cut him, or if those wounds weren't the result of some crash, his face versus a windshield. Before stepping away, Santana touched his beard and eyed up mine, tossing me a validating grin. In between sets, I watched him jump rope, work the speed bag. He wasn't as muscular as me or Dominic, and he wasn't tall like Maddox. But the dude was rattlesnake fast.

Around noon I checked in on Than, and he was out cold. When I first opened the door and saw him motionless on the bed like that, I thought the worst. But up close, I could hear a raspy breath escaping from his open mouth, and I could see the thin sheet rising and falling across his chest. In the living room,

I lingered by the corner table with the bronze Buddha and wondered if I should pray for Than. Would my Catholic prayers reach a Buddhist heaven?

I remembered praying as a boy, my fingers folded tight in the darkness, for Jesus to come and intercede with my father, calm his savage temper. One Lent, I said a rosary every night before bed. A lot of good that did.

I moved away from the shrine and sat on the couch, my head full of questions. All day during my workout, my mind had been crammed with thoughts — of the ref I hurt, of Leonard in the boxcar, and Sunday's offer to be some sort of junior-level enforcer. Now I couldn't stop imagining my mother with her arm in a brace, and the shame was too much. I needed to shut my brain down for a while, so I decided to try Than's meditation again. I settled on the couch and gently, I closed my eyes. I summoned up a summer sky, blue like a robin's egg. It was nice at first, pleasant and calm. I even felt a breeze brush my cheeks. Inevitably though, my worries returned. I concentrated my attention and made each into a small cloud, focused so that by force of will it dissipated. I tugged them apart as if they were cotton balls. But the troubling images began to gather one atop the next, and in no time, my blue sky was darkened by storm clouds. I heard a thunder clap, and a lightning strike opened my eyes.

I met Blalock at Pancakes and Porkchops for a late lunch. This time, I ordered one of those cheesesteaks myself, and yeah sure, it was damn good. Under the table, he slid me an envelope thick with cash. He explained that there was a little extra included, a bonus from Sunday, "to give me a taste." This was clearly an attempt to encourage me to accept Sunday's offer, and Blalock didn't need to spell it out. Instead he talked about Santana, said he'd once seen him foot-sweep a guy to the ground so fast it looked like he'd been shot.

Just cause I was curious, I asked where the next fight would be, and Blalock got fidgety. He glanced around and leaned in over our empty plates. "That intelligence is disseminated on a need-to-know basis. As a security precaution it's necessary to limit access to our actual whereabouts. Even the high rollers only learn the location the day of the fight. Loose lips sink ships."

He looked deadly serious and I nodded just to let him know I wouldn't ask again. Whatever. Like I cared.

Before we parted, he also explained that the advanced online betting was looking good. Despite my dominant first victory, Santana opened as the 5–1 favorite but a lot of the money was following me. I was curious about the offshore website, how big the organization was, where the high rollers fit in, but Blalock was edgy, so there was no point in asking.

When Khajee got home after school, she found me crashed on the couch. The TV screen was filled with an MMA fight tape I found mixed in with the box of Muay Thai. The closing door startled me, and I watched her drop her backpack and a white CVS bag on the table, then she turned off the TV and came to my side. "Trying some sort of subliminal training regimen?"

I sat up and she asked, "How's he been?"

"Fine," I said. "Good. He rested the whole day far as I can tell."

She handed me a tiny octagonal jar that had "Tiger Balm" printed on it. "Strong stuff," she said. "Massage a little bit into your neck and it'll relax the muscle. But don't get any in your eyes."

She disappeared into the bedroom and I did as she instructed. The lotion was pungent and my flesh burned, but in a way I could tell was good.

When Khajee emerged, I thanked her and she said, "He's hungry but sleepy with fever. A bath should revive him." After she went in the bathroom, I heard the water running. The sound make me think of Khajee's singing, something I hadn't heard in a few days.

I asked if I could help get him in the tub and she shook her head. "We'll manage. He's a private man, very proud. You understand? You can find something in the freezer for dinner for us, yeah?"

"Sure," I said. "Of course."

My stomach was still full from that cheesesteak, but I heated up some frozen lasagna during the bath, and Than eventually made his way to the table with great effort, leaning heavy on his walker and hopping with difficulty. He greeted me and gave me a thumbs-up. "Good to get a first win under your belt!" he said. Khajee smiled, but I wondered if she'd told him about all that had happened, if he knew about the fire or how I lost control. Than ended up not having much of an appetite for the lasagna. Mostly he just moved it around with his fork and sipped some sort of protein shake that Khajee made in the blender.

Later, I did the dishes while Khajee paged through some

math, tapping on a calculator. I wasn't sure if this was SAT prep or homework. I settled Than in his easy chair and we started watching a VHS tape of Olympic judo. He was asleep by the end of the second bout.

After we got him back to bed, I joined Khajee at the kitchen table and asked something I'd been wondering. "How does samatha help him with his pain?"

Khajee cocked an eyebrow at me.

"He taught me the word. I'm coachable." I winked. "Seriously, so like it helps him ignore it?"

She shook her head. "No. Meditation clarifies things. But it's not a way to delude yourself. If you feel pain, if you have troubling thoughts, you acknowledge them, but then you move on. You let them go."

"That sounds hard."

"Yeah right," she said. "And it's harder than it sounds."

I remembered my mom imploring me to forgive my father like she had done, to accept that we're all sinners in need of Christ's grace. But my anger at him was such a big part of who I was. If I let go of that, then who would I be?

Somehow, this must've been showing on my face, since Khajee asked, "You okay?"

"Fine," I told her. Then I said something true. "I'm really worried about your uncle. I know how he feels about doctors, but I think he's getting worse."

"He's stubborn," Khajee said, looking his way. "Besides, doctors cost money."

Quietly as I could, I stepped into the living room and

reached under the couch cushion. I pulled out an envelope with the stack of cash I'd gotten from my fight. That afternoon I'd counted it on the kitchen table — $5,000. More than I'd ever had in my hands. "Money we got," I told her.

Khajee stared at me for a minute. "I don't —" she said. "I could never —" Then she dipped her head, swallowed, and looked back at me. "I'm not in the habit of taking handouts."

"It wouldn't have to be a handout," I explained. "We could call it a loan or —"

"I don't like being in debt. To anybody." At this she abruptly turned away. Without saying another word, she slid on her sneakers and got Rosie into her harness, clipped on her leash. Sometimes in a fight, you've got to know when to keep pressing, so I got my sneakers too, and when Khajee opened the door to leave, I followed.

In silence, we walked along the darkened street, past the cans and bags set out for garbage night. Rosie seemed to want to sniff each one, and Khajee had to yank on the leash, urge her forward. She snapped, "Come on!" and Rosie trotted on obediently, head hanging from the scolding.

"Hey," I finally said. "Don't take it out on the doggo."

Khajee flashed me an angry glare and we walked on, but she let Rosie linger more at trees and hydrants. We crossed Front Street and made our way along the bike path, trotting by a mom pushing a stroller. I took note of the "exercise stations" the city installed in the name of public fitness, most of which looked like misplaced pieces from some strange playground.

The lights were on over at City Island, which was weird since the Harrisburg Senators were surely out of season. In the summer, they shoot off fireworks after a win. Some nights when Mom didn't have a shift, she and I would walk up to Negley Park overlooking the west shore. It was fun, trying to follow the game from afar, rooting for a win so we could watch them color the night sky. This memory dislodged another, one I'd lost track of: my father leading me by the hand to our seats inside the stadium, a special treat one year for my birthday. We shared nachos, did the wave, craned our necks to see the cascading fireworks. On the way back to the car, I was so tired he carried me.

Khajee paused at a bench I thought was already occupied. Then I realized the figure I saw was only a statue, another "improvement" the city made when they renovated the waterfront. The bronze man sat with his legs crossed, comfortably reading a bronze newspaper. I stood next to them and the Susquehanna flowed south. Two joggers padded by us wearing lights on their foreheads, like miners. The half-moon glowed plenty bright so we could see the ripples. I said, "Look how the water —" but cut myself off, remembering her odd reaction down at the creek.

Maybe Khajee sensed my thoughts, and I guess the evening was thick with the past, because out of the blue, she spoke in a quiet voice, facing the river. "When I was eight . . . one of my mom's friends invited us to spend the weekend at Chincoteague Island down in Virginia. The first night, I remember, we all chased ghost crabs on the beach with flashlights. So much fun. But then Saturday —"

Khajee choked on the next words, and I had a feeling where

this was going. I remembered that her parents had died, but she'd said nothing about them other than that. I wasn't sure why she was telling me this, but I could tell it was costing her. The sentences were like stones she was heaving up from a deep well. She sniffled and straightened. "Saturday, even though the sky was gray, they took us out on their new sailboat, about six adults altogether and me. I can still feel my mom tightening the straps of my orange life vest, the same one she made me wear when we went tubing on the creek."

She got quiet and I didn't know what to say.

"The rest is murky. The waves got bigger, sharper, tossing us around. I threw up. Some of the adults started arguing. I remember lightning and my mother crying, my father clutching me, the ship pitching, bucking like a wild horse. Then I was splashing in the water, alone. It got really dark then, black as midnight."

I imagined a child on her own in the ocean, and I wanted to tell her I knew something about that darkness. In the riverside air, impossibly, that familiar smell of the closet came to me on the breeze. "Khajee," I whispered. I reached out for her.

"No," she said, shaking away my touch. "Just let me finish this now or I might never get back to it. After forever, the storm subsided. There were lights in the sky then a rescue boat and a woman rubbing me with a towel, telling me, 'Let's get you warm.'"

"Sweet Jesus," I said, a curse and a prayer.

"My uncle took me in," she said. "He moved here from Atlantic City. He's always been a sort of jack-of-all-trades, master of none kind of guy. He's been a fisherman, a bricklayer, a bartender, an electrician. But he's a terrible gambler, and he got in way over his head with Sunday. My uncle had no assets to take, and there was no use beating him, so Sunday put him to work. He was an errand boy for a while, then graduated to being his personal driver. When Brawlers got going, he started training fighters in Muay Thai at that ratty gym."

I wondered how much they owed Sunday and asked, "What kind of debt are we talking about here?"

She knuckled her eye sockets. "The kind that keeps accruing interest. By the time my uncle's health took a turn, Grunt was driving and my uncle was mostly training fighters, so Sunday said he'd keep paying our bills if I stepped in. If I were a boy, I'd be in the ring making real money, not just chipping away at what we owe."

"No doubt," I agreed. I was pretty sure that one-on-one, Khajee could take most of the guys on my wrestling team. "But this is crazy," I told her. "Like you're some sort of indentured servant."

She shrugged. "No offense Mac. I mean, I like you and all, but still. You know I'm not training you for charity or to beef up my resume."

That hurt, but the words *I like you and all* sort of glowed in my mind.

"Sunday pays our rent, gives us money for food and a little extra. I'm not even sure what we still owe or how long I'll be paying it off. If I go to the cops, who will pay the bills next month? How will I buy groceries or medicine?"

Khajee was a proud girl, and I knew it pained her to tell me all this. I remembered my mom pulling the packet of food stamps from her purse at Karns, always keeping her head down when she handed them over.

"I understand," I said, knowing I really couldn't. Not fully. I wasn't supporting an adult and trying to get through school at the same time. Khajee began to weep quietly, and Rosie put her head on her lap, which was more comfort than I could offer. But I knew she'd shared something important with me, and it felt wrong not to share something back. "I only saw him once."

Khajee sniffled back tears. "What now?"

"My father," I said. "You asked if I ever saw him in prison. The answer is just one time. And even that was across a parking lot, through a cyclone fence. After he was in there for like a year, my mom convinced me to visit him. But when we got there I sort of freaked. I refused to get out of the car."

Khajee seemed to take this in. I wondered what screwed a kid up worse, having parents die like hers or having a dad like mine. I figured us both for pretty much lost causes.

"And you never went back?" she asked.

I shook my head. "Nothing there for me."

She fixed me with those green eyes. "You father has nothing you want?"

"What's he going to do? Explain how he's sorry for what he did? That's not going to happen."

"How do you know?"

"People don't change. Even as an inmate he kept screwing up, got a few years added to his sentence for fighting or something. Trust me. The only thing I'd want from him is a chance to kick his ass." Sunday's proposal drifted through my head. For Khajee, I added, "But that seems kinda unlikely, given the prison guards and all."

"Yeah," she agreed. "I guess crime is frowned upon in prison."

I stood. "It wouldn't be a crime to give that man a beating. It'd be justice."

She waited for me to say something else, and I heard the tone I'd used, the heat rising in my voice. "C'mon," I finally said. "My legs are getting stiff. Let's walk."

In awkward silence, we retraced our steps. A dad with three kids was helping them climb over the bars of one of the exercise stations. A homeless woman in filthy clothes leaned against a tree, stroking a cat on her lap. Eventually we wandered back into the neighborhood, with Rosie sniffing every stack of garbage bags as we passed. We traveled along a row of bars, doors open and music spilling out. Some of it was live. Some lady was butchering the Johnny Cash tune "Ring of Fire," and I turned to Khajee. "That better be karaoke. Nobody that bad should get paid to sing."

"She's not so bad," Khajee said. "A little pitchy on the edges."

"Are you kidding?" I asked. "You sound way better."

Khajee halted, nearly choking Rosie. "I sound better?"

I searched for the right words. "You know. In the house." I really didn't want to say shower. "When you're getting cleaned up."

Khajee's cheeks flushed and she started walking fast.

I rushed after her. "You're kidding me with this, right? The mighty warrior chick is embarrassed? That's so sweet."

She swatted my chest with a backhand, smiling. "Lay off. I didn't think you could hear me. But of course you could. I won't do it again."

I set a hand on her arm, stopping her. "That'd be a shame. You have a wonderful voice."

We held eyes for a second, then she looked away. "That's not what everybody thinks."

"Everybody like who?"

"Like Mr. Wertzman." She tugged her arm free and said, "Drop it. I'm not interested in rehashing the past."

A garbage truck rumbled by, and Rosie barked at it. I could tell Khajee was riled up by this Wertzman guy, whoever he was, but for the moment, I knew best to respect her wishes. To break the silent tension, I said, "So what's so terrible about my elbow strikes?"

Khajee had a bit of a spasm, suppressing a laugh. She looked up at me and wiped her eyes. "Everything. The only nice thing I have to say is that you elbow strike better than you kick."

I thrust a foot into the air, barely waist high, and she shook her head. "It hurts to see you try that. Please stop."

I laughed and together we walked on. At the mouth of an alleyway, Rosie took a sincere interest in some scent and she dragged us inside. She sniffed at a leaky dumpster. There was nobody else around. I said, "Seriously. We've got Santana at the end of this week. How about some pointers?"

"Fine," she said, and handed me the end of Rosie's leash.

She settled into a fighting stance with her knees bent slightly and her fists raised, close together up by her chin. "This is how you should be," she explained. For emphasis, she snapped her elbows in a series of rapid uppercuts, then threw a few looping hooks. Lastly, she turned sideways and thrust her right elbow out, like you would to break a window. "All these begin with your hands close together. This defends your face and keeps the strikes tight." She showed me again, resuming her initial stance. "But you," she said. "You look like this." Slowly, she moved her hands apart six inches. "This leaves a gap a mile wide, especially for a strike artist like Santana. It also kills the torque for your elbows, weakens their impact."

She took the leash from me and secured the dog to a pipe running down the brick wall, then stared my way. I realized this was my cue. So I crouched down, shrugged my shoulders in, and brought my fists up the way she had. "Better," she said. "Now throw some elbows."

Even though we were right there in an alley and anybody walking by could see us, Khajee didn't seem self-conscious about any of this. Me, I felt a little weird but decided to play along. As I swung at the air, she frowned. "Twist at your waist. You don't just throw a punch with your arm — it's your whole body throwing it . . . keep your hands closer together, it'll give you more power."

Figuring we were going to be a while, Rosie curled into a heap, still leashed to that pipe. Khajee began to bob and weave in front of me, and I understood she wanted me to echo her motions, so I became a living mirror image. When she jabbed with her left and followed with a right elbow, I did likewise. In slow motion, she floated a right hook across my face, and I pulled back on instinct. With her arm still extended, she said, "Even when you miss, sometimes it creates an opportunity." She popped her elbow gently into my chin, and I knew if she really drove it home, it would have felt like a hammer shot.

"Set up your shots. A knee to the side will lower a man's guard. Think in combinations." She leaned in and lifted her knee into my left rib cage. I hunched into it, dropping my arm a bit, and her right elbow tapped my skull, just above the ear. "Flow from one action to the next. Don't think of them as individual moves. Picture the whole constellation, not the stars."

I straightened up and we began sparring again. She said, "Once you've hurt your opponent, a feint is as good as a strike, yeah? But you have to commit to it with your eyes, make him believe the attack is real." She stepped into me and drove a fist straight toward my face. I leaned back and she dropped down, wrapping both arms onto one of my knees. She was quick as Santana. "A guy like you, with your strength and skill set, you can do a lot with a leg."

"Ground and pound," I said.

She released my leg. "Exactly. I'm telling you right now, you can't stand toe to toe with most of these guys. In a straight boxing match, you wouldn't stand a chance. Never mind the fact that they can kick too. But once you get them down, the advantage should be yours."

I nodded because she was making sense. Like the best coaches, Khajee was finding words to express what my body already knew. But she was also helping me form a battle plan for my next match. Even though Sunday's debt was forcing her to do this, she was damn good at it. "C'mon," she said, lifting her hands. "Practice faking a strike and then sliding into a single or double leg."

We began to circle each other again, falling into a natural rhythm, and our stiff movements melted into something fluid. Though she was half my size, Khajee was an awesome sparring partner, overreacting and staying open, letting me see my mistakes, but she was playful too, now and then tagging me on the chin with a slap or sticking a foot into my gut. "Your guard, your guard," she'd say. "Stick and move. Stay on your toes. Don't get caught flatfooted."

We got lost in the action, like you always do when it's good, and time passed without us noticing. Now and then when I did something right, she'd flash me a smile of approval, and I got distracted by how lovely Khajee's face was. She always struck me as sort of cute, but somehow when she was fighting, her real beauty came out. This recognition mixed with what she said about liking me spawned a stray thought, the notion that me and her might be more than friends. This stole my attention long enough for her to slip in a swift jab to my chin, which she followed with a ferocious fist to my sternum. I stepped back, catching my breath, and she said, "Lose concentration like that in a match and it's all over."

I charged forward, driving her back into the side wall of the alley, grinning playfully as I posted my hands on either side of her, trapping her inside my arms. Our faces were close now. She tilted her head and looked at me sort of curiously, like she wasn't sure just what I was thinking. Of course, neither was I really. But whatever was about to happen or not happen, we never got the chance.

Below us, Rosie snarled and got to her feet, tugging on her leash. Then I heard a deep voice ask, "What exactly are we looking at here?"

Through the darkness, I saw three figures silhouetted, just black shadows with traffic passing behind them. In the center, the tallest of the three spoke again. "Looks to me like a lover's quarrel."

I pulled my arms away from Khajee, and Rosie showed her teeth, hackles rising. Khajee bent to rub her head while I squared off, assuming the gunslinger's pose. If my boyhood taught me one thing, it was the sound of a man's voice when he's itching for a fight. And judging by this guy's tone, he was drunk and mean and on the prowl. Though I was sure I'd never met him before, his voice sounded familiar, and I decided right then that if he and his buddies were searching for trouble, they'd come to the right place.

12

*N*ext to the tall man, a shorter dude in boots lifted a bottle to his lips, tipped it, then said, "Don't let us stop you. Y'all look downright adorable."

The trio advanced a few steps, side by side. I scanned the walls surrounding us. A fire escape zigzagged down the one brick building, but the ladder was twelve feet off the ground. The only way out was through them. Rosie growled and Khajee said, "Easy girl," and her voice showed no sign of concern. She unstrapped her leash from that pipe, looped the handle around her wrist.

As they came closer, I saw they were all middle-aged. "Keep that mutt under control," the tall guy said. "Or we'll do it for you."

Rosie barked now, bearing her teeth. The third guy, with a ball cap tucked down low on his forehead, slurred out, "Same thing goes for her." He aimed a shaky finger at Khajee. "She's a cute little ninja, isn't she? Feisty. I like me a feisty gal."

I stepped toward them, shielding Khajee with my body. No way did I actually expect to talk my way out of it, but still I raised my hands and said, "We were having a little impromptu lesson. Just heading out."

The three of them stood shoulder to shoulder, making a

wall, and the short one in boots said, "Lessons? Where do we sign up?"

My eyes flashed across their faces to see if any were close to making the first move. I said, "Look. You're all drunk, and there's no need for this to turn nasty. You're about to get hurt if you don't drag your sorry butts back to the bar you crawled out of. Or even better, home to your ugly wives."

"Funny man," the tall one said. He drained the last of his beer and gripped the empty bottle by the neck. His buddy with the ball cap pulled something from his back pocket. It was too dark to be sure, but I saw a glint of something metal and figured it for a knife. We all could feel it, the tension about to pop. Rosie was snapping like wild now, straining against her leash, and I turned my head sideways, keeping one eye on the crew. I told Khajee, "I'll keep these jokers busy. You two make a break for it."

But Khajee bent down, patted Rosie on the head, and said loudly, "The answer is about seven inches."

"Come again now?" the tallest drunk said, head cocked. I had no idea what Khajee was talking about. The whole charged atmosphere had shifted.

She stood and stepped around my protective arms. At my side with Rosie ahead of us, she said, "The needles they use. To treat rabies."

The three guys traded confused expressions.

Khajee set a hand on her belly. "It's actually a series of injections. Deep into the abdomen. Usually four to six over a period of weeks. Very painful from what I've been told."

Rosie tugged on her leash, her front legs pawing at the air. The guy with the ball cap backed up but the tall leader set a hand on his shoulder. "She's full of it. That mutt ain't got rabies."

"Probably not," Khajee said. "But this dog was raised in a fighting pit, where her owners used to beat her. From the look of her, I'm guessing they smelled a lot like you." Rosie's jaw snapped madly at the air, and even in the alley's half-light her teeth glistened. Khajee went down on one knee, let her hand trail the leash to where it attached to Rosie's collar. She fingered the clasp. "She just needs to break the skin."

"Forget this," the shortest one said as he backed away, still facing us.

The leader said, "Come on Pete, don't let this little —"

Khajee lifted her hand and Rosie launched forward, bounding toward the men, barking ferociously. They practically fell over each other as they turned and ran. Rosie was right at their heels when they reached the street, and Khajee shouted, "Yùt!" Rosie came to a sudden stop. She trotted back to Khajee, licked her outstretched hand, and allowed Khajee to reattach her leash.

It all happened so quickly, I didn't have time to react. I said, "We should get out of here before they come back."

Khajee gave me a look. "Those cowards? They're not coming back. But yeah, I need to check on Uncle."

We passed by a small huddle of patrons outside the bar and followed the cracked sidewalks through the neighborhood.

Khajee was oddly quiet, given what just happened, and I said, "That was crazy back there. Where'd you come up with such a story?"

"I don't know," she said, walking just in front of me. "Guess I'm a good liar."

"I'll say," I told her. "You practically had me convinced. But, you know, I had things under control."

She stopped and faced me. "No," she said. "No you didn't. There were three of them and they were drunk. There's no way to have that situation under control. Anything could have happened."

Her expression was flat, her tone objective.

"Come on," I said. "I would've mopped the alley with those jerks. I could've taken them without breaking a sweat and that's not even —"

Khajee spun on one heel and marched away from me, pulling a reluctant Rosie. When I caught up to her, she didn't look my way. "I can take care of myself," she said. "This isn't a fairy tale and I'm no damsel in distress."

"I didn't say that you were," I said, trying to defend myself. "What did you want me to do? Let them beat us?"

She shook her head and increased her pace to put distance between us. I didn't want to jog to keep up and make a scene, so I trailed her for a block. Traffic was heavy at a red light and she had to wait, and when I came alongside her she finally gave me an answer. "You saw absolutely no other alternative? Either they beat us or you beat them? You were practically egging them on, and you know it. Not every problem needs to be fixed with your fists, Mac."

The light turned green and the little walking man appeared on the street sign, but Khajee didn't move. "I don't know what it is with you guys," she said. "Maybe violence is just in your blood or something."

"What are you talking about?" I asked.

"Come on," she snapped. "What you said before, about fighting your father? You can't even tell the difference between justice and revenge."

She looked at me then, waiting for some response. I couldn't tell Khajee then that for years on the mat, when I was bludgeoning some wrestler, I imagined it was my father I was hurting. It was his arm I was cranking, his cheek I was forcing into the mat. So I stayed silent. And when she turned and crossed the street, I just stood where I was. Others passed me by, and soon the flow of people tugged me along.

Fists in my pockets, I roamed by an all-night convenience store with a shoeless guy begging for change out front, and I walked past a couple leaving a fancy restaurant arguing about who forgot to make the reservation. There were young skateboarders practicing tricks in the cones of parking lot lights, a pack of evening joggers wearing neon-yellow safety vests. An ambulance screamed along the street, sirens wailing. All these things I took in, but mostly I was wrestling with Khajee's words.

Deep down in my blood, I knew I'd find my father's DNA.

Khajee hadn't meant it quite so literally, but it made me wonder if I had any choice in who I was. If some genetic code had decided that my hair would be black, my eyes crystal blue, then how was this any different than other parts of me — my instincts, my temper? Maybe that's why it's so easy for me to steal a glimpse of the future sometimes, because all of it is already predetermined.

My path back to the apartment was hardly a straight one. I took my time, wandering in that general direction as I tried to think things through. I had no answers for Khajee, but I'd decided that at least, as a start, I should apologize.

But when I turned onto the street of her building, there was an ambulance out front, lights silently strobing red/white/red, backed up to Khajee's place with the rear doors open. I charged into her apartment to find two paramedics kneeling over Than, lying on a stretcher on the living room floor. His eyes were closed. Khajee stood above them, crying, and the TV was on, playing the *World Series of Poker.*

The paramedics positioned themselves front and back and lifted Than. I heard him groan low, but at least this was a sign of life. From the bedroom, Rosie barked wildly. "What happened?" I asked in the confusion.

No one answered me and the paramedics carried Than through the door. Khajee grabbed her backpack and followed them, but paused long enough to get out, "When I got home, he was just on the floor." Her green eyes were shiny with tears. She looked at the rug. "They said something about respiratory failure but can't be sure. They're taking him to the ER."

At the open doorway, she paused and looked back at me. Beyond her, I could see inside the bright ambulance, where the paramedics were leaning over Than. Khajee rubbed her hands together and glanced side to side, like she was trying to find something she'd lost. Then she took a half step into me and asked, "Mac, could you come?"

Hours later, we were sitting next to each other in the emergency room waiting area at Harrisburg Hospital. I've long had a phobia when it comes to hospitals, and I felt like I was holding my breath, diving deep underwater. But Khajee needed me, and I sucked it up. She sat next to me in the waiting room. In front of her was the full cup of coffee, cold and untouched, that I'd gotten earlier from the cafeteria.

The wounded and sick wandered around us. A young dad paced with a wailing baby, a tubby businessman yelled into his cell phone right beneath a sign that forbid all cell phone use. A Latina woman sat calmly reading the newspaper with her swollen leg propped up on a table. The TV hanging in the corner was playing one of those shows where a panel of second-rate celebrities judge everyday people trying to break into showbiz. There was a guy juggling flaming rings while riding a unicycle, a team of three female magicians who changed themselves into men, and a Nebraska farm boy complete with overalls who broke into a rap about country life. He was a big hit.

I caught Khajee smiling at him and said, "Think he could be a winner?"

She shrugged. "He already won, if you ask me." Restless, she pulled out her cell phone and glanced at the screen. Earlier, a nurse had explained that Than was out of immediate danger for now but being admitted. They'd get us when we could see him. Right away Khajee texted somebody. I didn't ask who, but I could tell she hadn't heard back. She shoved her phone back in her pocket and stood. "What the hell's taking so long? I'm going to go ask."

I set a hand gently on her arm. "There's no point. Harassing them won't get us an answer. All we can do now is wait."

She looked down at me, more upset than angry. I was dwelling on the same thing I figured she was, the meaning behind a phrase like *out of immediate danger for now.*

As she settled in next to me, another singer took the stage. I knew it was a touchy subject but figured a distraction was worth it, so I said, "Tell me about this jerk Wertzman."

"What now?" she asked.

"Wertzman who thinks you can't sing."

A frustrated grin cracked her stony expression. "Sterling Wertzman. He directs the plays at our school, thinks he's God's gift to the Harrisburg theater scene."

"You're an actress?"

"Last spring, I nailed my audition for Cinderella. I mean, objectively, I owned that song. It was mine."

"And what, this guy didn't give you a part?"

"Mouse #3," Khajee said. "Not even a damn wicked stepsister. Cinderella went to Jenny Haskel, who can't sing worth a damn but happens to be very tall, and very blonde, very beautiful in all the best ways — like all the leads. That's just the way it is, right?"

What Khajee had said back in the woods, when we were talking about Hollywood heroes, made more sense to me now. She went on. "This . . . friend of mine, she said we should quit in protest, so we did. Me and Mouse #2. Not that it made a difference — they found other mice and the world kept right on spinning. This year, I didn't even bother trying out. Neither did she, and she can really dance."

"Their loss," I said. "I meant what I said before. You're a great singer."

"Everybody sounds good in the shower," she said, stretching that grin. After a few seconds, she added, "But hey, thanks for saying it."

It was a weird moment, one that felt close but odd too, like back in the alley. Once again though, we were interrupted. A male nurse came striding up to us. "Can you follow me please?" he asked.

Together, we stood, and I was surprised to find Khajee reach for my hand. He led us down a hallway and we took an elevator to the second floor, then down another hallway. Every step I was aware of her fingers in mine. With nothing but the unknown ahead, I was an anchor for her. It felt good to return the favor.

Finally the nurse turned into a room and we saw Than resting in a bent bed, eyes closed, skin pale. A plastic mask connected to a green tank covered his mouth and nose. Khajee collapsed onto him, sobbing, and the male nurse said, "Dr. Ngoyo will be in as soon as he can."

I nodded and the nurse left us. Rain splattered the window. Beside Than, a clear bag of something hung, dripping liquid into a tube that curved down and into the crease of Than's elbow. Khajee scraped a chair across the linoleum and sat at his side, holding his wrist. She whispered to him in Thai.

The doctor, who was thin and brown-skinned, strode in a while later. He greeted us, checked on a monitor with green numbers, then turned to Khajee. She said, "What happened to my uncle?"

"We're dealing here with a bacteria called pneumococcus. Unfortunately, it's not uncommon in diabetics, though there is a vaccine. I suppose your uncle never had it."

I thought this was a cruddy thing to tell her. What was the point? The doctor went on. "This has led to pneumonia, something we'll try to address with breathing treatments, and a condition called sepsis, basically a body-wide infection. We have antibiotics that will clear that up, hopefully."

"What do you mean hopefully? Will all this cure him or not?" Khajee shouted these questions, and the doctor looked at me for some sort of help. Khajee lowered her voice and asked, "Please. Is he going to die?"

Dr. Ngoyo said, "I don't decide that. But his condition is very serious. He'll be admitted, of course. You could be looking at a prolonged stay."

"We have no insurance," Khajee said, dropping her face.

The doctor tried to hide his frown. "Legally we can't discharge him, regardless of your ability to pay. But I'll be honest with you, his care isn't going to be inexpensive. Even if he recovers, his kidneys might be damaged. If they fail, which is likely, then we'll be looking at dialysis."

A chime sounded in the doctor's pocket and he pulled out a phone, glanced at the screen. Then he said, "When the time is right, someone can talk to you about payment plans, options for all that. For now, stay with him as long as you'd like."

He tucked the phone back in his pocket and left us. I moved behind Khajee with my hands on the back of her chair. For a while we said nothing. We listened to his ragged breathing and the hum of the machine at his side. The rain stopped. Now and then an announcement drifted in on the hospital PA. There was a Code Armstrong on the fourth floor. Khajee squeezed his hand. If Than noticed, I couldn't tell.

I leaned over and touched her right shoulder. "The money I have," I told her, "it's yours."

She bent that arm and patted my hand, then held my fingers. "That won't be enough. I know what these places cost. Dialysis. Can you imagine? We have no credit cards, don't own a damn thing worth selling. I'll quit school I guess, try to find a steady second income."

I moved around to the side of her chair, still holding her

hand, and bent a knee to the cold linoleum. Khajee's face was streaked with tears. "Everything's going to be okay," I told her. "I can fix this."

She shook her head, looked at me like I was naïve and foolish. "We covered this, Mac. It's not your job to save me. I don't need you to be my hero."

I got to my feet. "I know that," I said. "But I can be your friend."

13

So that's how I ended up agreeing to do "side work" for Sunday. The same night Than took that ambulance ride, I got word to Sunday through Blalock and heard back quickly that he was happy I'd seen the light. I was told Grunt would call on me when my services were needed. Tuesday and Wednesday I waited, trying to prepare for Santana's fight as best I could on my own. Each day I forced myself to stop by the hospital, pushing my anxieties down. The nurses let Khajee linger long past official visiting hours, keeping vigil by his side. She told me Than came around a couple times, sweaty and delirious, but he never showed any sign that he recognized her or knew where he was. According to Dr. Ngoyo, his condition hadn't gotten worse, and we tried to see this as good news. "He's too stubborn to die," Khajee told me. She wasn't happy when I explained that Sunday and I had reached an arrangement regarding the hospital bill, but she was too exhausted to really fight me about it.

Late that Wednesday night, I left Khajee to let Rosie out, and when I got back to the apartment, eager for sleep, Grunt was standing on the front steps, jacket buttoned, arms crossed. We made eye contact and he nodded solemnly before walking without comment to a black van. On its side were the words, "Home Improvements, Renovations, Demolition. Free Estimates."

I let Rosie back inside, then followed and climbed into the

passenger seat. Without saying a word, he drove off. After a few miles I asked, "So what's the deal? Where are we going?" In response, Grunt reached one hand across my lap and popped open the glove box. Inside, I saw the gray metal of a gun.

I reached for the weapon, and it felt cool in my palm. When I pulled it out, I was surprised at how light it was. During a middle school stint in Cub Scouts encouraged by one of my mom's temporary boyfriends, I'd learned how to shoot a rifle. Part of the safety program involved pistols like this one. I popped out the magazine and saw that it was empty.

"No bullets?" I asked.

Grunt smirked and shook his head. This was no mistake. Maybe I wasn't trusted yet, and they just wanted me to have a prop for whatever errand we were on. Or maybe they'd never think I was worthy. Regardless, I knew it was a slam on me, but I really didn't care. In fact, I was relieved. I'd been awake the last two nights, bathroom door cracked pretty wide, thinking about the boxcar and my father's genes, worried about what Sunday might ask me to do.

Grunt drove us to a truck stop off Route 83, and we parked in the darkness beyond the gas pumps. Before we got out, he showed me his gun, tucked down inside his beltline under his coat. I did the same and zipped up my jacket. He nodded and we headed inside. As we crossed the black asphalt, I said low, "So what's up? What am I supposed to do?"

He glanced back at me and said nothing.

Inside we moved through the convenience store, where two old ladies held up the line bickering about which lottery tickets to buy, a gray-bearded trucker considered the hot dogs rotating beneath a plastic lid, and a father yelled at his kids to hurry up and pick out snacks because "all the jackholes I passed are passing us now."

Grunt led me down a long thin hallway, past a refrigerator with a vault-like door. We had to step around a mop tilted into a yellow bucket on wheels. The water was gray and foul.

At the end of the hallway was an office with the door open. When we walked in, a stubby man with a grease-stained white shirt rose up from behind a desk covered in papers. He and Grunt shook and he eyed me up, not extending a hand. "Mr. Sunday's getting them kind of young these days, eh?"

Grunt shrugged, and the man returned to his desk, pulled back a drawer, and withdrew an envelope. He gave it to Grunt, who passed it to me and rubbed his thumb into two fingers.

"Come on," the clerk said. "You can trust me."

I cleared a corner on the desk and laid out the twenties, counting as I went. I made three stacks of five and then announced, "Three hundred even."

Grunt reached out for the man's shoulder and patted it, then turned. I collected the bills and fell into his wake. Behind us, the man said, "Okay, guys. Take care. Listen, you want some of those taquitos or a drink or something, it's on the house. Anything at all. Just tell Lucy I said."

At the cooler, Grunt paused. He pulled out a Yoo-hoo, then looked at me. I shook my head, and he let the door close. As we brushed past the line at the checkout, Grunt twisted the top and guzzled the drink. I glanced over at the woman behind the register, frozen. Her eyes trailed Grunt. On her shirt, a worn name tag read, "Lucinda." I wanted to say, "I'm sorry," but I knew I had a part to play, and that didn't involve apologies.

After that first stop, we made a few more. There was a pool hall in Harrisburg, a VFW club in Enola, a steakhouse along the river, even a funeral parlor down in Mechanicsburg. Each place was about the same. Lots of nervous eyes and shaky hands, a kind of courtesy that felt false. Equally phony was the calm I projected as I stood behind Grunt with a steely gaze, a mask of pure badassery that covered my turning stomach.

Between jobs, Grunt listened to AM radio. He never stayed on one station for more than a few minutes. One program had a conspiracy nut ranting about the government putting passivity chemicals in bottled water, then a call-in show where the host gave financial advice. We listened to a twangy country singer lament his lost love and then Grunt settled on a rock station. I recognized David Lee Roth's voice belting out the chorus of "Running with the Devil" and I anticipated the upcoming lyrics about living life like there's no tomorrow, but Grunt abruptly shifted to some preacher. Through the static of a distant station, he proclaimed, "None of us can fully know the love and grace of Jesus. But He tells us that salvation comes to those who seek Him. You need only walk the path of righteousness, and in that holy pursuit, you will find Christ!"

Grunt snapped the station off, and we drove for a while listening only to the tires hum on the highway.

Halfway to Carlisle, we pulled up to a warehouse as big

as an airplane hangar. Inside we were greeted by a trio of muscle-headed goons. They looked like the type who'd played offensive line together in high school and were okay with that being their life's crowning achievement. Two crossed their arms like Grunt did, shoulders back, chin up. The third held a gun at his side. If Grunt noticed, he showed no concern. They brought us to a huge room with crates stacked thirty feet up. A woman drove a forklift past us, and we came upon a geeky-looking man, complete with pencil tucked behind one ear and clipboard. Like all of them, he acted happy to see Grunt, shaking his hand with a big grin. "So listen," he began. "I've got a bit of a situation."

Flanked by his stony henchmen, the geek went on to tell a long story about a truck breaking down in Scranton, a supplier getting nervous about local cops, and his wife being sick with the flu. How they all connected to each other wasn't entirely clear to me, but somehow his conclusion was that, as he put it, "I'm a little short this time. Tell Mr. Sunday I'll make it up to him. He knows I cover my debts."

Along with his excuse, he offered Grunt an envelope. Emotionless, he passed it on to me and nodded. I counted what was inside and said, "Twenty-seven hundred."

Grunt's eyebrows rose up a bit, and the man said, "You'll tell Mr. Sunday my unusual circumstances, right? This is a once and done situation."

Grunt lifted a paw and dropped it hard on the guy's shoulder, then gripped it till he winced. The bodyguards looked at each other, like they weren't sure what to do, and I was right with them, uncertain of my role. Instinctively, I took half a step closer to the one with the gun. I unzipped my jacket, just enough to expose the handle of my own, a total bluff. I figured if he lifted his weapon, I might double-leg him, take him to the ground and see what happened next.

But Grunt released his grip and grinned, and I breathed again. When we walked away, everything seemed copacetic. Only then, sitting behind the van's steering wheel, Grunt took out his phone and texted somebody, I presumed Sunday. It was a long text, and I wondered if he was telling him how I was doing, and if so, what he thought of me. If I was handling myself or not.

There was silence, followed by the ding of a new message. Grunt stared at the screen grim-faced, then tucked the phone back into his pocket. He didn't start the van like I expected. Instead he climbed out and went around to the back. I met him in the rear as he opened the big back doors, and he bent into the dark interior, reaching with both hands. He straightened, holding a sledgehammer in one hand and a crowbar in the other. Extending his arms, he offered them to me, and I stared at my choice. "What are we going to do?" I asked, trying not to sound rattled.

He pumped his hands and looked toward the warehouse, where I could see a second-story window with the light on. We were being watched and had to move quickly. I closed my fingers around the cool shaft of the crowbar and felt its flaky metal.

Grunt left the rear doors open and strolled away from the

van, along the other vehicles in the parking lot. We passed a souped-up Camaro with huge back wheels, a pickup truck, and a Jeep. Next to them, though, closest to the door and just beneath that lit window, was a hot little Miata. It was red, immaculately clean in the mix of moonlight and shine from the industrial lamps above the lot. With one hand, Grunt brought the sledge up and drove it down onto the center of the hood, crunching it like the lid of a cardboard box. Adjusting his grip to both hands, he eyed up the windshield but I beat him to it, shattering the glass with the curved tip of the crowbar. This sort of mayhem felt familiar, even comfortable. Bright jewels exploded into the air, like water cascading from a fountain. We moved along either side, taking out the windows and then the taillights, and it felt as if we'd rehearsed all this elegant devastation. Grunt and I acted in concert, mirror images of destruction.

The warehouse door opened and we turned together. A figure was silhouetted by the light from inside, but whoever it was didn't take a step in our direction. Grunt's hand had slid inside his jacket. After a tense few moments, the door closed and we got back in our van, drove away.

My blood was pumping from the thrill of what we'd done. I didn't know if that dude deserved to have his car trashed and I didn't care. His problem, not mine. There's something about just unloading, letting it all rip, that nothing can compare to. That's always been the satisfaction of wrestling for me. You don't have to hold back. All the anger that nobody wants to see can come out, and suddenly you're rewarded for channeling all the dark ugliness inside. There's no rush like it. I wanted to celebrate with Grunt, at least talk about what had happened, but he was as silent as ever.

After the warehouse, I thought for sure we were finished, but it turned out we had two more stops. The first was in Dillsburg. We pulled into a strip mall that housed a barbershop, a bagel joint, and a place called "Battery Galaxy!!" that somehow stayed open. How many nine volts and double Ds do people need to buy?

Grunt rolled past the empty anchor store, which had a big "Will Remodel for New Lease" banner across the front. He drove around back and parked by a huge loading door. On the radio, a former NASA specialist talked about the possibility of life on Mars. Grunt glanced starward and changed to some music.

Sitting there with the radio on, I thought again of those rock 'n' roll marathon drives with my mom, crisscrossing the network of Harrisburg highways when I was a boy. Looking back, I doubted some of those hazy recollections. Were there really nights she tossed a suitcase in the trunk? Did she really slow down at unfamiliar exits, activating the turn signal then racing on without taking the ramp? Maybe she was flirting with an escape from my dad. I can't be sure. The mom of my memory was as unreadable to me in the back seat of that Subaru as Grunt was next to me in his van. Who knows what the heck was going on in the depths of his squared skull? Nothing seemed to bother him.

Take for example the police cruiser that appeared at the other end of the alley behind that strip mall. It slowed as it neared us. We both had guns and Grunt had a bag stuffed with cash we couldn't account for legally. But Grunt just stared at the cop over the dashboard as he parked fifteen feet away. "Let's bolt!" I said under my breath. "Go! Go! Go!"

Grunt didn't move, so when the cop got out and strode in our direction, I opened my door, ready to make a break for it. But Grunt's right hand latched down hard on my left thigh, locking me in place. He lowered his window, making it easy for the cop, who aimed a flashlight inside the van. It landed on me and stayed there for a few long breaths, long enough for me to assume he'd recognized my face from some APB. The ball of illumination swung to Grunt, and the cop said, "License and registration."

Grunt reached into the bag, which was resting on the floor between our seats. He selected one envelope, counted its contents, then pulled a few bills from another and added them to the first. This he handed to the cop, who took it with a grin and used the envelope to give a little half salute. "Tell Mr. Sunday we all appreciate the steady tithing."

He disappeared from the window and walked around the rear of the van, pacing slow as if he were inspecting it for clues. When he came to my side, the door was still cracked open, and he swung it wide. "And who the hell are you now?" he asked.

I looked at Grunt, who stared my way impassively. The cop said, "Don't worry, boy, I'm not out to make trouble. I just like to know who I'm doing business with." Up close, and without the light in my eyes, I could see the cop was on the far side of middle age. He was pudgy and had a mustache in bad need of a trim. Taking my cue from Grunt, I said nothing.

"Don't tell me Sunday's gone and hired himself another damn mute! What's your name?"

I couldn't tell if he didn't recognize me or was testing me, seeing what I'd say. But he wouldn't quit eyeing me up, so finally I turned, got into my role as fully as I could, and told him, "Call me Wild Child."

He laughed. "One of those," he said. "Shoulda figured." With that, he walked back to his car and drove off. I wondered just how far Sunday's circle of friends extended.

By our final stop, it must've been nearing 3 a.m. After sending a quick text, Grunt followed tree-lined side streets from that strip mall, through suburban neighborhoods. We passed a school and a playground, lots of picket fences and minivans, the promised land of book clubs and low interest second mortgages. My eyes lingered on one house with a For Sale sign out front.

Finally Grunt pulled into the driveway of a nice looking Colonial. It seemed a lot like every other middle-class house on the street, hard to even distinguish one from the next. All the windows were dark.

Grunt killed the engine, and a row of stepping stones in the lawn led us to the front door. A ceramic leprechaun grinned at us from under a hedge. All around us there was only quiet. Grunt thumbed the doorbell and the chime echoed really loud. He waited just a few seconds and then banged his fist into the door, and now a light flashed on inside. The door swung open to reveal a sleepy-eyed guy in his thirties. He was wearing a Penn State T-shirt and zipping up a pair of jeans. He stopped when his eyes found Grunt's face, and he'd barely gotten out,

"You!" when Grunt pushed in the door and stepped inside. I followed.

"Come on now," the guy said. "This is my home. This is where I live." All the while, he was backing up and Grunt was advancing. I stayed in his shadow.

The guy retreated to the bottom of a blue-carpeted staircase and bumped into the banister. His face was white and sweat dotted his forehead. "I explained this to Mr. Sunday. I explained!" he said. His voice trembled and his eyes, hopeless with dread, reminded me of Leonard from the boxcar.

At the head of the stairs, a woman appeared in a white nightgown. She held a phone in one hand, and as she came down the steps, she said, "Get the hell out of here, whoever you are."

The man said, "Melissa, no! Put that down."

She paused, midway down the flight, and Grunt jabbed a thick finger at me and then at her. I understood. A couple quick strides brought me to her, and I snatched the phone away. I smashed it into the wall, and only after it burst into a thousand plastic pieces did I ask myself why. It simply seemed the thing to do, the next action in the script I'd somehow committed to.

The wife went to run upstairs, but she only made it up a few steps before I snagged her one wrist. She twisted and tugged, and I thought of my mom on the hill outside Perkins. "Quit struggling," I snapped quietly. "I don't want to hurt you." This was totally true. Yet something in my tone when those words came out, something whispering even in the back of my head, promised to us both, *but I will if I have to.*

The wife, sufficiently freaked out, stopped squirming and asked, "Marty, what the hell's going on?"

Marty held both hands up, then rubbed one through his hair. "I can handle this. Please."

I couldn't be sure if he was pleading with Melissa, Grunt, or both.

Grunt pulled a slip of paper from his pocket and gave it to Marty, who read it and said, "He can't be serious. There's no way I can make this happen. It would mean —"

The slap came swift and fast, Grunt's open hand snapping Marty's face sideways. He looked shocked and his wife screamed his name, but Grunt did it again anyway. I thought it was especially insulting, to be slapped instead of punched. But if Grunt unloaded on a guy like Marty, there would be permanent damage. Marty hunched and held a hand to his cheek. "Beat me all you want," he said. "I can't make money appear from thin air."

After a quick scan of the foyer, Grunt took hold of one of the wooden spindles of the banister. He snapped it free and held it in both hands, a yardstick-long rod of carved curves. With a backhand swat, he drove a hole in the drywall above Marty's head, and now Melissa said, "Oh God." Something in her tone turned my head, and I followed her eyes to the second floor.

There, out on the landing, looking through the railing, stood a girl in footy pajamas. Her feet poked through the spindles, toes over the edge. She gripped an upside-down stuffed animal by a leg and said, "My throat is still scratchy."

Her mother tried to pull away from me, stretching her arm and leaning up the stairs, but I anchored her. And then Grunt was plodding our way, boot by boot, eyes on the child. The mom screamed and blocked his path and there was a second when I could've gotten in his way, but I didn't. I let him pass me and he latched a huge paw on the mom's face and shoved her down, hard, so hard her head banged on a step with a sickening crack.

"Mom?" the little girl asked, and the woman began crawling up the steps after Grunt, still gripping the splintered wood.

I froze.

The husband cried out, "Okay! Okay! Tell Sunday it's a deal. I'll find a way. I have no freakin' idea how, but I'll find a way damn it."

Grunt smiled. He stepped over Melissa and deposited the broken banister spindle in a tall bucket that held umbrellas just inside the door. Then he looked at me and tipped his head toward the exit. I started down the steps. The little girl bumped past me, joining her father on the ground by Melissa, who had begun to sob.

Again I felt the urge to apologize, but doing so would've opened up something inside me I knew I couldn't touch, not with who I had to be then. So when I spoke, it was with a voice I didn't recognize. "This is all your daddy's fault," I said. The little girl looked up at me, and I told her, "He needs to take care of things better."

Grunt opened the door and I walked out into the cooler night air. We drove away from the family, and Grunt turned off the radio. It was clear that we were finished for the evening and heading back, and I was grateful we were done. So we rode in silence, back to the highway and then down toward Camp Hill.

All the while I couldn't stop thinking about that little girl, how lodged now in her brain was a memory of two scary men who invaded her home while she was sleeping and attacked her parents. She'd never get back to sleep that night. She'd lie in bed between her parents, clinging to that stuffed animal, and wonder who the men were, why they came, and if they'd come back. Decades from now, maybe the memory would fade, or perhaps she'd categorize it as a nightmare. But for now, that child knew something more about grim reality, and I'd helped introduce her to it. And what would've happened, I wondered, if Grunt had signaled me to climb those stairs? What if he'd sent me after the girl? Sunday's line came to me, the one about wolves and sheep.

"Pull over," I told Grunt just as we approached the exit ramp for Camp Hill. "Now."

Maybe something in my voice told him what was up, because he did what I asked. The van came to rest just before the overpass, and I lurched out onto the shoulder. I made it to a patch of weeds, just in time to double over, grip my thighs, and retch. My gut clenched and I threw up again, hard enough that I dropped to one knee. A truck roared by overhead, thundering, and my vision swam. A last spasm emptied my stomach and then I just stayed there, trying to gather myself. When I finally rose to return to the van, I nearly passed out, but soon enough my steps grew steady. At the open door, I leaned into the roof, but I didn't want to get back in. "Go on," I told Grunt. "I'm going to walk. The fresh air will do me good."

It was miles, though Grunt clearly didn't care. He shrugged

and tapped his own belt, and I pulled the gun from my waist, returned it to the glove box. I asked him, "Will you need to tell Mr. Sunday about this, or can we keep it between us?"

Grunt's impassive face gave me no answer, and I wondered when I would learn to stop trying to communicate with him. I leaned back and slammed the door. He merged into traffic and drove off.

On foot, I followed the swoop of the exit ramp, walking along the solid white line. In the darkness, I couldn't make out the roadway beneath it, and it felt as if I were balancing on a thin beam, treading over a bottomless black chasm. I found myself trying to remember some poet's line from DJ's class, something about gazing into the abyss. Another line came to me too, from some British guy, about how when we wear a mask, sometimes our face grows to fit it.

―――

For a long stretch my legs carried me through Camp Hill, and I didn't care that I had no destination. In fact, wandering felt just right. Up on the bypass, I drifted past the Panera where Mom always got me smoothies after a trip to the dentist when I was a kid. Without pausing to pray, I crossed the moon shadow cast by the steeples of St. Sebastian's, where Mom had surely been praying for me for weeks. Block to block, I zigzagged through the sleepy neighborhoods. I went by that fancy house for sale, where we'd pretended for the last time. At the high school it's true, I wished it were open. Not so much so I could hit the weights, just so I could walk the halls again, go back to my locker, get jostled in the rush of students in the hallway. I wanted to bitch with Shrimp about the horrible cafeteria food, debate LeQuan about music, worry about the atomic number of palladium. Having lost the life I had, I didn't find it quite so miserable. Maybe that's called nostalgia.

And I guess it was this sense that drew me to the yellow house on Seventeenth Street. I had to lean into the steeply slanted hill it's near the top of, but this reminded me of the sloping yard behind it, perfect for a young boy's sledding adventures. When I stood in front of the house, I saw that not much had changed. The front porch still had a swing, the azaleas were even more overgrown. The new owners had the fractured sidewalk fixed, so my old bike ramp had been flattened out.

Just like at the high school, I felt the impulse to go inside. I wanted to walk into the basement, with its dehumidifier rumbling and musty smell and table full of Legos. I wanted to climb into my old bed and set my cheek on my mom's chest, feel her heart beat as she read to me about Narnia or Hogwarts. And when I didn't know a word, I wanted her to reach for the dog-eared paperback dictionary. I wanted to feel the cool linoleum floor in the kitchen pulse with bass as my mom paused from cleaning dishes to crank the classic rock station and spin me around in an impromptu dance party. I wanted to be alone with my father in the garage, my chin barely reaching the workbench, and have him hand me each tool, listen to him explain the difference between socket wrench and needle-nose pliers. "You can't do a job right with the wrong tool," he told me, and I remembered thinking, I will never forget this simple moment.

As I climbed the wooden stairs, even the creaks felt familiar and perfect. It was like I was walking back in time. And the screen door's whiny protest told me no one had WD-40ed the hinges in forever. I gripped the smooth doorknob and took the deepest of breaths. What exactly was I doing? I didn't know. But I found myself in the grasp of the strangest of fantasies. Because what I imagined then was that I would open the door and stride not just into my old home, but into the past itself. I would walk into the living room, where the Civil War documentary would be playing on the TV and my father's beer would be on the coffee table. He would be in his armchair and my mom and me on the couch. She would have already asked what year the war began and if Lincoln really wrote the Gettysburg Address on the back of an envelope, not noticing his rising irritation. When she asks the third question, something about why all the generals had such long beards, the boy I was will have his first prophetic vision. He will know with certainty that his father is about to upturn the coffee table, that our mom will flee from his rage, down the hallway, hoping to lock the bedroom door behind her. The boy will see that she will be too slow.

And he'll be powerless to stop it. Everything will happen just as he foresaw, and the screams will be horrible.

As it happened that fateful evening, he'll try to help. But tonight, he won't be alone. Because as my fourth-grade self, gangly and awkward, charges down that slim corridor, I'll be at his side. Together we'll barge into their bedroom and see the dresser mirror already smashed, the nightstand toppled. The boy

I was will jump onto the bed, and from there he'll see what's on the other side, our father's hulking shape on top of our mom. Her face is already half covered in blood, and she's wailing and contorting, but our father's one hand has a hold of her hair, pinning her to the ground, and his other is shaped into a fist, and he's raising it up and bringing it down, deaf to the cries of his wife and son.

I know from memory, from the hundreds of times this scene visited me in my nightmares, that the boy is about to leap onto his father's back. I know he'll wrap his skinny arms around his father's thick neck, try in mighty desperation to pull him off his mom. And I know that when the father rears back like a bucking bronco, he'll toss the boy across the room, that he'll crash in a heap in the corner near the upturned nightstand. When his father faces him, with his eyes wild and his teeth bared, Mac will see him as part man, part beast.

Rather than trying again to stop this creature, he'll run and hide in his boyhood closet. Plenty of times he's seen his father lose his temper before, and more than once his mom's had black-and-blue marks she explained away as falling down the stairs or being clumsy. Little by little as he got older, the boy had learned. At six, he'd seen him slap her hard in the garage. At eight, coming back from a Christmas party, the boy had sat in the back seat cowering as his father pulled the car over and banged her head into the window. So by ten, he knew the truth behind his mom's bruises — and he'd faced his wrath himself. There were plenty of nights he could feel things escalating, and he'd try to defuse the bomb by acting goofy or even draw fire to himself by acting bad. Sometimes it worked. But many times he'd wake from sleep to sounds straight from the land of nightmares. His head board was up against the wall to their room, so he'd leave behind the warm blankets, drag his pillow to the darkness of his closet, crouch amidst his snow boots and old stuffed animals and try to pray. The darkness stank of mothballs.

So now, he'll rise from the corner with the overturned nightstand, and he'll flee. In the mothball dark of the closet, he'll hear his mother crying out for her husband to stop, crying out for help, and the boy won't run to the kitchen phone and punch three simple digits. Instead he'll quiver and feel that shameful release, the warm wetness soaking his pants.

Some random neighbor will do what he couldn't, and that call will summon sirens and Officer Harrow and an ambulance and everything will change forever, but the boy will never escape the truth. The truth that he is a coward.

In my fantasy though, the dreadful script is revised. I fix history. The boy never leaps from the bed. I am there, and I set a hand on his frail chest to steady him, and I nod to let him know I'll take care of everything. I say, "Don't worry. I got this."

I grab the overturned nightstand with two hands, heft it over my head and crash it down on the back of my father's skull. He collapses on my bleeding mom, and when I roll his body off her, he is groggy and helpless. And I can feel it now, the power I never had then, swelling in my blood and filling me with a calming rage I can't describe. She is safe now and he can't defend himself, but I know I am not done. The act is not yet complete. There must be something else. I don't care if Khajee calls it revenge or retribution or violence. But I will punish this man, and he will know it is me. I'm trying to decide the exact nature of his pain when a sleepy female voice from the other side of the yellow house's front door says, "Who are you? What do you want?"

I released the doorknob and stepped back on the porch, shocked to be in the present.

The tired woman asked me more questions, threatened the police, but I was already retreating, down the steps and down the hill. The foolishness of my fantasy made me feel silly. It's the dream of that ten-year old boy, paralyzed with fear of his father's wrath.

That night, huddled in the bitter stink of my own soaked clothes, I vowed to myself to become stronger, strong enough so no one could hurt me or threaten my mom. We would be safe and I would be her hero. My plan was to fix everything. That's what was supposed to happen. But instead, I found myself now running away from the yellow house and my past, with no clear idea of where the hell I was supposed to be going.

14

*T*wo nights after my shift with Grunt and my return to the yellow house on Seventeenth Street, Blalock drove me and Khajee down into New Cumberland. It's a sleepy town on the banks of the Susquehanna, not far from Three Mile Island. For a long time, when people moved into the surrounding area, they were given potassium iodide capsules to take in the event of a nuclear accident, something to minimize radiation poisoning. That quick fix always seemed strange to me, a false comfort. Disaster strikes? Take a pill. Then everything will be all right.

I'd told Khajee she didn't have to come to the fight with Santana, that I could handle myself. But after four days in the hospital, Than wasn't showing any change, and according to Khajee, he'd have wanted her to be there. "Besides," she told me, "I could use a good distraction." Dr. Ngoyo had suggested that sometime soon, they might be looking to transfer him to a hospice. I thought this was a good sign, and said, "That's great," but then Khajee explained to me what I guess they explained to her, that hospice care is meant to ease your suffering. No one expects you to leave there alive.

Blalock steered along the quiet main street, where most of the shops were closed at this late hour. We passed an old theater that somebody had converted into a movie house. Out front, on the marquee where there should have been a title, red letters spelled out "For Sale. Great Potential." To my surprise, we cut down the next alley and parked in the back, amidst a dozen expensive cars that by now were familiar. At the rear entrance, I greeted Grunt with a raised hand and he actually opened the door. If this was a sign of some respect or a sort of mocking gesture, I couldn't tell.

Before leading us backstage, Blalock offered me a series of clichés, the kind of thing only guys who never fought would say like "Don't forget how much effort you've put forth, how hard you've worked for this," and "Give it your all." Once he was gone, I said to Khajee, "I'm so glad he said that. Otherwise, I might not have tried." When she laughed, I realized it had been a while since I'd heard that sweet sound.

The first match was between an unknown guy from Virginia and a jiujitsu artist Khajee had seen around. They were warming up on two-thirds of a mat rolled across the stage, where I suppose at some point people put on plays. Out in the audience, the crowd settled into their seats. Khajee and I were watching from offstage, behind these huge musty curtains. Across the way, on the far side of the mat, I saw Santana and Badder side by side. They were looking at me, and Badder made one of his warrior faces. I hooked my fingers inside my cheeks and puffed them out like a kid, stuck out my tongue and waggled it. Badder scowled and started forward, but Santana held him back. Again, Khajee laughed. "Come on," she said. "They'll start soon. You should change."

"But I'm perfect just the way I am."

My third-grade joke fell flat, maybe because we both knew how far it was from the truth.

We bumped around backstage, past a paper-mache space-ship, an enormous plywood rainbow, and some old-style garbage cans painted blue. Behind a grand piano covered in dust, we found a quiet corner, and I slipped off my sweatpants, exposing the gym shorts I was wearing beneath. I tugged my shirt over my head and began to stretch. The air was chilly.

"How you feel?" Khajee asked me.

"A little tight," I said. "But ready."

"Good," she said. "Cause I'll tell you this about Santana. He's a damn dirty fighter. You've got to keep an eye on him."

"Dirty how?" I asked.

She told me about a time, a few months back, when she'd seen him bend a guy's fingers until they broke. Also, she warned me that if he was riding on top and could sneak a hand around to the chest, he might jab a finger into the nerve cluster just inside the rib cage. "As for his fingernails," she said. "He keeps them sharp like that so he can scratch you or gouge your eyes."

"Nasty," I said.

"Nasty and quick," Khajee said. "Santana's even faster than Dominic. So listen. No games with this guy. Any way you can, get him down. Don't stand toe-to-toe with him, don't lock up. Stick and move, glide away."

"I don't glide so good, Boss."

"Just stay out of his range until he gets frustrated, tries a spinning back fist or something fancy. Then shoot in, take out his legs, and bring him to the mat. That's where you'll have the advantage. Ground and pound."

I twisted and felt my spine crackle. In the back of my head, I wondered if Khajee knew how Santana earned those scars crisscrossing his face, but it seemed an odd thing to ask. "When are you going to let me box?"

Khajee rolled her eyes. "When you face a wrestler. If you find yourself up against Badder, box all you want."

I swung my arms in great loops, cracking my shoulders loose. Khajee trailed a finger along the dusty top of the piano. "That was Marco's problem," she said quietly, her voice little more than a hush. "He didn't know the kind of fighter he was."

I'd never heard this name before, and I gave it some thought before speaking. "Marco was Blalock's last fighter," I guessed.

Her finger came to a dead stop and she nodded once, heavy. "You trained him like me?"

"Pretty much."

"And he stayed with you and your uncle."

"He did. Same couch and everything. You get exactly one more question."

This whole time, Khajee avoided eye contact. I wasn't sure of the source of tension in the air, but I decided to take a stab at it. "You and this Marco guy, you were kind of . . . special friends?"

Khajee's eyes flashed to mine, and her face looked incredulous. "Like I was his girlfriend or something?" She was smiling coyly. "I'll tell you, Mac, you're not so good at reading people, are you?"

"What?" I asked. "What am I missing?"

She shrugged and told me, "I don't like boys like that. Do you understand?"

The truth dawned on me. "Oh," I said. "Oh. Oh. Sure, right. Great. Yeah, I wasn't up to speed on that. Sorry and all."

"It's all right," she said. "Not like lesbians all wear a big sign or anything."

I chuckled uncomfortably, not because it was funny but because it felt like I was trespassing suddenly. "Course not. So like, are you seeing anybody right now?"

She grinned a funny grin. "Nah. I broke a girl's heart last summer. Or she broke mine. I guess both."

She was quiet then, and I turned to the wall and started doing a little shadow boxing, in part to move us back to safer ground. But Khajee didn't seem to feel awkward. She set a hand on my bare shoulder, causing me to pause. "I'm glad you know," she told me.

"Me too," I said, not sure how else to respond.

"You didn't get mixed up with Sunday's side work because you . . . thought there was something between us, did you? A couple times lately, you seemed —"

"No way," I said, facing her as I fudged the truth a bit. "You're my boss," I said. "My coach and my friend. I'm glad to help."

She seemed relieved by this, for a moment. Then she bit her lip and said, "But you shouldn't keep doing this. Sunday is dangerous. He's worse than crooked. He's malevolent."

I thought about this, then said, "Your SAT vocabulary's impressive, but I think I'm pretty clear on who I'm dealing with."

"I'm not kidding around," she protested.

"Me neither," I said. "And I'm not just doing it for you." Long term, I still hoped for a payday to change Mom's life, but for now, Than came to mind, the way he'd just taken me in without asking any questions, accepted me into his home. The guy fed me and sat with me for hours trying to share what he knew about fighting. "I haven't known him long, but Than treated me good. Like a father really. I owe him."

I fell quiet and felt heat rise across my neck.

Khajee said, "When you talk about your dad, you seem so angry."

"I am angry," I snapped. "Want to know something I never told anybody before? Sometimes during a match, when I'm pounding somebody good, I imagine it's my old man. Some of those kids I hurt on purpose — not to get points, just to inflict pain — it was my father I was thinking about."

Khajee considered this, didn't take her eyes off me. "You realize how messed up that is, right?"

"Why do you think I haven't told anybody?" Ms. Flintock, our school counselor, would crap herself with joy at details like this.

Khajee stepped closer, took my hand in both of hers. "I was mad at my father. My mother too. I was mad at them for leaving me alone, for dying."

I turned to her.

"I know," she said. "It doesn't make sense. But I was a kid. For all his faults, Than helped me let go of that. You've got to let go too, Mac."

Sunday's voice came booming from the stage area, and soon

the gong sounded with the now familiar opening. The first match was about to begin. I pulled my hand away and said, "We should get going."

"Okay," Khajee said, and we headed that way. We joined a small huddle of folks off to the side, right where we'd been before. Khajee fitted my gloves on and I slid off my sneakers, just so I was ready to go. Across the way, Santana and Badder hadn't moved. Next to Khajee, some senior citizen in a Hawaiian shirt was applying tape to a kid's shoulder. The kid had sideburns and a somber face. I took him to be Badder's opponent. Khajee and I found a good spot to watch the opener from just behind a tripod camera. Since we were around people now, I realized I couldn't ask a question that had cropped up in my mind. Where was Marco now?

The first match went long, like fifteen minutes. The two guys locked up and spent a lot of time trying foot sweeps as set-ups, basically kicking each other in the ankles and shins. They'd break, box a bit, then lock up again and go back to it. A handful of rowdy fans in the balcony began to boo, and finally, out of desperation, the shorter brawler tried a hip toss that failed miserably. The thing about wrestling is that every offensive move, if done poorly, exposes you in some way. In this case, after the kid missed his throw he basically dropped facedown, with his opponent riding him to the mat. After a lame attempt at a choke, the brawler on top turned and went to work on one of his legs. He folded it up, heel to butt, then wrapped it inside a double arm lock and cranked the leg back into his spine. It looked like he'd snap him in half. The kid on bottom howled and slammed the mat with both hands, signaling his submission. The fans suddenly were in love again. They applauded and cheered and cried out for more. In this case, more meant me and Santana.

After the mat was cleared, Sunday didn't waste much time getting out there into the spotlight. He worked the crowd a bit, then swept a hand toward stage right, where Santana was waiting in the wings. He bellowed, "Bow your heads and put your hands together to welcome . . . The Saint!" Not one to miss his cue, Santana tore onto the stage executing his favorite kata, more choreography than fighting, but still, he was impressive. From his performances at the gym, I recalled the routine's moves — the opening punch, the elbow strike, the leg sweep and front flip, all with the same battle cries. Maybe he thought he'd intimidate me, and Lord knows the audience ate that crap up, but I wished I had a scorecard from *Dancing with the Stars* so I could hold up a 6 and frown.

Khajee slipped in my mouth guard, retightened the Velcro straps on my gloves. Sunday waved an arm in my direction and yelled, "And fresh off the hottest debut in Brawlers' history . . . the unpredictable Wild Child!"

I had no fancy entrance prepared, and I considered doing a moonwalk just to mock Santana. But I figured Sunday might not like it, and besides, I'd never tried it in my bare feet. So I plodded toward center stage without fanfare.

At the mat's edge, Santana took a long draw from a blue water bottle, and I noticed he didn't wear a mouth guard. Maybe he figured he wouldn't get hit. Anyway, he joined me in the center, and accompanied by the gong, the audience cried out, "No mercy! Prepare! Brawl!"

Instead of a full-out assault though, Santana greeted me with a gesture I recognized. He held one hand flat like he was praying and set his other hand, locked in a fist, into that palm. Like this, he bowed at me deeply, showing respect. Caught off guard and not thinking, I echoed his movement. For this courtesy, I was rewarded with a whipping front kick right to my face, and I snapped back just in time to miss a follow-up spinning back fist, which slid within inches of my chin. Santana took an angular fighting stance and raised his eyebrows. Game on, I thought.

He orbited me, arms constantly windmilling, staying out of range. Every time I advanced, he retreated. I tried stepping side to side to cut off the mat, but he was too quick, and he just slid away. This went on long enough that the rowdy balcony bunch began to complain. Antsy from the previous bout's absence of action, they wanted us to mix it up.

But Santana reacted in a way that shocked me. He stopped moving, stood totally still, and waved me in. This was a trick, I thought, but he adopted a standard wrestling pose and came slowly forward, arms extended and hands out. Cautiously I slid into the lock up, each of us dipping forward. Our heads rested on the other guy's shoulder, one hand gripping a neck, the other cupped to a tricep. We tugged each other and I began to probe for my opening, which I could feel would come quick from this familiar position. Santana shoved his cheekbone into mine, nothing more than irritating but enough of a distraction that

I shoved back. We were crouched low, eye to eye and nose to nose. He lifted his chin, pursed his lips, and I had the absurd thought that he was about to kiss me. One of my prophetic flashes rushed over me but made no sense, because all I saw was pitch black. How could the future be only darkness?

The next instant, something splashed across my eyes. A stinging burn forced me to wince, and I took a knee. I blinked back the tears and looked up, but my vision was engulfed in a sightless sea. Instinctively, I tapped my hands together in a "T" shape, signaling the ref that I needed an injury timeout, but all that came from the black void around me was a chuckle. Santana said, "You forget where you are? This is Brawlers, and there's nobody here to save you."

The first shot was a foot or a fist smashing my cheek with enough force that I dropped to all fours. In the next instant, something sharp and hard — an elbow? a knee? — ignited my ribs, and I rolled sideways. On my back, I tucked into my guard position, but I kind of played possum a bit, acting more hurt than I really was. I even moaned. I was hoping to lure him into attacking me on the mat. If he came down here, tried to get an arm bar or something, I could get hold of him. And once I had a good grip, even in the dark, I had no intention of letting go.

But Santana didn't press his advantage. Instead of grappling on the ground, he circled me, swinging a foot into my arm, my thigh. All I felt were the impacts, and I just did my best to protect my head. This whole time, my vision didn't clear at all, and I wondered what the hell he spit at me — lemon juice? Whatever it was, my world was nothing but darkness. In that blackness, I could sense the fear taking shape. It was right on the edge of the dark, eager to swarm in, consume me as it had my boyhood self. Knowing it was all in my head didn't make it easier to keep it at bay.

Another blow to my head brought me back to reality. Somehow, maybe because I wasn't tracking Santana's movements as he took his cheap shots, the fans caught on to my predicament. Somebody yelled, "Hey! Wild Child can't see!"

This brought a mixed reaction from the audience. There were scattered applause and a few whoops, I guess of excitement, but there were more than a handful of serious boos. Santana was losing the crowd. He stopped kicking at me, and I thought maybe there'd be an official break in the action. But then I remembered what Khajee had told me. Once a brawl began, it only stopped when one fighter submitted or was unable to continue. It occurred to me that in my state I might be disqualified, so I rolled my arms toward my chest and yelled, "Come on! Come get some!" just to let them know I still had fight in me. The crowd responded with a surge of clapping, and somebody called out, "Saint sucks! Can't finish off a blind man?"

"Keeya!!!" cut through the crowd's banter, and things got quiet. I realized that, angered by the crowd, Santana had decided to go for a kill stroke. He was going to focus his chi by executing his kata and finish me off. I was in the dark, helpless, and sure that childish dread wanted to flood my world with terror. My heartbeat sharpened. But also, on the fringe of that abyss, I thought of something Than told me — that sometimes you see things better in the dark. With this thought, I relaxed, focused, and a new future took shape.

I could hear Santana's feet stomping the mat, then his screams of "Hu! Hu! Hu!" In my mind's eye, I pictured him doing his kata, now retreating after the front kick and elbow blows. Moments later, I heard the silence that meant the foot sweep, and sure enough something cracked into my head, a worthwhile substitute I guess. Dazed and groggy, I managed to get to all fours, and I knew the finale that was coming — that front flip into a downward stomping kick. And I tried to gather myself, thinking if I timed it right I might explode upward, arms extended, and catch him in midair. But in that split second, the darkness surged, and doubt dragged me down, dragged me back — into the mothball closet, huddled in the corner listening to my mom cry out for help while I did nothing. While I did *nothing*.

Santana's blow landed like the judgment of a just and angry God, and my head nearly came off. I collapsed, curled up on my knees with my forehead on the mat, and he began pounding my back and ribs — with elbows or knees I couldn't tell, but it felt like my organs were being grinded. Somehow these blows mirrored the beating I imagined my mom took while I hid in safety.

I tried to calm myself and clear my mind, tried to think of Than and just breathe, but I couldn't stop the images, couldn't help but hear her wailing, and the pain of this was more than I could bear, worse by far than any beating. Right there on the mat, I began to weep, and I covered my face to hide that shame.

Maybe I thought about giving up, it's true. Maybe I deserved to be hurt, and this punishment was my penance. But something else happened because of those tears. My vision came back to me. It was blurry, sure, but as I blinked I realized I was looking at a fuzzy Khajee, just off stage kneeling down, yelling, "Mac! You've got to get up! Get up!" Yet with the darkness dispelled, I was back in control and my mind had cleared, so I knew her advice was wrong.

Instead, I slumped down, flattened out, and even extended my right arm as bait. Santana saw his chance and halted his assault. Faced with a defeated opponent, I knew he'd gloat, and sure enough he stood over me, considering his next move, which I'd already planned for him. He couldn't resist the arm bar, and when he leaned down and reached in, I was ready. I sprang to life and spun, snatching his hand and yanking him down. As he fell, I drove an elbow up to meet him, and it caught his jaw flush. It didn't suck to hear that popping sound.

We traded places as his body collapsed to the mat and I rose to my feet, never releasing his arm. Lazily, he kicked up at me, and I decided to upgrade. I let go of his hand and snagged an ankle, tight in my grasp.

Santana flopped around like a fish on the rocks, desperate to get back to the creek. I worked my way down that leg and once I saw my opening, I dropped heavy and hard on his back. He let loose a "whumpf!" and I wrapped a thick arm around his waist. I had him now.

He reverse–head butted me, which stung my nose good but also got me focused. I needed to quit screwing around. Time for ground and pound.

With my left forearm, I pinned his neck to the mat, and with my right fist, I began to hammer on the back of his head. When he tucked his arm up to deflect my blows, I snuck in a few punches to his temple and cheekbone, nailing his ear a couple times too for good measure. At least, that's what it felt like. My eyes were streaming tears, but my vision wasn't totally clear.

Now that I'd taken the fight out of Santana, I shifted my chest so it rested on his head and dug my right arm under his neck, all the way through to the other side, so my radius pressed into the artery that runs under the ear. People think you choke somebody by squeezing their throat, and while that might hurt like hell, the throat's for eating. You want somebody to go lights out, you need to cut off the blood supply to their brain. So with my right forearm in place, I scooped that fist with my left hand and began to tug. You don't need to do it all at once. It can be slow, gradual, like an anaconda squeezing its prey. Patience is key with a chokehold, Khajee had helped me understand. And so I was patient.

Beneath me Santana bucked and fought. Following a standard defense, he tried getting purchase on my elbow to tug it off his neck, just release a little pressure, but my choke was set deep, and he knew he couldn't last more than thirty seconds. In desperation he rocked back and forth, and I rolled with him, tumbling us sideways. From my back, with him splayed out on my belly, I actually had even better leverage, and now I could really apply pressure. I also hooked both his legs with mine, secured him tight. I was in total control.

Me and Shrimp used to mess around before practice with

chokeholds, arm bars, other things we'd seen on MMA. Coach Gallaher had some judo training and showed us a few techniques after practice, just monkeying around with moves he warned us never to use in a real match. Mostly he used to always demonstrate on me, because I was the toughest SOB in the room. In my stubbornness, I refused to tap one time when he had me in a rear naked choke. It's a crazy feeling, having your brain shut down like that. The edges of your vision go dark first, and then you have a tunnel you can see through. All the sounds of the world go quiet, and you can only hear your heart. Then the tunnel begins to narrow until there's just a pinpoint of light, and when it goes out, you're gone. The party's over.

I could tell Santana was close. He'd stopped flailing and I expected at any second to feel his tap out. I was surprised when he twitched with a last surge of energy, made one last grab at my elbow with both his hands. He didn't really weaken the choke, but he did manage to make enough space so he could turn his head, tuck his chin down into the crook of my right elbow. I was impressed but hardly concerned. I just had to work the radius back to position, return pressure to that vein, and finish him off.

Santana had other plans.

He sank his teeth into the fleshiest part of my forearm. I heard myself scream and head butted him from behind, tugged even tighter on the chokehold. But because I wasn't on the right part of his neck anymore, it didn't have the effect I was looking for. He didn't let up. Indeed, I could tell my yell had given him some hope, and he ground his teeth hard on my muscle. Because of how we were positioned, the crowd could see what he was doing. I shouldn't have been surprised when this schoolyard tactic was met with thunderous applause.

It took every bit of willpower I could muster to not release my grip. Above us, the stage lights were clear now, and I could see the hazy shape of his head, my bicep. Was that blood trickling down it? I couldn't be sure.

Just offstage, I could hear Badder hollering, "That's the way! Chew your way to the bone!"

The pain was rising, like a white-hot knife. And damn I needed to wipe the cleansing tears flooding my eyes. But they were clearing out whatever crap Santana had spit. I flung my head around, found the outlines of the group watching from the other side of the stage. There, in the front, the small shape that could only be Khajee. I spit my mouth guard clear and yelled, "Son of a bitch is biting me!"

Khajee's voice was calm and quiet, yet it pierced the crowd and reached me with crystal clarity. "Bite him back."

I blinked away the tears, rubbed my eyes into my shoulder the best I could without losing the grip, and tried to focus my vision. Though it was still a bit hazy, I could see the side of Santana's head now — and there, right in front of my mouth like a prize — was his ear.

I snapped down hard and fast, taking in about half that curvy flesh. Like an animal, I chomped and I gnawed, and I could feel my top and bottom teeth nearly meeting. While holding Santana's head fast in the remnants of my choke, I yanked my face away, still gripping his ear. A chunk of it came with me, a meaty little oyster in my mouth. I turned toward the sound of the cheering crowd and spit it in their direction as tribute. They roared.

Santana let loose a sound I'd never heard before, something between a painful banshee wail and a defeated battle cry. His hands were slapping the mat, my arm, everything, but I held on to him for another few seconds, just to display his helplessness and be sure everyone watching was clear that he'd surrendered, that I, Wild Child, was in control.

When I did release him, he slumped away off the mat. I could see colors now but not faces. I rose and rubbed at my bicep, came away with a thick swab of blood from where he'd bitten me. With my other, I wiped my face and again found more blood, though this was my enemy's. I could taste it on my lips. I lifted my arms over my head, both palms bloody as if I'd been crucified, and I screamed to the cheering mob, "Who's next?! Who else you got for me, Sunday! Who? Who?"

I bathed in their applause, and I heard a few folks holler out "Badder! Badder!" One voice from the balcony cried, "Badder versus Wild Child!" I thumped my fists into my sweaty chest, whipping the congregation into a fury. And maybe I'd have stayed there longer, drinking in their adoration, but Khajee appeared at my side, touching one elbow gently. "Mac," she said, "let's take care of your eyes."

She led me backstage, and unknown hands slapped my shoulders in admiration. Unknown voices congratulated me. In a bathroom she had me bend into the sink and ran the faucet, splashed water over my face. It was cool and cleansing, and I dropped to my knees and cupped my hands, doused my eyes until I was no longer blinded. My vision fully restored, I looked up at Khajee and said, "So tell me again why you think he's a dirty fighter?"

She laughed and Blalock pushed in through the door. "Edward!" he said, hands raised. "Most impressive exhibition!" He swooped in as I rose and embraced me in an awkward hug. "This is an occasion for celebration! Santana was sixteen and three and your victory was decisive."

Khajee added, "Also kind of gross, you know?"

I told them both, "I didn't have many options." I considered making a *tasted like chicken* joke, but decided against it.

"Well the fans adore you. Badder's contest is about to commence. I'll secure an audience with Sunday. We need to have a constructive dialogue about how best to proceed."

"Just get our money," I said, and he left us.

After I slid back into my T-shirt, Khajee and I roamed through the labyrinth until we found the stage, where the main event was well under way. Badder and his opponent were trading playful jabs, bobbing and weaving, dropping head feints. We went out onto the floor with the crowd, standing off to the side. A few folks saw me and there was a bit of a commotion as those nearby applauded and chanted "Wild Child! Wild Child!"

"More like a brat!" came from the stage, and when I looked, Badder was staring our way. He was ticked that I'd distracted his audience, but he was the one who should've worried about distraction. His opponent executed a textbook front snap kick, planting all his weight on his left leg and extending his right, driving that foot into the side of Badder's turned head. It's the kind of blow that'll typically knock a guy out, maybe even cause a concussion. Badder took a half step back.

He turned away from me, stone-faced, and I saw his opponent's eyes go wide. Badder charged like a bull, wild and blind — something I took note of — and his opponent retreated, circling backward and to the side. When he stumbled, Badder collapsed on him, unleashing a flurry of elbows and hammer fists to his face. The guy was taking a beating, and taking it badly. This went on for a minute, and Badder only stopped because he was sucking wind. He spit into his opponent's bludgeoned face, raised a victorious fist, and contorted his expression at the crowd and me, tongue lolling, eyes crazed. I figured the match was over, but Badder had other ideas.

He bent down and hoisted up his opponent's limp body, cradling him like some gigantic sleeping baby. The guy must've gone 250, and dead weight is damn hard to lift, but Badder strode across the stage like he was carrying a bag of groceries. That old guy in the Hawaiian shirt, a trainer, a manager, ran out to block him, and Badder swung up a front kick that dropped him too. Once the path was clear, he made his way right to the edge of the stage, standing above me not five feet away. I pulled Khajee behind me but didn't retreat.

Without saying a word, Badder shifted his grip and pressed the other brawler's body up over his head. I'd seen muscle boys before, various impressive feats of strength, but this stunned me, nailed my feet to the ground. Badder's arms trembled at the strain, but he managed to take one huge step forward and heave his cargo in my direction.

The defeated brawler's body landed on my feet with a crash, and I tumbled into Khajee. As I scrambled to get up, Badder leapt down and drove into me. He slammed my back into a wall, and I banged my open palms together like cymbals on both his ears. That tends to get a guy's attention, and Badder was no exception. He staggered back, shaking his head and getting his bearings. All around us the crowd scattered. Even Khajee bolted for cover. Badder and I squared off, but then a huge shape stepped into the space between us, dark and blocky. It was Grunt, who crossed his arms and eyed us each in turn.

Above us on the edge of the stage, not far behind him, Mr. Sunday appeared, looming. "At ease, gents," he calmly ordered. Sunday waved one of the cameramen to get in position in front of him, and then he addressed the lens and the theater crowd simultaneously. "We've just witnessed some savage brawls, and I know you'd like to see these guys tear each other apart. Well, I'm a man of the people, and I'll give the people what they want!" This announcement was met with enthusiastic cheers, fists pumping the air. Sunday glanced at Badder, then me, grinning, before going on. "I'm hereby setting a championship match for three nights from now. Then we'll see who brawls supreme."

As the applause rose, he nodded at the cameraman, who lowered his lens. The crowd around us shuffled away, and Sunday descended the stage stairs. Grunt stepped out from between me and Badder, and Sunday took his place. He put one hand on my shoulder and the other on Badder, drawing us together. "You boys both made me proud tonight, and you'll be rewarded." Badder kept scowling at me, and I was ready for him to make a move. In a lower, nontheatrical voice, Sunday continued, "Come Monday, you can kill each other, but you'll do it in front of a new paying audience, understand? Hands off till then. For now, this show's officially over."

Sunday swooped one arm around Badder's neck, maybe holding him back, and the two of them turned away from me and walked toward the door that led backstage, trailed by Grunt. Sunday was still talking to Badder, but I could no longer hear him.

I looked around and found Khajee on the ground behind me. She was kneeling over Badder's opponent, who I'd forgotten about completely. His face was pulverized, with blood oozing from his lips and nose, and an open wound around one eye. Across from Khajee, the guy in the Hawaiian shirt was cradling the brawler's limp head. "Oh, son," he said. "What did they do to you?" I realized then how much the two of them looked alike. And this bothered me more than anything else.

15

*T*hat Sunday morning, alone in the apartment, I slept in late. Only Rosie's need to go outside finally drove me from the comfort of the couch, dragging myself into the new day. On Saturday afternoon, even though I'd been aching from the fight with Santana, I'd made it to Than's sick bed and sat for a while, quiet and still. When I got ready to leave, Khajee told me she was going to spend the night and I promised to come back. But the truth was, I didn't want to. I still couldn't shake my uneasiness being inside a hospital.

So yeah, I felt guilty when I stalled and took my time making breakfast Sunday, when I lingered in an extra-long hot shower. On the two-mile walk to the hospital, did I need to pause by the churches I passed? Not really. There must be a half dozen in downtown Harrisburg, planted all around the capitol. St. Stephen's Episcopal, Our Lady of the Blessed Sacrament, Pine Street Presbyterian, Salem United Church of Christ. As I strolled in front of them one by one, my hands stuffed in my pockets, I could hear the rising songs of the true believers inside, and each time, I felt the urge to join them. I can't say why.

The tug got so strong that by the time I neared St. Patrick's Cathedral, where Mom and I used to attend before we moved across the river, I mounted the stony steps. Mass was under way, but I pulled back the big door and slipped inside, found an empty pew in the back.

The priest, a young guy with a bright smile and a neatly trimmed beard, was well into his sermon, so I'd missed half the service. And he was clearly energized about his message that morning, something about the pilgrim's journey, hope and renewal. After he left the pulpit and moved on to the preordained script, my mind wandered. Sometimes it fixed on my upcoming bout with Badder, or the notion that I was a wanted man, or my predicament with Grunt. But mostly I worried about my mom, about Than, and Khajee. I even thought about why I hated hospitals. It sure wasn't because of all the sick and dying folks. Was all this a kind of prayer, focusing on your problems in the presence of God, hoping for a solution to present itself?

As the congregation recited the Our Father, I tried to concentrate on the words that held the most meaning for me. "Thy will be done." "Forgive us our trespasses." "Lead us not into temptation." Could be I found some brief consolation, but no grand epiphany about my dilemmas came to me. And when my fellow pilgrims rose to receive the Eucharist, I reflected on some of my recent activities. I stood with them and went to the end of my pew, but rather than joining the line headed for the altar and communion, I turned away and shuffled back out into the gray morning.

At the hospital, I found the scene in Than's room unchanged from Saturday. He was propped up in bed, pale and sagging. Buried deep in the pillow, his frail face was covered by an oxygen mask, and the respirator at his side made a constant shushing sound. The thin tube snaked from the crease of his elbow, twisting up to a clear bag of fluid suspended from a hook. On a white board on the wall, thick Sharpie letters announced, "Hello!!!! Today is Sunday!! Your nurse's name is Wendy!!!" Though it was nearing noon, the curtains were still drawn, and Khajee was curled up on a chair, huddled beneath a thin white blanket. I stood in the doorway and felt like an intruder. Maybe this was an excuse to skip my visit. But then Khajee stirred, lifted her head, and I realized she was awake. "Hey," she said.

I entered the room and took a seat near her. "How is he?"

"Same as yesterday. Same as the day before. It seems they can keep him from getting worse, but they can't help him get better."

"That sucks," I said.

Khajee nodded. "It's like he can't recover but can't quite die."

"Did Dr. Ngoyo say —"

"The doc's a good guy," she snapped, cutting me off. "But at a certain point, it's more faith than science. They're just giving their best guesses."

I couldn't think of how to respond, and we listened together to the hiss and sigh of oxygen pumping from the green tank into Than's lungs. I wondered if this experience made Khajee want to go into medicine more or less.

After a while, Khajee sat up and folded the blanket, split the curtains to let in the clouded sunlight. She set a hand on Than's arm, bowed her head in what I took to be prayer, then came back to her seat across from me. She stared, unapologetically, and when I returned her gaze she asked with a slight smile, "Mac, how come you keep coming back here?"

"What do you mean?" I asked, a little hurt.

She had a slight smile. "You're clearly not comfortable. You're fidgeting, sweaty even. You don't need to come you know."

"I want to," I told her. "I should be here. I want to support you."

"Not if it rattles you like this."

"I'm not rattled," I said, to which she cocked a single accusing eyebrow. I shifted the conversation. "Has he been awake at all?"

She nodded. "For a while last night, after you left. He came to for fifteen minutes or so. He was pretty disoriented, kept calling me Buppha — that was my grandmother's name. And he kept asking me to open the window more, to let in some air. I tried to get him to eat some Jell-O."

I could tell by her face that the effort hadn't been successful. "When was the last time you ate?"

"I'm not hungry," she said. I was going to tell her she had to keep her strength up, a line I'd heard my mom use in the kitchen at New Horizon with newcomers, but it felt token.

On the hospital loudspeaker, a calm voice said, "Code six in room three-thirteen. Code six in three-thirteen."

In the hallway, nurses rushed past, followed by a sprinting doctor. I'm not sure Khajee noticed. "Last night," she began, "when he was awake. He wanted me to help him get dressed. He said we were going to be late for the train. Isn't that the weirdest thing?"

"I guess," I said. "Maybe he'd had some sort of dream."

"Maybe," Khajee said, looking out the window. "Do you think it means anything?"

I could tell she really wanted this to have significance. "I don't know," I told her. "Could be he's ready to go? Like to heaven. Is that a comforting thought?"

Her eyes swung up to mine, and there was a mixture of surprise and frustration. A nurse in polka-dot scrubs rushed into the room. She stopped when she saw just us and said, "Where's the code six?"

Without turning to her, Khajee said, "Room three-thirteen."

After the nurse left, Khajee pulled out her phone and checked something. "I tried calling the apartment last night. It was almost midnight and you didn't answer. Do I want to know what you were doing?"

The truth was that I'd been out with Grunt again Saturday night. We'd picked up some supplies at a Lowe's and delivered them to an apartment building super, stopped by a liquor store and bought two cases of bourbon, filled up the van and a plastic red tank of gas at a Sheetz, a handful of errands like that. In Boiling Springs, Grunt went into a firehouse, and I sat in the van alone for an hour. On my cracked MP3, I listened to an entire Rolling Stones album, *Emotional Rescue*. Down in Dillsburg, Grunt used bolt cutters to break through the chain link fence at a used car dealership, then handed me a knife.

Together we sliced the tires of two dozen cars, silently crossing the darkened parking lot. I didn't even ask why. When we finished, he took that red tank and poured gas around the office trailer, then handed me a packet of matches. I looked around then ignited one, tossed it to the glistening ground. Flame rolled like a wave rushing toward shore, along the asphalt and up the vinyl side of the building. I turned to Grunt and he was already walking steadily toward the van, so I followed. As we drove off, I didn't even look back at the results of my handiwork. With all this on my mind, I looked at Khajee and said, "Me and Grunt went bowling."

Her smile was crooked. "You're a terrible liar."

"Lying and front kicks," I said. "It's good to know where I've got space for improvement."

"Speaking of which," Khajee said. "I forgot to ask if you tried the wall yesterday."

"I didn't make it to the top yet, if that's what you're asking."

"That's not what I asked. Did you try?"

"Yeah," I told her, a bit defensive maybe. "I try every time I jog that route."

"Results come from effort. Right effort leads inevitably to right results. Wrong effort leads to wrong results." She said these words staring at Than.

"That's part of Buddhism?" I asked.

She nodded. "Sort of," she said. "But it's also common sense." Now she turned to me and held my face with her eyes. "Whatever you're doing at night. It has to stop."

I looked over at her uncle. I had no idea what treatment like this cost. "I'm doing the same thing you are, working for a guy I don't like to earn money I need."

Khajee shook her head. "You're digging yourself deeper into something I'm trying to crawl out of," she said. "That's a big difference." I considered her words, and she went on. "Than. He wouldn't want this. You have to know that."

My eyes dropped to the oxygen tank, and I wondered again how long it'd been since she ate anything. Her cheeks looked gaunt. I stood up. "It's lunchtime," I told her. "Want to hit the cafeteria?"

She nodded her head and stood. "Actually that sounds good. But for me, it'll be breakfast."

One silent elevator ride later, and after wandering around the café-style cafeteria, we sat down across from each other. I had a bottle of water and a chicken salad. Khajee went in a different direction. "Who drinks coffee with pizza?" I asked. "Let alone black?"

"Just me, so far as I know," she answered.

I dug in with a plastic fork, and she started in on her droopy slice of pepperoni. "So have you been in contact with any of your teachers?" I asked.

"What's the point? School isn't really high on my list of things I'm worried about right now."

"Sure," I said. "That makes sense. What about your family?"

She chewed, swallowed, but looked like she didn't understand.

"Back home in Thailand," I pressed. "Isn't there anyone else?"

"My home is on Third Street," she said. "There's nobody in Thailand, not really."

I shoveled my salad around, flicked out a piece of lettuce that was brown on the edges. Khajee held her coffee cup on the table with two hands. "Buddhists don't believe in death you know. Not in the way you do."

"What do you mean?"

"For a Buddhist, existence is a long cycle with each individual struggling to attain nirvana — perfection. Based on your actions during a single lifetime, you generate karma, and depending on your karma, your consciousness comes back in the next life in a new form. You get to try again."

"So like reincarnation?"

"Not exactly, but you're in the right ballpark."

I liked this notion of infinite new chances, always starting over fresh. And I thought for a while about the questions I had, trying to find the words to not be disrespectful. But then Khajee said, "You're wrong about Sunday."

"Wrong how?"

"You think you've got it under control. But you're wrong, just like Marco. Working for that man, doing the things we do, it's bad karma."

I glanced around the cafeteria. There was an older couple a few tables away and a doctor looking at a laptop in the corner. No one was near enough to hear us. I pushed my plate to the side. "Where is Marco now?" I asked, sort of afraid of the answer.

Khajee sipped at her coffee. "Don't know for sure. According to Blalock, Grunt broke all ten of his fingers and they loaded him on a bus heading to Chicago. He's been exiled from the Eastern Seaboard."

"Exiled for what?"

"Refusing to obey orders." Here she leaned in too. "Every now and then, Sunday fixes a fight."

I sat back, almost like the news was a punch I wanted to avoid. "You serious?"

She nodded deeply. "I don't have any proof. But I've seen fighters do some strange things. Uncle told me that a guy like Sunday could make a fortune with the betting on those websites if he knew the outcome ahead of time. It all makes sense."

"And Marco?"

"I think Marco wouldn't play ball. Too much ego and not enough greed. He never told me anything, was sort of quiet like you. But I had my suspicions."

I looked down at my plate, mostly empty. "You think I'm quiet?" I asked.

"You keep your secrets, that's all I mean."

This landed on me funny, and I didn't want to let it stand. So when I finished the last of my salad, I said, "I don't want to have secrets from you. What is it you want to know?"

She eyed me up, like she was deciding where to begin. "For starters, how come you hate hospitals so much?"

My mind flashed to the tumble from the monkey bars when I was five, the sharp pain in my arm, the emergency room X-ray, the doctor's questions about the other bruises on my back and legs. Even at that age, I knew what my father did with his belt wasn't right, but I thought I'd brought it all on myself, by leaving my wet towel on the floor after my shower or not finishing my applesauce at dinner or by wandering into their bedroom in the middle of the night, searching for the source of those angry sounds. Sitting on that exam table, feet dangling as the doctor wrapped my arm in a cast, I worried that I'd inadvertently betrayed my father. So I lied and answered, "From when I fell at the park." I don't know if that doctor believed me or didn't want to get involved, but before we left, he talked to my mom alone in a room for a long time.

Khajee reached across the cafeteria table and touched my forearm. Her fingertips were warm from the coffee. "I'm sorry. I can see you're getting upset again. I shouldn't have pried."

I put my other hand over hers. "Don't apologize. I was just remembering this time when I was a kid. I broke my arm."

"It was a bad experience at the hospital?"

"Sort of bad, yeah. But not bad like you're thinking. Way worse was something else. Another time. Basically another part of the same damn story."

"You can tell me if you want."

I took a long swig from my water, then set it down. "This was the night the police took my father away, the night he beat my mom so bad I thought he killed her. This cop, a nice lady named Harrow, she sat with me at the hospital while they operated on my mom, and I worried the whole night she was going to die, that I hadn't saved her."

"That's a lot of pressure on a little boy."

It felt strange to be telling this story, but something about Khajee drew the words from me. "When I was finally allowed to see her, half her face was wrapped in gauzy bandages. I hugged her and asked when we could just go home. Harrow, she said something about helping us find a new home, making a fresh start. Something about this made my mom start crying, which was a mess because of the injuries to her face. I just kept telling her I was sorry."

"What were you sorry for?"

I took a deep breath. Too much to explain that I'd had a vision of her getting beat that night but hadn't been able to stop it. Plus, it was more than that. "I don't know exactly. Maybe I felt guilty because I hadn't protected her. Or maybe I felt guilty because I thought if she didn't have me, she'd have left him long ago. I was pretty screwed up."

Khajee thought for a while, drained the last of her coffee. "And when you fight Mac, the anger that takes over? You don't connect any of this to that rage?"

I didn't like the answer, which came to me right away of course. But I stayed silent.

And she was about to say something more, but just then that polka-dot nurse came hauling into the cafeteria and ran up behind Khajee. "We've been looking for you," she said. "It's your uncle. Come quick!"

We skipped the elevator and sprinted up four flights of stairs, then down the long white hall. As we approached the open door, I was worried that we'd find the old man dead. I felt guilty for drawing Khajee away. But when we got to the room, I was shocked to see him sitting up in his bed. He was no longer wearing the breathing mask, and he turned to us. "Hello," he said with a little wave of his hand, bright-eyed and smiling.

Khajee rushed in and embraced him. She said something in Thai and he said, "I'm not ready for that just yet."

The nurse said she'd track down Dr. Ngoyo and left us alone. Khajee poured a glass of water from a pitcher and made Than drink some through a bent straw. He spoke to her in Thai and she answered. I couldn't understand, but I was surprised to hear the energy in his voice. At one point, in the flow of sounds I couldn't understand, I heard the word "Sunday," and then, a minute later, "Santana."

Than's eyes widened at me, and he extended a shaky thumbs-up. "Santana's a legitimate badass. Khajee must be rubbing off on you."

"He's not tiger tough," I told him, and this made him grin.

Khajee said, "He's fighting Badder tomorrow night."

Than took this in, scratched at the stubble that had grown along his jawline. "He's the kind of guy who thinks no one can beat him. Worst thing for him is making him doubt that."

"Doubt," I repeated.

Than nodded. "Like a crack in a dam. Hurt him early."

This made sense to me. Coach Gallaher had cautioned me more than once that nothing was more dangerous than feeling invulnerable. He called it a Titanic mentality.

Than and Khajee beamed at each other and talked a little more. He asked about Roosevelt, and we assured him we'd been taking care of the dog. He wanted to know how school was going and she lied, saying she'd aced a chemistry test on Friday.

Dr. Ngoyo showed up and gave Than a once-over. He consulted a tablet and tapped at the screen, asked him a few questions. While he talked with Than, he smiled and patted his forearm. "I'm glad you're feeling well," he told him. But when he turned to leave, the doctor caught Khajee's eyes with his own, and we followed him into the hallway.

He walked down to a nurse's station and leaned onto the counter. "Just one sec," he said as he entered something into the tablet.

Khajee grew impatient and asked, "When can I take him home?"

This stopped the doctor, who turned to Khajee. "Your uncle's condition remains serious. I'd even say grave."

Khajee tilted back into me. "But you saw him. You said you weren't even sure he'd wake up. He's totally himself. Laughing and —"

The doctor held up a thin hand. "I saw exactly what you did, yes. However the fact remains that his kidneys are failing. His lungs are in terrible shape and he's still in severe respiratory distress. The breathing treatments have helped beat back the pneumonia, but that was only brought on by the terrible condition of his lungs in the first place. The sepsis is rampant."

Khajee's body went kind of lax, and I held her by the shoulders from behind. "What are you telling me?"

"The same thing I tried to get across the other day. We're at the stage where we can make him comfortable, but I don't want to hold out false hope."

"How can hope be false?" Khajee asked quietly, clearly not expecting an answer.

The doctor looked around the hallway.

I said, "He seems so alert."

He nodded. "I'm not sure if this will help," he said. "But sometimes, as a sort of prelude to the final stages, a patient like this gets a burst of energy. They seem healthy and even supercharged. In my experience, it's best to enjoy their company during this period. You should go to him, okay?"

Khajee mumbled something and stepped out of my grip. She wandered back toward Than's room, and I looked at the doctor, who said, "The truth can be a hard thing to accept. I just thought she deserved to know."

I went after Khajee, who was leaning into the wall just outside Than's door. She was crying softly, making no noise. When I got to her, she sniffled and stood up straight. She wiped at her eyes and said, "Doctors don't know everything. He's going to be just fine. A week from now, we'll all be home."

Even as she said these words, I could tell she didn't believe them. She was just trying to convince herself. And I wished I could control my power to see what was to come, to peer into tomorrow and confirm her dreams. But in my heart of hearts, I knew that if I could glimpse the future, I probably wouldn't like what I saw.

I understood when Khajee told me she couldn't leave her uncle for my fight with Badder. She wanted to be nearby in case Than, who'd slipped away again, returned for another lucid spell. Monday afternoon, she'd bolted home for a songless shower, a change of clothes, and to check in on me and Rosie. "Don't let Badder get your arm," she warned me in the doorway of the apartment, a night bag slung over her shoulder. "He's got some ferocious submission holds. I've seen him snap an elbow like a chicken wing."

"He'll never get past my front kick," I boasted.

She shook her head. "You don't have a front kick. But it's true. He won't be expecting your lame version of one."

"Total secret weapon."

"Something like that. Use it wisely."

"Will do, Boss," I said. "The championship belt is as good as ours."

"Don't get cocky," she snapped. Leaning into the frame, Khajee didn't seem to want to leave. She slid one foot over the doormat. "This guy is dangerous for real. Sunday's up to something."

"Sunday wants to make money. And Badder doesn't scare me."

"Maybe being a little scared wouldn't be a totally bad idea."

I shook my head. "I'm not real good at being scared." Some inner part of me laughed.

"For real," Khajee told me, brushing a hand along my bicep and pulling me from the past. "Take care of yourself tonight."

It was good that we'd cleared up she wasn't looking for a boyfriend like me, or any boyfriend at all. Otherwise, I'd have interpreted her concern as something more than it was. "You too," I said, pretty sure she might have a harder night ahead of her than I did.

———

On the far end of that Monday, I found myself standing over a sign collapsed in a patch of waist-high weeds. "28 Days without an Accident at This Worksite!" I wasn't convinced that four weeks of safety was worth bragging about, and I wondered what the circumstances were that shut the place down.

Blalock had driven the two of us south into an industrial park with hangar-like buildings and no streetlights. At the end of a mile-long winding road we came to an isolated construction site, at the center of which was a partially completed building that looked to me like a gigantic Erector set. There were four stories of I-beam girders stretching up into the sky but no floors or ceilings or walls.

Blalock went to find Sunday and I checked out the fighting area. At the base of the structure, a foundation had long ago been dug into the earth. Like most basements, the pit was lined with cinderblocks. From two corners, bright lights on tripods illuminated the concrete floor, and cameras in the other corners angled down, waiting. Leaves and debris coated the pit, and one of Sunday's cronies had scrambled down on a ladder with a Hefty bag to tidy up.

Some of the high rollers crowded around me at the edge of the pit. They patted my shoulders, asked me how I was feeling. I said, "Extra wild," and this made them grin. But I could tell by the look in their eyes, by the way they glanced at each other and exaggerated their smiles — most of them had bet against me. Badder was considered unbeatable. I could only take so much of their false admiration, and I excused myself and walked away, out into the darkness that rimmed the site.

That's where Blalock tracked me down, standing over that sign. "The evening's initial bout has begun," he said. "Maddox and a young pugilist from Maryland are engaged in a heated display."

"And you think that sounds appealing to me?" I asked him.

He looked around. "What exactly are you occupied with out here?"

I stared up into sky. "Trying to see the stars."

Blalock turned his eyes upward. "I suppose there simply aren't any out."

"Of course they're out," I said. "We just can't see them."

He adjusted his glasses, pinched his nose where they rested. "You sound oddly philosophical. The warrior poet is more myth than reality. I suggest you focus your concentration on the evening's main event, as it were."

I said, "Yeah."

"You deserve recognition, Edward. You've accomplished more in a short period of time than any other brawler."

"With everything else going on in the world tonight, you'll forgive me if I want to think about more than a fight."

Blalock went quiet. Behind him, a cry went up, some big move in the match.

"Than's situation is deeply regrettable. He was a good man."

I didn't like Blalock talking about him in the past tense and threw him a nasty look. "Still is," I corrected.

"Undoubtedly," he said, a little rattled. "Sans caveat."

With him off-balance, I took a shot with an unexpected question. "What happened to Marco?"

Blalock twitched and looked out into the darkness beyond the construction site. "Marco happened to Marco. The young man had significant potential but an inflated sense of self-importance. He failed to grasp the crucial concept that in life, one is sometimes compelled to do things that may seem unpleasant or distasteful."

"Things like what?" I pressed him. "Things you don't want to do?"

Behind Blalock, another cry went up, followed by applause.

"The first match has concluded. We should retire to the pit."

The second match was barbaric, two certified hard-asses from Pittsburgh trying to settle a grudge. They stood toe-to-toe, no finesse, no style, just trading haymakers without even pretending to defend themselves. I'm not sure I'd ever seen anything quite so brutal. Finally they both collapsed together, bloodied, and one crawled on the other, pinning him down and raining tired punches. Even exhausted as he was, he managed to land a couple shots, enough to drive his opponent into unconsciousness. To prove the guy was out, the victor lifted one limp arm and dropped it. The winner could barely climb the ladder out of the basement, and they had a hell of a time carrying out the groggy loser.

With all the blood left behind, somebody had the bright idea of blasting the concrete with a hose, and the water swirled down a drain in the center. During cleanup, I saw Badder across the pit from me. His groupies surrounded him in a gang, but he brushed them off, locking eyes with me over the opening in the earth, which felt like a giant grave. There was something different about the way he was carrying himself. He wasn't scowling or making any of his crazy faces, which didn't make a lot of sense. Maybe we both knew it was time to get down to business and settle this thing between us. We were past the point of games.

Sunday emerged from the crowd and took a position in front of one of the cameras. Through a mic attached to a speaker, he welcomed everyone to the main event, did his usual schtick about the purity of hand-to-hand combat, the warrior spirit, etc. As if from a distance, I heard him yell, "The champion Badder versus the upstart Wild Child!"

I secured the Velcro straps on my gloves, then dug my mouth guard from the pocket of my gym shorts. Before stuffing it in, I turned to Blalock. "Any last words of encouragement?"

The glow from his phone bathed his face in a blue light. "Perhaps it will serve as some motivation that the oddsmakers underestimate you. You're currently an eight-to-one underdog. Prove them wrong."

I climbed down a metal ladder, one rung at a time. On my bare feet, the concrete was cool and slick. Above me, Badder pointed my way and yelled, "You're mine!" then jumped down, I guess to show how tough he was and everything. Eyeing each other, the two of us made our way to the center, where we found ourselves ankle deep in a puddle of bloody water gathered around the clogged drain. Up close for the first time in a while, his tattoos looked different than I remembered, like the swirls on his cheeks were bigger or something. I dismissed this stray thought and turned my attention to the fans rimming the edges of the pit, pumping their fists and chanting.

Sunday produced the gong, and as he banged it out all present roared, "No mercy! Prepare! Brawl!"

For all this bravado, Badder was cautious at first. He circled, kept his distance and tossed out a few tentative jabs from outside. I pursued, eager to mix it up, but I kept my guard raised. Hunched behind my fists, I sidestepped and cut off the corner. Badder backed into the wall, then without warning charged into me like a mad bull. Too late to sprawl, I scrambled backward with his arms wrapping around my waist, his head planted in my gut. He couldn't quite get ahold of my legs to drop me, and I couldn't quite get free, and we shuffled diagonally across the fighting pit. In the far corner, he slammed me into the wall hard enough to snap my head into the cinderblock. I tasted blood and went dizzy.

Bent before me, Badder pummeled his fists into my ribs, left and right and left again, swinging wildly. I raised an elbow and spiked it into the back of his skull three, four times, then launched a knee up into his face. Reflexively he sprang up, and I was ready with a left jab, poking it into his nose and driving him back. Advancing now, I missed a looping right hook that passed just over his ducking head, but still it gave me a chance to slide away from the wall. He pursued me, crouching, and I circled, a little wobbly. I found it hard to get a full breath without a pain shooting across my midsection, and I wondered if he'd cracked one of my ribs. Badder maybe saw me wince and banged his palms together, pounded his own thick chest. He screamed to the audience and they yelled back their approval, inspiring him to turn to me and contort his face into the Maori grimace — eyes bulging, tongue extended. In that moment, he was flatfooted, with his head stretched away from his body and his arms draped at his sides. My opening couldn't have been clearer. It was an amateur mistake, a gift.

In the heat of battle, you don't often think. It's not like a game of chess where you plot out different courses of action, weighing the pros and cons and making a deliberate decision. Mostly you react, rely on your instincts, and go with your gut. Sometimes you realize your body is in motion before you even know for sure what it's doing, as if the warrior inside has taken control and bypassed the conscious self. When I saw Badder exposed like this, I didn't think anything. The pain in my ribs disappeared and I just found myself bolting forward. As I charged in, I pivoted to the side, planted my left leg, leaned back and drove my other foot into his chunky torso. It was a side kick that would've made Khajee proud, and it doubled Badder in two. His face was now at waist level, and I twirled a full 360 degrees, catching him flush on the cheek with a spinning kick I didn't know I had in me. Badder dropped to a knee, and I felt like I was chopping down an enormous tree, one axe swing at a time. Standing before him, I took a thick handful of his bushy hair in my left hand and raised my right fist up to my shoulder. He glanced up at it, and his eyes were bright, more aware than I thought they might be. I released that downward punch like a thunderbolt from Olympus, connecting with his chin, then looped a left hook in the other direction, whiplashing his face. How he didn't go down, I had no idea.

I backed off a bit, wondering why he hadn't collapsed and trying again to catch my breath. My ribs complained but I ignored them. In frustration I swept in again, swinging my foot at an imaginary bull's-eye on his face. I pictured punting his head up into the crowd, maybe Sunday catching it. But Badder's two thick arms crossed in front of his chest, blocking my kick, and he captured that foot. Gripping it viselike, he rose to his feet, leaving me hopping on one leg. The crowd exploded.

When a guy's got your leg, you're basically at his mercy. Odds are he's going to take you down unless you can get out of bounds, but that wasn't an option in the cinderblock pit. I turned and mule-kicked, trying to yank my trapped leg free, but Badder was way too strong for that, and he tugged me back, hoping to slide his grip up past my knee. I remembered that crazy move Dominic pulled, and the next time Badder jerked me toward him, I went with the momentum, lifting my planted leg up and catching him flush in the chest with my foot. He released my leg and I crashed to the concrete.

I scurried to my feet while he was still staggered, sidestepped a sloppy kick, and tagged him in the ribs with a nice combination, followed by a knee to his gut. Badder retreated into a corner and covered up, ducking his face behind his raised forearms. Rather than trying to punch my way through his defense, I shifted gears and locked up with him, wrestling style. We each had one hand on the other's neck and one hand on an arm. Our heads bent into each other's shoulders.

Facing the floor, both of us grappling, Badder said quietly, "You're doing great," which I sure as hell didn't understand. Was he trying to psych me out? Get in my head with mind games? Whatever his motivation, I was distracted by his words, and even when he telegraphed his attack with, "My turn now," I wasn't ready for the foot sweep. He shoved my body to my left, then blocked that foot, sending me tumbling to my side. I splashed in the nasty puddle and tried getting to all fours, but Badder was on me too quick, riding me from behind. He chopped my arm and broke me down, flat-bellied into the water, and when I tried to rise, he slipped in a full nelson, arms snaking under my armpits, hands locked on the back of my skull — same move I'd dropped on Kowalski. Bad karma indeed.

Pressing down with all his weight, Badder forced my face toward the water. I strained my neck, shoved back into him, but he had too much leverage and was just too freaking heavy and strong. First my chin dipped in the cruddy pool, which smelled rank and foul. As my lips got close, I twisted my head sideways, but Badder kept the pressure up. Soon my cheek was wet, and then half my face was submerged. Had the water been just a bit deeper, he probably could've drowned me. As it was, I had to keep my lips locked and breathe through my nose. Badder must've realized he couldn't completely cut off my air. In frustration, he rocked back, drawing me up with him, then slammed us both forward, pounding my forehead through the pool and into the concrete floor. I was dazed, exhausted, and he pressed his face in close to mine, bringing his mouth along my ear. He whispered, "Just so you know the real score, all right Baby Blue?" With this, he hoisted my head and drove it down once more, but then he did something entirely unexpected. He let me go.

The weight was suddenly gone from my back, like a boulder lifted from me, and I turned to see him above me, and the stars now above him, visible through the intersecting beams. He was raising his hands in victory, rotating slowly to bask in the crowd's adulation. For a second I thought that maybe they had the impression I'd tapped out, which I hadn't, but then Badder kicked me and yelled, "Come get some more." This guy was so cocky he'd given up a perfectly good hold, one I couldn't escape from. He was treating me like I'd treated Dunkirk back at the Giant Center, craving a showboat victory. As I got to my knees and regained my breath, I vowed to myself I'd make him pay.

Once I took my fighting stance, he kept his distance, regarding me from ten feet away. He pointed at me and laughed, getting into a mirror image of my stance to mock me. He looked away, egging the crowd on, but I recognized his feint as a dead giveaway, and right then, my vision came to me, and the future revealed itself. So when Badder spun and exploded in my direction, I'd already slid three steps away from him, and as he roared my way with his arms outstretched, poised to tackle me into the wall just behind me, I held my ground, letting the moment stretch out. Anyone watching might have thought I was caught flatfooted, that I was about to get plowed over. They'd have been dead wrong.

As his chest slammed into mine, I scooped one arm under his shoulder and lifted while with my other I gripped his opposite elbow and tugged down. I absorbed his momentum and tilted back, but my feet were planted firm, and as we tumbled, I twisted and arched my back, torqueing my waist so Badder's body drifted up and over mine, weightless. On the mat, this move is called a pancake because you end up slapping the guy flat on his back. And that would've been good in my fight with Badder. But even better, I'd backed up enough that halfway through this headlong flip, his back collided into the cinderblock wall. We crumbled awkwardly down, the top of his head crashing into the concrete floor, and when we settled he was on his back and I was leaning onto his chest. My wrestling instinct told me to slide into a headlock, stick his shoulder blades so the ref could call a pin, but there was no judge in that pit but me. So instead my arm slipped just around his neck, forgoing his arm, and when I began to squeeze, it was clear why this move too is totally forbidden in high school. In the crook of my arm, pinched between my bicep and the bone of my forearm, this throat felt fleshy and soft. Badder gasped and his eyes bugged out. He thrashed and his arms flailed, pounding my back, my head, but they had no power and wouldn't deter me. I tightened my grip and felt his struggle slowly dwindle. It was almost like he was going to sleep. And I knew — I was totally aware — that I was strangling him, that this was more than a chokehold but something indeed that could kill him. That power surged through my blood and I tasted the thrill of invincibility.

Even after Badder went still, I held on for a few seconds more. I didn't want to kill him, but I wasn't upset by the notion that everybody watching knew I could. And one of those bearing witness stood directly over me. Up above, towering with his arms crossed on the edge of the wall, Grunt looked down on me with an expression I could only read as approval, even admiration.

I released Badder, gasping. When I got up onto my feet and he remained flat, his chest barely rising and falling, I turned my face to the cheering fans. Their applause was like thunder, the sound so strong if felt like a physical thing taking shape in the air around me, a swirling wave of glory. As I rotated and soaked it all up, I had the strange sensation that somehow, I would be raised up, my body lifted into the starry sky.

———

An hour later, I was still riding that high, though of course it had faded some. Blalock brought me to a greasy spoon on Route 11 and I ate steak and eggs and listened to him prattle on about the future spread out before me, the one I wasn't sure I was at all interested in. He drove me back to Khajee's and handed me a wad of cash bigger than any I'd ever imagined I would hold in my hands — $10,000 — more money than my mom could make in three months as a waitress. This was equal to what I had stuffed under the couch cushions back at Khajee's, the combined winnings from my fights with Dominic and Santana. "Mr. Sunday thought it an appropriate time for a bonus of sorts," was the last thing Blalock told me before driving off.

I was so caught up in the excitement of all that was unfolding that I didn't ask myself why the light was on in the apartment when Khajee was supposed to be down at the hospital all night. I was surprised by the unlocked door, and when I stepped inside there was no Rosie to jump all over me. I followed the glow of a lamp into the back room, where Khajee was standing over a cardboard box on the bed. Papers and old photos were spread all around it. Rosie was curled up on the pillows. "Khajee," I said proudly, lost and clueless. "We won! I'm the champ."

When she lifted her eyes to me, they were dull, lightless.

The picture she was holding slid from her fingers, and as it rested on the mattress I saw it was a portrait of Than.

We stood in the room in silence, and the reality of what happened settled over me. I walked around the bed to Khajee, folded my arms around her, drawing her into my chest. I couldn't think of what to say, and when I finally told her "I'm so sorry," the words felt hollow and stupid. Khajee didn't hug me back. She just leaned into me. And I held her gently, waiting for the tears I wasn't sure would ever come.

17

At my wake, I want the funeral home to be packed. And afterward, I hope the church is standing room only.

Back when I was thirteen, one of the ladies staying at New Hope — a "guest" was the term my mom always preferred — took her own life. I don't know if that woman slit her wrists in a warm bath or swallowed too many pills and just went to bed. That wasn't something I asked. I also didn't ask if the woman had been abused by a husband or boyfriend, since this was pretty much a standard feature in all those stories. What I did want to know, and what I did ask the morning we were getting ready to attend the woman's funeral, was if she had any kids. This was because I had the habit of picturing every wandering soul in that sanctuary to be some version of me and Mom. In this case though, I was wrong. The woman in question had come to that place seeking refuge alone, and alone she had died.

So it should have come as no surprise to me that when we arrived at the funeral, the pews of St. Sebastian's were essentially empty. Oh sure, the director of New Hope was there in the front, and three old lady parishioners huddled together in the back. They bent forward together in whispered prayers, and I remember they reminded me of witches, all dressed in black with lacy doilies on their heads. But all the other dusty pews were vacant. I asked my mom if we'd come too early, but she told me that we were right on time. Up at the front of the aisle, the coffin waited before the altar.

There was no music at the mass, no choir and no piano, so we didn't sing. The somber priest seemed in a rush to get through the service, and he gave a brief sermon about obedience to God and the sanctity of life. As he finished, I realized he was scolding the dead woman for what she'd done, that her final act was a mortal sin in the eyes of the church. According to him, if I understood correctly, there was a good chance even God had turned His back on her. All this made me terribly sad, and I couldn't help it when the tears came.

My mom slid an arm around me and patted my back. She misunderstood why I was upset, and I didn't correct her. Later, when we got home and she went off to work a shift at Perkins, I ripped a sheet of loose-leaf from my seventh-grade binder and wrote out the name of everyone I thought would come to my funeral if I died that day. I figured all my friends would show up, and most of my classmates, even if they were just curious. I also included a couple neighbors, and Mom's estranged sister in Erie, though I didn't think she'd drag along my bratty cousins. Fleetingly, I wondered if they'd let my father out for the day on a special pass or something, if he would stand over my grave in prison orange. When I added in a few teachers, my total came to forty-five, and that seemed sort of pathetic. If nobody remembers you after you die, it's a pretty good bet your life didn't mean much. Then I decided that some parishioners might show up who didn't know me, like the trio of crones I'd seen that day, and it occurred to me that my classmates couldn't really come alone, that they'd have to be driven by a parent or two. With this in mind, I recalculated and decided I might get close to a hundred. This wasn't a lot, but sitting alone in our apartment picturing that church with just five congregants, a hundred seemed pretty good. Good enough.

All this was in the back of my mind two days after Than's death, as Khajee and me rode in a taxi to Than's midday funeral. Khajee sat next to me in the back seat, wearing a simple black dress. She was calm and collected, and her hands were folded neatly on her lap. Earlier that morning, she'd told me she was going to meditate in the bedroom for a while, but not long after she closed the door, I'd heard some weeping, short and stifled. I felt weird going to a funeral in just normal pants and a buttoned-up shirt, but Khajee told me I shouldn't go buy a tie or a fancy jacket. "It's not our way," she told me.

In the taxi, she told me that typically Thai funerals aren't for a week or so after the death, to give the spirits a chance to adjust and prepare. But she thought Than had waited long enough.

"Long enough for what?" I asked.

She turned to me and said, "For whatever comes next."

The sunlight caught her face and I noticed the damnedest thing. "Your eyes," I said. "What happened?"

Khajee looked at me, curious.

"They were green," I explained. "How can they be brown now?"

"They were always brown," she told me. "Last year on St. Patrick's Day, I put in green contacts as a gag. This friend of mine, someone special, told me they were cute, so I got used to wearing them. They just became part of my look. Today, it just didn't feel right."

"Sure," I said. "That makes sense." There's so much about people, even ones we're close to, that we just don't know.

When we got to Scherr's Funeral Emporium, there were only a few cars in the parking lot, but we were very early. I held the door for Khajee and inside, we were greeted by a tall, gray-haired funeral director. She said, "The preparations are nearly complete. If you'll just follow me." She led us down a broad carpeted hallway to a room with a few dozen folding chairs, all empty, all aimed at the open coffin up front. A man wearing saffron robes shuffled back and forth between crowded tables on either side of the coffin, and he turned when the director cleared her throat.

The monk, who had a shaved head and a gentle face, said, "Very good," and walked toward us. We met in the aisle splitting the rows of chairs, each of which had a white booklet centered on the seat. Facing the monk, Khajee pressed her hands together and bowed slightly, lowering her eyes. She turned to me and said, "This is Eddie, my friend. Eddie, this is Arthur. He's from the Buddhist center in town." Unsure of what the etiquette was, I went to bow, but he extended a hand. We shook, and his palm was warm. The funeral director asked Arthur if he needed anything else, and the two of them disappeared back into the hallway. Khajee and I were left alone with Than.

For a few moments she just stood beside me, frozen, staring at the coffin. I told her, "We could just sit for a bit. We don't have to —" but I don't think she heard anything I was saying. She continued up the aisle slowly, like a hesitant bride. It didn't occur to me to let her go up there alone, so I stayed close without crowding her. She stopped in the open space before the coffin, placed her feet tightly together, pressed her hands palm to palm, and solemnly brought them to her chest. In a fluid motion, she lifted them to her forehead, then bent down, kneeling and then folding so far her face was in the carpet. Slowly she rose till she was standing, then she repeated the whole thing two more times. It looked like some sort of exercise, but I recognized it as a form of prayer. I wasn't sure what to do, so I watched in silence.

When she finished, she took a few tentative steps forward. From over her shoulder, I saw Than's body in the coffin. It was in casual clothes, a dress shirt and simple khakis. I was surprised to see they had stuffed the one pant leg with some material, giving the appearance that his amputation had been made whole somehow. There was even a shoe propped up, though I knew there was no foot inside. Than's arms were folded at the elbows so his hands could clasp on his chest. Khajee slipped a hand into her dress's pocket and leaned in, bringing a black plastic comb to her uncle's wispy hair. She brushed it a few times, making the part distinct, then straightened. The room felt very quiet, and I said, "He looks peaceful."

Khajee returned the comb to her pocket, stared for a few heartbeats, and then said, "He's not in there anymore." It wasn't with a judgmental tone — more of a simple observation.

With that, she moved to the table beside the coffin. A half

dozen golden statues sat cross-legged, their bare chests exposed. Some had their fingers contorted in complex signs; some were cloaked in robes like the monk. Before them was a row of glasses filled with colored gems, and a bowl of white flower buds. Khajee lifted one out and nodded at me, so I took one too. When she passed by the coffin and set her bud on her uncle's chest, I did the same.

On the left side of the coffin there was a high-backed chair with a red pillow on it, then a second table. This one had a gold-framed portrait of Than, a shot of his face from when he was young. His smile reminded me of Khajee. She selected a single incense stick from a small pile next to the portrait, brought its tip to the flame of a white candle, then jabbed the other end in a pan of sand. The gray smoke curled into the air, and I smelled something sweet, like sandalwood.

At the very end of the table was a bottle of water and a dish piled high with grapes. This surprised me, and I grew even more curious when Khajee pulled from her pocket an oversized York Peppermint Pattie. She set it down and glanced back at Than, offering a tight smile. Also on the table was a white paper flag, the same size as the one they give out at July 4th parades with a little wooden stick and everything. Only instead of the stars and stripes, the flag was just a white field with an "R" made in red marker.

We took two seats at the end of the row of chairs up front, and I spent some time flipping through one of those white booklets. Inside there was a series of prayers that looked like poems. On the cover, I read this:

The end of collection is dispersion.
The end of rising is falling.
The end of meeting is parting.
The end of birth is death.

Over the next half hour, about three dozen people entered either alone or in small groups. Some were former brawlers, easy to pick out with their gnarled knuckles, cauliflower ears, and loud voices. Others from the Buddhist community repeated the same ritual that Khajee had done in front of the coffin, and I noticed a few leaving items on the table with the food — a small bag of peanuts, a glass jar of jelly beans. Someone, I imagined his secret supplier, left a pack of Newports. Most lifted white flowers from the bowl to Than's chest, and a few lit incense sticks. Everybody stopped by Khajee and shared their condolences, but for the most part she just nodded and they moved on.

She did rise when a group of teenagers showed up, friends playing hooky from school I presumed. Not wanting to be rude, I stood too, thinking I might be introduced. Khajee hugged each in the gang of five, and lingered in the arms of the last one, a slight girl with a nose ring who seemed especially upset. This girl's cheeks were streaked with tears, and she couldn't seem to stop sobbing. When even the other teens averted their eyes, it came to me that this was the girl with the broken heart from last summer, the one who'd found Khajee's green eyes cute, the friend who'd quit the school play in solidarity. This was Mouse #2. I decided I should give them all some space.

I excused myself and went to the bathroom where I was surprised to find Badder at the sink, glancing down as he washed his hands. I was considering slipping out to avoid a confrontation when he shut off the water and looked up, making eye contact in the mirror. I was so shocked by what I saw that I spoke without thinking. "Your face," I said, staring at his unadorned cheeks in the reflection.

He turned and shrugged. "Yeah, Sunday makes me do that crap as part of the show. My big sister has to use a damn Sharpie so they don't sweat off. Total pain to get off." He slid by me and I heard paper towels being ripped from a dispenser.

Of course, I'd assumed his tattoos were permanent. Badder swung around in front of me, wiping his hands, and up close one cheek was puffy from our fight. Badder spoke in an unfamiliar, quiet tone. "Sorry for your loss. That Than, he was old school for real."

I wasn't sure how to respond, so I just said, "Thanks. I didn't know him long."

"Guys like that, you don't need to know them long to know them well, right?"

Smiling, I nodded, and it was clear we understood each other.

"All right," he said. "I've got to go pay my respects. Need to get home and watch my little brother." He offered me his hand and I shook it, unsure of how to talk to this very real person in front of me, so far from who I faced in the ring.

As Badder headed for the door, he paused and looked back. "Those tribal tattoos," he said, "they're sacred to the

Maori. I feel bad using them as part of an act, you know? One day, I want to get them for real."

I was surprised by his confession. "That'd be cool."

"Yeah." He just stood there for a second, like he was deciding something. "The other night," he finally said, "we did good."

"Sure thing," I told him, still a bit dazed. I felt the urge to ask him something more, but he turned and pushed through the door.

When I returned to the viewing room, Blalock and Sunday were along the back wall, standing with their arms crossed just inside the door. I joined them, and Blalock brought his face in over my shoulder. "Being in the presence of the dead forces one to consider their own mortality. I'd rather be anywhere but here."

I pulled back, and Sunday shook my hand. "Good to see you, Champ." He said this with a tone I couldn't quite name.

Blalock went into a long story about the wake of his ex-wife's sister. Apparently some little kid recited a sappy poem, and then a nephew decided to sing their favorite song. "The entire affair resembled a third-rate talent show," Blalock declared, loud enough that some in the back rows turned their faces to us. "What?" Blalock said. "We're not allowed to talk?"

Sunday shook his head and tilted into me. "You're coming to the reception later, yeah? I got everything set up. We need to send old Than off in style, am I right?"

Khajee had told me Sunday had offered to foot the bill for a gathering after the ceremony, something I interpreted as a power play. I said to Sunday, "I wouldn't miss it."

He stroked the tip of his white beard and said, "Excellent. We need to talk."

I was about to ask what we needed to talk about, but then the monk returned, shuffling past us in his robes. Everyone fell silent and got to their feet. Blalock and Sunday exchanged a look and took the opportunity to make a break for it, clearly not interested in the ceremony itself. As they snuck out, Blalock leaned in and whispered, "I'll gladly provide transport to the reception. We'll gather in the parking lot after."

Standing before the coffin, the monk prostrated himself the same way Khajee had, three times bringing his face to the ground and rising up again. Once he was finished, he stepped to that tiny flag with the red "R" and dipped it to the white candle. With the flag aflame, he lifted it for all to see. The fire did its work quick, incinerating the paper and leaving just a stick with a charred tip. He nodded and inserted it into the sand with the incense, then positioned himself cross-legged on the red-cushioned chair. The congregation lowered into seats, and I found an empty one nearby. I craned my neck to see Khajee, and the nose ring girl was sitting at her side. This made me glad.

The monk spoke in a clear voice, loud enough to get everyone's attention. "For the Buddhist, there is no death. There are no endings. Only transformations. Only changes. We gather now not to mourn Aawut Thanasukolwit, but to help his consciousness leave this form and move on to its new one. We pray to give him positive energy, so his consciousness ascends to a higher level in accordance with the merit he earned during this life."

With this, he opened one of those white prayer booklets and began chanting. It wasn't like singing or humming, but a low guttural sound, something generated from deep in his throat, even his chest. I picked up a prayer booklet and followed along the best I could.

After the ceremony was complete, a few of the guests wandered back over near Khajee, laid a hand on her shoulder or lifted an open palm as they passed. Most just shuffled into the hall. Khajee embraced the nose ring girl, who then ambled off with the other teens. Khajee saw me waiting and made her way to me, and as we left the funeral home, she leaned heavily onto my arm. Crossing the parking lot, her knees were shaky, and she kept her head down. At Blalock's SUV, he opened the big back door, and all this time, Khajee held it together. But once she was out of public sight, once the two of us were in the back seat and the tinted windows shut out the rest of the world, she came undone. The tears came in great waves now, and sobs wracked her tiny body. In between, she muttered something in Thai, but of course I didn't understand. All I could do was hold her, rub a hand over her back and try to comfort her. The problem is that everything you try to say at a time like this is all cliché. Sometimes words just make it worse.

From the front seat, Blalock asked if he could help.

"She'll be fine," I said. "Just give her a few minutes and we'll head over."

"No," Khajee choked out. "I'm not going. Just take me home."

Blalock put his eyes on me through the rearview mirror.

"Mr. Sunday won't be pleased. Not attending might be interpreted as an insult."

I said, "I'm not sure his vote matters right now. She's not in good shape."

"Mr. Sunday's vote always matters. He went through a significant effort clearing out the banquet room and making arrangements. And he was just sharing with me his desire to converse with you, Edward, alone. The time has come to talk about what's next."

By this point, Khajee was spread across the back seat, resting her tiny head on my lap. She'd calmed her crying but her body, curled into a ball, was still quivering. "Fine," I told Blalock. "I'll go talk to him. First we'll swing past Khajee's and drop her off. Then you and I will go to the reception. I'll handle Sunday."

Blalock shrugged and started backing out of the parking spot. "As you wish," he said. "Your funeral." He winced as he tapped the brakes. But I doubt Khajee heard.

From what I'd picked up from my nights with Grunt, I knew Sunday owned a piece of a dozen legitimate businesses — a beer distributor in Lemoyne, a pool hall in downtown Harrisburg, a car wash, even a bowling alley. So it's no surprise I guess that among them was a restaurant, Santalucia's. It's a steak house three blocks from the capitol building, where I could imagine senators and lobbyists meeting to make deals over thick Delmonicos.

When we got there, Blalock led me through the main dining area, weaving through the tables with regular customers and avoiding a busboy carting dishes. At the back wall, we took a flight of stairs up to an open room the size of school gym, big enough to house a small wedding. There was a high ceiling with four dull chandeliers, tall windows along the front wall that could've used a good cleaning. A dozen round tables draped with white cloths were arranged across the floor. Some of the people in their fold-out chairs turned when we walked in, but if anybody noticed Khajee was absent, they didn't say anything.

Blalock said, "I'm starving," and headed to the buffet table along one wall. I wasn't really hungry, but I followed him just for something to do. He loaded his plate with asparagus and mashed potatoes, and at the cutting station at the end, he got a hunk of ham and a slice of roast beef. I settled for a split dinner roll and a sliver of turkey. He stared at my plate disapprovingly. "To each his own," he told me.

We found seats at a table with a few of the other brawlers including Maddox and Dominic, all in front of plates heaped high with food.

"Freaky ceremony," Maddox said.

Dominic closed his lips and sat back, somber-faced, then did a terrible impersonation of the monk's hum chant. A cloud of bright red blood streaked the whites of one of Dominic's eyes, surely a hemorrhage from our fight. And it was hard not to notice he'd cut his dreads, trimming the singed edges. I scanned the room for Santana, looking for a bandaged ear, but he wasn't there. I'd heard it took six stitches.

I was surprised when Grunt appeared behind Dominic, smacked the back of his head. Dom shot up, turned to confront his attacker, and stopped dead when he saw who it was. Dressed in his usual black pants, black shirt, black tie and jacket, Grunt seemed especially at home at a funeral. Once he stared down Dominic, he pointed a thick finger my way and then turned.

"Good luck," Blalock said.

I got up to follow and behind me heard Maddox. "You think he'll come back for this sandwich?"

Grunt never looked back as he went down a narrow set of stairs in the rear, then through a swinging door with a circular window. The kitchen bustled with clanging pots, flames leaping from grills, chefs topped with white hats. No one turned or made eye contact with us. The waitresses and busboys just slid left or right, making way for Grunt's thick form, and I drafted him. He stopped outside a wooden door with a sign displaying a series of drawings detailing what to do if someone was choking. I stood in front of it for a moment, blank-faced, then when I went to knock, Grunt just grabbed the doorknob and pushed it open. I stepped inside.

Sunday sat at a desk at the far end of his windowless office, which had walls lined with bookshelves. When he saw me, he was on the phone, an old-fashioned one with a squiggly cord and everything, but he waved me forward with lifted eyebrows. I closed the door, shutting out the clattering of the kitchen. As I slowly moved inside, I scanned the titles of the books. One was about gardening, another the art of war, a third the history of bridge design. It occurred to me that Sunday had never read any of these, but just purchased them in bulk to use as decoration.

Near the chairs that faced his desk, a table held an oversized birdcage, and I peeked inside. It was empty. The newspaper lining the bottom was clean, but a couple years old.

His desk was crowded with piles of papers, a stack of three-ring binders, and an old computer with a huge tan monitor. Directly before him was a cleared-away space occupied by a plate with a half-eaten steak. Holding that phone receiver to his head, he nodded at me and dipped a finger at one of the chairs, so I sat. It was short-legged, or the cushion gave too much, or something, but I ended up so low that I had to lift my head to see over the edge of the huge desk.

"Fine, fine," he told whoever he was talking to. "I don't need to know how the sausage gets made. Just see that what I want happens and tell me when it's done." With that, he banged the phone down and turned a smiling face to me. "Why can't people just honor their commitments? Is that too much to ask in this world?" He reached for a glass of red wine. After taking a long draw, he lifted his knife and fork, began sawing at that hunk of meat. It was rare, bloody, and a pool of red juice gathered on the white plate. As he raised a forkful to his open mouth, he paused and said, "You had something at the buffet, yes?"

I nodded.

He asked, "You want something else? I can have Kendall cook up one of these bad boys for you in ten minutes."

"I'm good," I said.

Sunday seemed distracted by something and for a few minutes, I awkwardly watched him eat. He chowed down on the steak, jabbing with his fork, and made his way through a baked potato, ignoring the bowl of salad. A couple times, he glanced at the computer screen and grimaced. When he finished eating, he snatched the phone, punched in some numbers, and said, "On second thought, Friday morning's not going to work for me. Thursday night. No excuses."

This time when he hung up the phone, it was gentle, and he seemed calmer. There was a smug, satisfied look on his face as he shaved the sweet meat close to the bone. He lifted a red cloth napkin from his lap, dabbed at his white beard, then turned to me, as if he just remembered I was in the room. "All right," he said. "How are things upstairs?"

"Upstairs?" I said. "They're fine."

He lifted his wineglass but didn't drink. "How's the girl?"

"Khajee's upset," I told him.

"For good reason. When my old man died, I went a little nuts. Got so drunk the day of the funeral I picked a fight with the cop directing traffic to the cemetery. Can you believe that?"

"People do weird things when they're stressed out."

He eyed me up and aimed a fork my way, loaded with a thick strip of dripping red meat. "You know Kid, when you put your mind to it, you can be diplomatic. That's a rare talent. The question now is, can you be pragmatic?"

"I'm not sure what you mean."

He chewed, not bothering to keep his mouth shut. After he swallowed he said, "I mean it's time for you to play ball. I'm setting a rematch with you and Badder. And this time it's a fight you're going to lose."

I could tell from his tone that this wasn't a prediction but an explanation. Still, I said, "I beat him before and I'll do it again."

"Actually no you didn't. Beat him, I mean. The big man laid down on my orders, but only after I promised him he could get his championship back inside a week."

I felt a rush of heat on the back of my neck. This didn't seem possible, but suddenly some tumblers fell into place. That look Badder shared with the kid he wishboned, the way he released me during our match, what he said as we left the bathroom at the funeral home, they all made sense now in a way they hadn't before. "Why?" I asked. "How come?"

Sunday put down his utensils, wiped his mouth again with that napkin and tossed it on his desk. "Three reasons: money, money, and money. We play this right, we can milk the rivalry between you two for a while. Don't get all sanctimonious on me now, Kid. I'm not entirely sure what exactly you want out of life, but I'm betting money can get you a lot of it. Am I right?"

I thought about the things money could get me, how at one point that meant college and then a better house for my mom, a better life. I still wanted those things, though they seemed farther away than ever, beyond a distant horizon.

"Money is why you got into this and money is what this means. Losing can be very profitable — this is an important life lesson."

When I said nothing back to him, Sunday went on. "I'll double your payday. You ever make twenty thousand in a night before? That's after Ray's cut. I'll even pay you half up front, sign of good faith and all. I mean, it's not like I don't know where you live."

I stood up, thinking of Khajee and bad karma. "No. I want no part of this. I'm out." With that, I stomped toward the door.

I hadn't taken but a few steps when I heard Sunday rise behind me, the screech of his chair pushed back. "Out is an interesting term. And tell me, once we're no longer friends, why would I not make an anonymous call to the police? What would prevent me from sending them a copy of the video of you beating poor Leonard in the boxcar?"

I stopped and turned to see him coming around his desk. He approached me and set a hand on my shoulder. Sunday sucked on something stuck in his teeth, some bit of beef, and said, "Explain to me in clear terms why you think betraying me now wouldn't come at a cost, that Grunt might not just beat some sense into you, or some horrible accident might not befall dear old Mom?"

I swatted his arm away. "Don't threaten my mother again."

"Tough words," he said, motioning for Grunt to stand his ground by the door. "Maybe you could back them up. But all that sounds so unpleasant, retaliation and consequences. I'd rather talk about rewards and gifts. What if I could offer you, as an added incentive, something more than money?"

His grin was sly. I asked, "What are you getting at?"

"Not long ago in a certain trailer, I suggested the possibility of a reunion between you and your father. I've made those arrangements. Just waiting on a green light from you."

Sweat warmed my forehead. My fingers tightened into fists. I smelled mothballs and I heard my mom cry out. I thought about all the fantasies that had come to me in my private moments for nearly a decade, beating my father, taking the pain he'd given me and returning it to him tenfold over. Yet now that the chance was here, it didn't feel right. This seemed someone else's revenge. I felt like I was on the edge of something, a cliff I should be backing away from.

But Sunday was offering his hand to seal our arrangement,

locking his eyes on mine. "Wolves and sheep, Kid. It's time to pick."

I felt almost hypnotized, and I couldn't find it in myself to refuse him. I saw my hand extend toward Sunday's grip, pump it once, and I heard my voice say, "You got a deal."

It was a mistake to tell Khajee.

The morning after her uncle's funeral, she invited me to go for a jog, said she needed to clear her head. So with my bearded face shrouded by my hoodie, together we ran the Camp Hill route, over the bridge, me with one eye out for cops. We ran down through Seibert and along the forest path. Standing at the base of the rock wall, I bent with my hands on my knees and sucked in air.

She said, "Let's see if you're finally worthy of the Tiger Claw secret." It was the first time I'd heard a smile in her voice in days.

"Let me catch my breath."

"No," she snapped, shifting into a serious tone. "Now, when your body thinks you're exhausted. You have to learn you have reserves you haven't tapped."

I knew what she was trying to do, using her coaching voice, disappearing into that role, because she didn't want to be a mourning niece. But me, I wasn't ready to play along with that script. My head was in a different space. "Look," I said as I straightened, "I've got something to say, and you're not going to like it."

She listened without speaking, no expression as I told her about my arrangement with Sunday. Flatly, I explained about the fixed fight with Badder. As I went into my end of the bargain, the beatdown I was planning on administering to my father,

her eyes — green no more but their true brown, deer-like — grew wide. This part felt like a confession, since I was still waffling between regret for accepting and anticipation of the chance to face him. When I finished talking, Khajee shook her head, took a few steps away from me, and said, "Revenge is all wrong. You aren't the kind of person who would do this."

I thought about all the things that sportswriters had written about me. *Out of control. Brute Boy. No good.* "Maybe I am that kind of person. Maybe I've been that kind of person all along."

"Mac," she said, facing me again. "The kind of person you are, that's not just one thing set in stone. It's not something you discover. It's something you decide."

We walked toward each other, and there was a weird vibe in the air, like maybe we were two brawlers squaring off, about to start swinging. I could see her trying to mask her disappointment. Up close now, I said, "Well, this decision's already been made."

She nodded and looked at the rock wall behind me. "Every decision has a consequence Mac. You'd do well to think that through. I'm going to jog home and try and get my head back in the game, get back to school. I need to restart my life, figure out a few things."

Khajee, always with a better plan than me. I could tell by the way she said what she did that she was imagining running home alone. "That sounds good," I told her. "Go do your thing. I'm going to do what I have to do."

She winced. "Don't do that, Mac. Don't pretend you don't have a choice when you do. I gotta go." With that, she started trotting back up the path, and I watched her until she disappeared around a bend.

I wandered the other way, following the trickling water down to the Conodoguinet. On the banks, I bent for a handful of slim rocks, and for a while I skipped stones just like I did when I was a boy, watching the circles radiate across the water and dissipate. A memory of me and my dad together having a good time floated through my mind, the two of us not far from this place, catching crayfish for fun. I needed two red Solo cups but he just used his hands, snatching them from the water with a pinch. I let go of these images and everything inside me they brought up. And for a time, I tried to think of nothing.

At first it felt a lot like what I'd heard at church, just being still and listening for the voice of the Holy Spirit. But after a while, all I heard was the buzz of traffic on the bridge overheard. Seems I was equally unskilled at meditation and prayer, and all I was really doing was wasting time chucking rocks in the water.

And so that night, in the same way Than's consciousness had traveled on its way to its next form, I found myself taking a trip, but my destination was much more certain: the Fort Indiantown Gap Correctional Facility. I was seated in the front seat of Grunt's van, and he had managed to drive the whole way from Camp Hill without uttering a sound. On edge and feeling a little crazy, I began playing a game with him. I'd say, "What's six hundred and eight minus six hundred and eight?" and when he stayed silent I'd say, "Right! Nothing!" For kicks, I also asked,

"What's Aquaman worth in a fight?" "What can you hear in space?" and "What's the meaning of life?"

I couldn't get a rise out of him, so I retreated to my MP3 player. A little Aerosmith goes a long way.

Finally we rolled into the parking lot where seven years earlier I'd refused to get out of my mom's dilapidated Subaru. I saw the high cyclone fence my father had gripped with his fingers, staring my way. Then and now, curling barbed wire lined the top. Grunt drove us toward a guardhouse, and two towers cast spotlights roaming the yard. It was easy to imagine the men in those outposts, holding loaded rifles at the ready, trained to shoot on sight.

The uniformed woman at the guardhouse seemed to have been expecting us, and as we idled up to her window she turned to a computer screen. The gate before us rolled clear of the road. While it slid out of our way, she pointed and said, "Deliveries are straight ahead, left at the T. You'll see the incinerator and beneath it, a big red door. That's you."

As we followed her instructions, I found myself trying to imagine my mom in this very place. About a year after his incarceration, not long after he got time added to his sentence for fighting, my father began writing her letters. She had joined a support group, stopped drinking, was volunteering at New Hope. Finally, accompanied by our parish priest, she agreed to visit. A half dozen trips later, she convinced me to go, said it would be good for all of us. "Forgiveness helps you as much as the person who wronged you, Eddie. There's just no point in staying angry like this." Once we arrived though, I looked at that barbed wire and remembered my father as he was on the night of the Civil War. I'm not sure what I told her about why I wouldn't get out of the car, but the real truth is that I was scared, plain and simple.

But I wasn't scared tonight. Instead, I was resigned. I didn't want to accept Sunday's claim, that I was a wolf at heart, but I couldn't reject this chance to face my father. So I'd decided before Grunt had picked me up to just smack him around, give him just a slim taste of his old medicine, and call it a night.

Grunt parked by a stark brick building, one with a huge chimney climbing skyward. Even in the blackness of the night, I could see the white-gray smoke billowing from its top. I wondered what dynamo was inside that structure, buried but burning still.

We left the van and headed for the red door, and when I pulled it back I was shocked to see Blalock standing there. "Good evening, Edward," he said. "Always a pleasure."

Grunt and I followed him along a cramped hallway lined with overhead pipes and drooping wires. We turned right and then left, passed through a shadowed area where I guess the light bulb had died out. I had the odd impression that we were descending into the guts of some vast mechanical organism. At one point, we crossed over a rickety catwalk and down below us, in a huge open chamber, great furnaces roared. Conveyer belts fed material into open mouths alive with flame, and even from high above, I could feel the waves of heat on my cheeks, the palms of my hands. When I inhaled, the air singed my nostrils. There were a couple men down there on the floor — shirtless with hard hats — but I couldn't understand how they survived. More than workers, they looked to me like sinners condemned to some unendurable penance.

At the other end of the catwalk, we passed through one more hallway and then entered a large room. Inside were two gigantic metal eggs, each twenty feet around and ringed with dials and valves. They rumbled low and angry. I took these to be boilers and decided we were positioned over the fiery machines below.

In the open space between the twin boilers, a group of men stood around a rough circle of fold-out chairs. I recognized Sunday, but not the other three. One wore a suit and tie, two were in prison guard uniforms.

Blalock said, "You should be grateful. Mr. Sunday called in a lot of favors to arrange this. But he's convinced it's worth it, giving you this. It represents a significant allocation of resources."

"That's fine," I said, mostly to shut him up.

As we neared Sunday, he broke from the others and extended a hand my way. I shook it, and he said, "Here's the man himself, the star of our show." I turned to see if the other men wanted to shake, but they kept their hands at their sides. One of the prison guards, a stocky guy, folded his bulging arms and stared at me hard.

I scanned the room and said, "So where's he at?"

"Patience," Sunday advised. "You'll live longer and won't seem so rude."

I couldn't give a crap how I seemed, but I knew there was no point in saying this.

Sunday slipped a hand over up behind my neck, a power display for the others. "A few rules before we begin. I promised you a chance to reckon with your father and I'm a man of my word. So no one here will intervene unless it's clear you're in over your head."

"Ain't likely," the thicker guard said. He'd been searching my face before, looking for a resemblance. I wonder what else he knew to make him say this.

"Be that as it may," Sunday continued, a little annoyed, "it's important too that you not inflict any damage requiring medical attention. You can rough up your old man all you want. Bloody his face. Give him a good stomping. Anything the infirmary here can handle we can contain, even a few stitches. But if we need an ambulance, the situation gets more complicated. Understood?"

I nodded. No need for them to know it, but this was all in line with my plan.

Sunday said, "This is important. I need to hear you say it."

"You betcha," I said, ticked at being pushed. "I'm not here to kill the guy. This is just going to be a friendly family get-together. I thought there would be cake and ice cream."

Sunday grinned. "Sarcasm is the language of the ignorant, Kid. Don't think so little of yourself."

After the pep talk, we all waited together. Sunday and the guy in the suit sat down and whispered. Grunt took a post by the door. Blalock checked his phone, illuminating his birdish face in the darkness. I paced back and forth by one of the boilers, feeling the radiant heat. That thick guard kept an eye on me and popped his knuckles.

When the door to the catwalk swung open, we all turned

as one to the two figures stepping through. The hallway light cast them in silhouette, so they had to come forward before I could see the big one in the back was a uniformed guard, holding a nightstick in both hands. The one in the front wore flip-flops and was dressed in an orange jumpsuit with short sleeves and had his hands chained at the wrist. But there was something wrong.

"That's not my father," I announced, before I had a chance to consider my words.

The man stopped walking about ten feet away. Frozen in place, he said, "Eddie?"

Sunday motioned with one hand, and the guard behind the chained man pushed him forward, closer to me. I took a few steps in his direction, and we stood face-to-face. He was silent while I looked him over. This man was forty, fifty pounds lighter than my father, and surely a few inches shorter. His hair thin, his cheeks gaunt, his eyes without fire. This man was wearing wire-rim glasses.

But when he spoke, when he licked his lips and searched my face and actually smiled a bit and said, "Eddie, what are you doing here?" I recognized his voice with absolute certainty. It simply didn't go with this body, like in a sci-fi movie where two people switch minds or something.

He leaned forward, and I think he would have tried to hug me but for the handcuffs, and I reared back. "You're thinking of the wrong scene," I said.

Now my father scanned the other people in the boiler room. His eyes fixed on one and he named him, his tone not hiding his disdain. "Sunday." But quickly he turned back to me. "I'd heard you were on the run."

I was surprised he kept tabs on me, that I was even on his radar, but I didn't want to give that away. "I didn't run far."

Sunday stepped forward, put a hand on my father's shoulder. "Don't worry Victor. We've taken him in and are watching over him. He's family."

My father's face, twisted in anger, suddenly looked quite familiar. "So help me God, Sunday, if you —"

Sunday waved a hand dismissively and stepped away, taking a position in front of Grunt. "Forgive me if I'm not in the mood for a series of empty threats." He shifted his gaze to the guard. "Lose the cuffs."

The guard stepped in between me and my father, yanked his hands forward by the chain, and pulled a key ring from his belt. I noticed the chunky guard who had been eyeing me up reach for his holster. With a thumb, he unsnapped the flap.

In turn, my father rubbed each wrist with the opposite hand, and I saw black-green ink covering his forearms. One displayed a huge cross, slightly lopsided, and the other broadcast the message "Christ Alive in Me!!" He saw me looking and I said, "You're freakin' kidding me, right? You're going to tell me you found Jesus in here?"

My father grinned and shook his head. "More like He found me."

"He who was lost has been found," I said. "Praise the lord and pass the cheese whiz."

"Don't mock the Lord, boy." This came from the old man,

the one in the suit, still seated. He looked at Sunday and said, "Can we get on with this? I didn't pay for a conversation."

My father's forehead knotted in confusion, and he looked around as if some answer could be found. Blalock saw the same thing I did and said, "Allow me to articulate your dawning epiphany Victor, in parlance you will comprehend: Your boy is here to even the score."

My father looked at me for confirmation, his eyes tightening, and I nodded. And with this, the whole endeavor returned to my mind. I was over the notion that yes, clearly he was physically not the man he used to be. I'd expected us to be equals, but certainly he was smaller. Still, he was larger now than I was in fourth grade, when he ripped an extension cord from the wall and whipped me with it, just cause the Raiders missed a field goal and I had the nerve to say, "Tough luck." He was larger than I was the day I dumped his liquor down the drain, an act of rebellion that ended with him smacking me with a damn spatula, chasing me in my socks out into the autumn leaves behind the yellow house. His size advantage had never stopped him then, and it wouldn't stop me now.

Sunday said, "Let's begin then, shall we?"

Everyone stepped back, leaving us in the center of a loose circle. I slipped off my hoodie and tossed it into a corner. My father watched this and said, "I don't understand. Listen Eddie, I'm not sure what this jerk's got you involved in, but you can't trust him."

A laugh rattled from me. "He's the guy I can't trust in this room? That's what you're going to tell me?"

"Enough talk," Sunday shouted, his voice agitated now. "Eddie, if you can't follow through on what we discussed, I'll have Grunt take your place."

I turned to the big man, standing with this arms crossed by the catwalk, statue-like. Then I told Sunday, "No. I fight my own battles."

"Fight?" my father echoed. "No way am I going to fight you, Eddie."

Hearing him say this, which somehow I'd been expecting since I saw him, tightened my hands into fists, and in the next instant I was streaking forward, plowing a punch sideways across his chin. It snapped his head hard to the right and he took a step back, shook it off, and then wide-eyed said, "That's one hell of a cross."

I slid easily into a fighting stance, the familiar blood rising. "I got a lot more than that."

But my father remained flatfooted. "Look Francis," he said to Sunday. "I'm not sure what you expected would happen here tonight, but if you think I'm going to fight my son for your sick thrills, you're out of your mind."

"I wanted this," I told him. "This was my idea."

My father looked at me, mouth open in shock.

"Oh yeah," I said. "This scene has kept me company on a lot of long nights." The adrenaline was taking hold of me now, and the thrill of all those violent fantasies settled in me like a fever.

As my father stared my way, something shifted in his eyes. Finally he said, "I understand now." With that, he knelt on the concrete floor, tucked his hands behind his back, and lifted his face. "I was a drunken man, fallen and wrecked, full of hate and spite. You and your mom deserved way better, and me getting locked up was a blessing for us all. I've begged forgiveness for my many sins, prayed a thousand nights for absolution, from your mother and from God. They've given me their answers, and I guess now it's time for you to give me yours."

The man with Sunday dabbed a handkerchief to his forehead and said, "What kind of maudlin BS is all this?"

I reached down and with both hands took hold of my father's orange collar. Twisting my fists I lifted him to his feet. "Be a man," I said. What he used to say to me.

Weakly, he stood before me, his arms still behind his back. "I won't hit you, son."

My left hand held him up and I cocked my right, like I was pulling back a nocked arrow. I was thinking of a cool line to say — *You picked the wrong night to be a pacifist — I'm not your son* — when my fist flew forward, flattening his nose and snapping his head back. Only my grip on his collar kept him from falling, and I'll confess a certain thrill at seeing his eyes roll. I decided I wanted some evidence of his pain, a trail of blood, a shattered tooth, and I drew back my fist again.

"Eddie," he got out before I pounded him to silence.

I could feel his weight as his legs went limp, and I released him, letting his body collapse to the concrete in a heap. "Come on!" I shouted. "At least put up a fight."

Facedown on his knees and elbows, he said, "I won't."

As he turned to look at me, I stepped in and swung my right

foot into his gut, which made a satisfying crunch. Could be I broke a couple ribs, and I didn't give a damn about Sunday's rules. My father doubled over, curled away from me. To my side, the man with Sunday mumbled something about "hardly seems sporting" but I couldn't have cared less. My plan of a soft beat-down was abandoned, and I fell on my father's fragile form, kneeling above him. I whaled away with righteous fury, no hint of pity or mercy.

The sounds he made were pathetic, but I found no further satisfaction in the beating. It came to feel more like an obligation than a pleasure. I paused to catch my breath, and in that break I recognized something. The chamber at the center of my heart, which I'd expected to surge with revenge or justice, remained empty. It was hollow.

His face, I thought. I just need to see his face. So I grabbed him by the shoulders and roughly flipped him to his back, with the full intention of mounting him and returning to his punishment. Only when I rolled him over, and the light above us flashed on his face, he wasn't crying as I'd imagined. He didn't look hurt or scared, or any of the things I'd hoped for. Instead his eyes were flat, deadened. I saw the stubble of beard covering his gaunt cheeks. My father looked resigned to whatever grim fate his future held.

This was a look I knew all too well. The man in the boxcar. My mom. This was a look I'd surely worn back in that moth-ball closet. I stood up, stepped away.

Those gathered around us stopped cheering, and only then did I really register that they'd been applauding.

I stepped over my father's body and walked to where I'd dropped my hoodie, snatched it off the ground. Behind me, I heard whispering, and when I turned the man with Sunday was leaning into him, looking my way. Sunday nodded, then said, "Eddie, you won't get this chance again. You should finish him off."

I looked at my father, sitting up now on the floor with his elbows draped over his knees. I shook my head. "There's nothing left to finish. He's done."

I headed toward the catwalk only to find my path blocked by Grunt, who planted his feet and squared his shoulders. My hackles were up and I didn't stop.

Sunday caught up to me from behind me and took me by the arm. He turned me so I was again facing my father, who had staggered up and was now standing on shaky legs. "You're going to let him off that easy? This is the guy who beat your own mother, disfigured her for life. He's at your mercy."

My father, bent slightly, took a few steps toward us, and Sunday ushered me closer. We faced each other and Sunday egged me on. "He deserves more. Did he ever go easy on you?"

I stared into my father's emotionless face, like some mask he was wearing. I watched it soften, grow tender, and the thinnest of smiles took shape. "It's okay, son. Do what you have to do. I'll understand. He's right that I deserve it. Later, just know that I'm sorry and that I'll always love you because —"

My hand flashed out, grabbing his throat and trapping his words. And I was shoving him backward, hard and fast, so quick his feet almost couldn't keep up. We charged straight past the old man who came with Sunday, straight past the prison guard with the nightstick, and only stopped when we hit a wall, which I smacked his head into. I pinned him against those thick bricks, still gripping his throat. "There's nothing you have to say I want to hear. There's nothing you can do to make up for what you did. I don't forgive you. I don't pity you. I don't hate you."

Here, I released his neck and he took in a deep breath. I said, "You're nothing to me."

I turned and walked past the others, zipped up my jacket and slid the hood over my head, then marched up to Grunt, still blocking my path. He eyed me hard, and I felt ready for anything. But Sunday raised a hand. "We've got a long drive home," he said. "The show here is over."

20

When I fought my father, or rather when I delivered his beatdown, I made at least one stupid mistake. Because I didn't wear gloves or even tape my hands, my knuckles were pretty swollen come morning. Before dawn, I woke on Khajee's couch with a pulsing pain and I stumbled to the kitchen. After wasting a few minutes trying to rig ice packs with plastic bags, I just filled a couple bowls with cubes from the freezer and eased my hands into them. The cold stung like it always does, but just on the other side of that burn, there's a dull numbness that registers as comfort. Sitting in the dark at the kitchen table, my tired mind tumbled to where my bruised and battered father was at that instant — in his cell bunk? On some gray cot in the prison infirmary? Was he thinking of me like I was thinking of him?

Part of me wished Mom could've witnessed what I did, how I avenged her. Maybe she'd feel justified, but more likely, I knew, she'd be horrified. If I could go back and replay my encounter with him, I wasn't sure what exactly I'd do differently. But I knew I wouldn't do the same thing.

I was grateful for the weight of Rosie's thick head, which dropped suddenly on my lap. She had padded out from the bedroom, leaving the door open behind her. I guessed that my attempts at being quiet had failed. The big dog huffed and nuzzled me, mooching for a few pats on the head. In the dim light from the stove, I saw the scar marks where her ear had been mauled and decided to pull one hand from the ice, though when I went to pet her, my touch was too cold. She recoiled and walked over to the front door, scratched at it with a paw.

Before I could get up, Khajee appeared in the entryway to the bedroom, tightening a belt around her pajama robe. Without speaking, she let Rosie out for her morning pee, then scooped out a cup of dog food from the bag under the sink. "Hey," she said sleepily, as she got a pot of coffee brewing.

Rosie came back in and bent to her breakfast, and after a couple percolating minutes, Khajee sat at my side with a steaming white mug. "Looks like you're getting a manicure," she said.

I pulled out a fist and let her examine the swelled flesh.

Peering down she declared, "That'll be two days."

"Just in time then," I said.

With all ten fingers, she tenderly lifted the mug, sipped. "Still think that's a good plan, huh?"

"A deal's a deal," I told her. "And I'm not seeing it as much of a choice, frankly."

She took another drink, slowly. "So you got what you wanted last night? With your father?"

I turned my hands in the ice. The throbbing pain had dulled some. "I got enough."

"You don't exactly sound convinced."

"I am," I told her. "Absolutely. One hundred percent."

"If you say so. Will you be around after school?"

I looked at her. "I can be."

"Okay," she said, standing. "There's just something I need to do. Something I don't really want to do on my own."

"I'll help however I can," I told her. My mom always said there were two kinds of friends, and you could tell the difference if you called them up at midnight and said you needed them to come over. One sort asked, "What's up?" The other said, "I'm on my way."

Khajee finished her coffee and showered in silence, then left for school with no further explanation. Given the shape my hands were in, there'd be no lifting weights, and I thought about going for a jog but couldn't summon the mojo. So instead, I took Rosie for a marathon walk along the waterfront, following the bike path all the way to the wildlife refuge. I found the underpass where Khajee and I first trained not all that long ago. It felt like a year had passed. Walking those wooded trails, I kept getting caught up at the forks, trying to decide which way to go. Looking back at my recent history, I couldn't shake the sense that I'd made a series of truly crappy decisions, award-winning screw-ups. Each one seemed to lead me further from the life I was supposed to live and deeper into something else. And now, this match with Badder felt like one more mistake.

Maybe worse, my involvement with Sunday seemed about to escalate. In the prison parking lot, leaning against Grunt's van, Sunday told me he was glad I'd given my father what he deserved. "Welcome to the pack," he said, flashing his teeth. "So look, Grunt needs to take a trip down to DC next week. We got word that a former associate is flying in, and he needs to be taught a particular kind of lesson. You'll be lead instructor." This was no request, I could tell. Sunday was giving me an order.

I felt my life racing down a dead end alley, and I needed a way to fix all that was wrong.

Back at the apartment, I iced my hands more and watched a couple hours of fighting tapes, trying not to stare at Than's empty seat. I wished he were alive, and I recalled him mocking game show contestants and bad poker players. I imagined telling him about my fight with my father and the deal I'd made with Sunday. I could hear his goofy voice, only from my memory, saying, "Not so good."

I made some lunch and watched a dumb movie about a scientist's college intern who accidentally activates a defective time machine. He keeps jumping throughout history — from the Revolutionary War to the time of the dinosaurs to the year 2176 — trying to get back to where he belongs. The harder he tries the more lost he becomes.

Instead of disappearing into the sci-fi storyline, I found my mind sliding to real-life images of my mom alone and crying, my father's ragged tattoos, the hilly campus in State College where now I'd never take classes. I thought of the future, the fight with Badder, the nights with Grunt, what I might be pressured to do down in DC. I felt like I was in a match against an opponent who was dictating the pace, blocking every move. A couple crazy ideas popped up, schemes that promised escape, but each seemed more farfetched than the movie's lame plot.

After the intern made it home with the help of a resourceful caveman ally, I decided to surrender to the lazy impulse that had been hounding me all day. I shut out the lights and pulled down the blinds, curled up on the couch, and plugged into *Led*

Zeppelin III on my MP3. I made it through "Immigrant Song" and "Friends" but passed out somewhere in the middle of "Celebration Day."

During my nap, I was visited by uneasy dreams. In one, the Perkins building was on fire and I was in the parking lot, watching the firefighters douse the flames with streams of water that had no effect. Someone yelled, "There's still somebody trapped inside. She's burning!" In another, I was a toddler, at the mall with my father. It was crowded, and he held my hand to keep from losing me as people bumped into us. There was Christmas music playing, and everyone seemed very tall. To make way for a woman in a wheelchair, I let go of his hand and immediately got hit by a swinging bag of presents. This spun me around and just like that, I'd lost him. I stood still for a moment, then began rushing through the forest of legs, thinking I was heading in his direction but really not sure. Panic drove me sprinting blindly, and as I banged into shoppers they looked down at me with annoyance and anger. A man with a black hat tried to grab me by the wrist but I wriggled free. And as I ran on and began to weep, the terror of it all settled over me. I might never find him. I might be alone.

I woke to the sound of Khajee coming in the front door, Rosie getting to her feet and woofing to greet her. "Hey girl," Khajee said, rubbing her head. When she saw me on the couch, she added, "Sorry to wake you Sleeping Beauty. It's three-thirty."

I looked around the apartment, grateful to not be a lost child, and wiped a little sweat that had been gathering on my forehead, the back of my neck. I asked her how school was, and she told me it was fine. She dropped her backpack by the TV and set a white cloth bag on the ground next to it. It looked sort of like a knotted pillowcase.

"How are your hands?" she asked as she stepped into the bathroom.

I sat up, rubbing my neck and wiping the sleep from my eyes. Those dreams had seemed so real, and I was trying to remember if the one with me in the mall was purely fantasy or if, as I was starting to think, it was a lost memory that had resurfaced. I glanced at my knuckles, still swollen but not nearly as tight. "Better than they were."

Rosie seemed curious about that pillowcase pouch. She bent her nose to it and sniffed all around the base. Khajee emerged from the bathroom and yelled, "No, Rosie! No!" She yanked the bag up and the dog retreated, tail drooped. Khajee cradled the sack, and now I saw her puffy eyes and wondered if she'd been crying.

I asked, "What's up with the bag?"

"It's my uncle," she answered bluntly. "All that's left of him."

"Damn." As soon as the word slipped out, I wished I had it back. "Sorry," I added quickly. "I guess I just wasn't expecting that answer."

Khajee carefully set the bag on the kitchen table, emptied the books from her backpack, and slid the sack into the largest pouch, zipped it tight. I stood and went to her side. I couldn't decide if I should put my hands on her shoulder to offer some comfort or just leave her be. With some people, it's hard to know. She turned into me and said, "So about that favor."

"Sure," I said. "Right. Whatever you need."

"This is a little embarrassing," she said, dipping her head. "The thing is, I never learned to swim. And I'm kind of afraid of water."

I pictured a kid Khajee in a life vest, bobbing on waves in the Atlantic. But I still wasn't entirely sure what this had to do with Than's remains and why she needed my help. I was about to find out.

On the long walk to City Island, we didn't talk much. I didn't ask her why we were going there, though a pretty good guess gradually came to me. At one point, while we were waiting for the light at Harvey Taylor Bridge, she adjusted the backpack straps and I said, "I can take that for you."

She shook her head and said, "This is mine to carry," then cut across the stream of traffic even though the light hadn't changed. I followed her, and cars laid on their horns. She didn't seem to notice.

City Island sits in the middle of the Susquehanna River. Around that stadium where the Senators play semipro baseball, they've got all kinds of touristy activities sprinkled on the outside: a mini-golf course, a train ride, a steamboat, an old-style arcade. Along the bank on the western side, there's a business that'll rent you canoes and kayaks. This is where Khajee led me, crossing a parking lot loaded with commuters heading home.

She approached a young guy in a booth scrolling through something on his phone. He looked startled to see us, and Khajee studied the prices on the board over his head. She asked me, "A tandem, okay?"

I told her it sounded good, and the kid passed over two life jackets. "Federal regulations," he explained. We also needed to sign waivers: We recognized that kayaking is a dangerous activity; we recognized that swift-moving waters can pose unforeseen hazards.

It was uncomfortable watching Khajee put on her life vest, knowing for sure where her mind was trying to take her. As for me, I had to fiddle with the straps to get the extra-large vest secured across my chest, but once I did, we walked down to where a half dozen brightly colored kayaks waited like beached whales. One had two seats and Khajee and I each took an end, dragged it to the water's edge. After removing the white sack, she tossed her backpack on the ground. When she settled into the front seat, she nestled the sack on her lap, cradled it like precious cargo. I passed her one of the double-edged paddles and shoved the kayak into the water, then hopped in and snagged my paddle from the dock. We were off.

To our right, a couple folks strolled along a raised metal walkway, one that ended after fifty feet. Directly across from it on the western shore, a similar structure waited. From the gap in between, I'd always figured that some accident had wiped out the middle section. It looked like a small drawbridge with no middle, two disconnected dead ends.

"Where to?" I asked her as we paddled into the river's flow.

"Away from people," she said. "We need something like privacy."

On the far bank, three restaurants faced us, their decks filling with patrons. "That means south I guess," I told her.

We dipped our paddles and aimed away from the broken bridge and put ourselves out into the current. Because we were moving with the river's gentle flow, mostly I just used my paddle to keep us straight, and almost right away Khajee lifted her paddle and set it across the boat. My hands were tender and puffy, but I could manage a decent enough grip.

We drifted beneath the Market Street Bridge, one that supports power lines, and one that handles trains. Just before passing under the Capital Beltway, we had to navigate down some mild rapids, just enough white water to make the boat rock back and forth a bit. She grabbed the rim of her seat and I said, "You all right?"

"Fine," she spit out, though I hardly believed her.

For about five minutes after that, Khajee didn't say anything, and now and then I thought I heard her sniffling, but rather than pester her, I let her be.

South of the beltway, the river opens up a bit, and there's a series of smaller islands scattered across the waterway. Each one is home to a scraggly forest, and I remembered the rumors when I was a kid about such spots, that these were home to a pack of wolves that swam across the water at night and prowled the streets of the big city.

I steered us into a wide lane between two strips of land, hiding us from any onlookers on either bank. A half mile behind us, traffic hummed from I-83, and to our south, the plumes of smoke from Three Mile Island billowed into the sky.

"Do you think this'll do?" I asked.

Khajee was quiet, and I saw she was cradling the white sack. Finally she asked, "This water, it leads to the sea, right?"

"Eventually," I said. "The Susquehanna runs down into the Chesapeake, and that runs into the Atlantic. So yeah, I guess so."

Khajee didn't reply.

I asked, "Is this a Buddhist thing?"

She turned around. Her cheeks were wet. "Loi angkarn is a Thai Buddhist tradition," she said. "It means 'floating the ashes.'"

The kayak turned a bit and Khajee shifted in her seat, making a space to work at her side. She unknotted the sack, withdrew a white plastic bag, and reached inside. Her hand came out with a fistful of white flower petals, and she tossed these into the open sack. Next she began to whisper in Thai. I couldn't tell if she was communing with her uncle or offering a prayer. "Crap," she said unexpectedly, shaking her head. "I forgot the incense."

After this, she took a deep breath and retied the cloth, then held it gently over the side, gripping it by the knot. The current tugged on the bag, and for a second I wondered if she might not change her mind, bring the remains back. But just then her hand opened and the sack slipped away, bobbing along the surface as it began to take on water. She shook out the plastic bag and the remaining petals flitted through the air like tiny butterflies. They settled on the rippling water and drifted with

Than's remains. After a hundred feet I couldn't see the petals or the cloth sack anymore, though I can't be sure if it sank or I just lost it in the tiny whitecaps.

"There's supposed to be incense," Khajee said, chastising herself again. "At least I think there is."

"It's okay," I told her. "All this is perfect."

Throughout the ceremony, I'd been steadily back-paddling to keep us where we were. I let the silence hang for a while, then asked, "Okay, what now?"

"Now we go home," Khajee said, and she grabbed her paddle. But before she dipped it into the water, without facing me, she said, "Mac. These last weeks. Today. I'm not sure I could've done this alone. I owe you."

"We're even," I said, believing it.

Together, we turned the kayak north and began rowing against the trickling current. It wasn't easy, fighting against the flow. We had to cut diagonally across the rapids and even after that, we had to dig and strain to gain ground. But I was glad for the distraction of the exercise, happy to have my mind on a task I could complete. When we were almost back, we hit an easy patch, and ahead of me, Khajee began to hum, a song both soft and low.

At City Island, we settled up with the kid in the rental shack and gathered Khajee's empty backpack. We hadn't walked far before Khajee sat on a bench and said, "Maybe we could just rest a minute. Would that be all right?"

"Sure," I said. "All good."

A horse-drawn carriage with no passengers clip-clopped past us. The driver wore a black top hat.

"You okay?" I asked Khajee.

She inhaled and let out a long breath. "I feel guilty for being angry at Than."

"Angry?" I asked.

She nodded. "For the dumb choices he made. All the money he lost. Not taking care of himself. He didn't have to die like this, not now. It's just messed up that my sadness is mixed up with being so upset with him, you know?"

"It's not messed up," I said. "It's human."

She went on. "For a long time, I knew he wasn't well. But I never really thought about life without him, what I'd do. I just wanted to focus on taking care of him like he always took care of me."

"You were a good niece," I said. "A good daughter, really. Nobody could've done better, especially with the attitude he had."

Khajee shook her head. "He was strong-willed, that's for sure."

"Stubborn," I offered.

"Bullheaded."

I thought for a second. "Uncompromising."

"Intransigent."

I raised my hands. "I surrender," I said. "I bow before your superior SAT preparations."

It was good to see her start to smile, but she blocked the pleasant expression before it took full bloom. Abruptly, she stood up and starting walking, and I followed. She led us over the walking bridge, which had a slim stream of late afternoon joggers and parents pushing baby strollers. A concrete sidewalk lines one side, but the bridge surface itself is made of these tight metal grates, so you can see down to the water passing below. The current tugged along tree branches, swirled in eddies around the pillars, flowed south.

About halfway across, Khajee came to a stop and held the railing, looking downstream. I was sure that bag of ashes was on her mind, and it seemed clear she was thinking about Than's spirit, or his consciousness, or whatever it was we'd call what he'd been, and what he was on his way to becoming. "How are you doing?" I asked.

"I feel strange."

"Strange in what way?"

"Hard to say. I just thought I'd feel different than this, after I did that. You know, more at peace, less upset."

Together we watched the waters roiling beneath us. Without looking at me, Khajee said, "You haven't said anything about the prison. All I know is your hands are swollen."

"What do you want to know?"

"Did you really get what you wanted?"

"No," I said right away. "Not really. Not at all." I remember my father on his knees, urging me to punish him. "I think I feel kind of like you do now. Like I was due some big release or something. I thought it would be an ending."

All this made me think about Mrs. DJ's class, how the books we read always had some big moral at the conclusion, a clear lesson the main character learned. I could feel my story taking shape, but I had no sense of impending enlightenment.

Khajee was quiet, but I felt certain she understood. A fishing boat puttered below, just one guy at the wheel. "There are no endings," she said. "Only transformations. Only changes."

I recalled the monk's words. For an instant, my tumbling thoughts came into alignment — a couple of those unlikely schemes merged — and I saw what was meant to come next. "Yeah," I said. "Changes sounds like the way to go."

Khajee turned to me. "What does that mean?"

"Do you have your phone with you?"

"My phone?" She shook her head. "It's back at the apartment."

"Let's go," I told her, leaving the railing and starting across the bridge. "I need to make a few calls."

21

*T*hat day when we floated Than's ashes, I ended up making three phone calls from Khajee's apartment. The first was to Shrimp. The instant he heard my voice, he began firing off questions like a machine gun, and it was hard to get him to shut up and just listen. Lured in part by the promise of a free Happy Meal, I convinced him to meet me at the McDonald's in Camp Hill late that night, where I saw it'd been a while since he dyed his hair that electric blond. Dark roots showed. We ordered and sat at a table like nothing strange was taking place. On the bench between us, I casually set down a shoe box with thirty-five thousand in cash, this the total of my winnings, the advance on my rematch, and the bonus money Sunday paid me for my "side work." In a low, clear voice, I explained to Shrimp exactly what I needed him to do, and he stopped dipping his nuggets in barbecue sauce. With his mouth half-stuffed with processed chicken, Shrimp said, "Too risky." After he finished swallowing, he continued. "Even for you, Mac. Too much can go wrong."

"Nothing's gonna go wrong," I assured him, then I stood to leave. "I've got everything under control."

Shrimp agreed because he's a good and loyal kid, but the truth is, my scheme was riskier than even he knew. I hadn't told him about Grunt, who I didn't think would hesitate to pull that gun and put it to use if there was trouble, which was very much what I was inviting into my world.

The second call was to my mom. I timed it so I knew she wouldn't be home and I could just leave her a message, which I thought would just be easier for all involved. How do you apologize for putting someone you love through hell? I told my mom how much I appreciated everything she'd ever done for me, believing in me when I didn't always deserve it. I told her not to worry about me. I told her I'd found a way to fix everything.

Just like with Shrimp, I tried to sound more confident than I really was. There were too many variables, something Khajee pointed out from minute one when I explained my plan to her, asking for her help too. She knew the risks, though just like me, she couldn't resist the rewards.

But with my third call, I set in motion a series of events that couldn't be stopped. It was the same as any move you make on a wrestling mat — the instant the decision happens, you need to commit 100 percent. In a match, half-assing it can get you crushed. In a scheme like I was plotting, it could get you legit killed.

The next day, Blalock arrived right on time to bring me and Khajee to the rematch with Badder, just around sundown. Khajee sat in the back, and I climbed in up front. "So where we headed?" I asked casually, hoping for a heads-up.

"Due south," Blalock answered, cagey as always.

I glanced in the rearview, trying to make eye contact with Khajee. We both understood how important her role was in all this, and I knew I could count on her.

Cruising down 81, Blalock described a series of investment

opportunities he wanted me to be aware of. One was a vape shop in Mechanicsburg, another was some sort of Internet security start-up. Clearly he pictured me as fat with cash and having no prospects. "The only way to ensure your future is to invest wisely. Sow your seed well so that you might reap the rewards."

"You sound like a preacher in need of a tent," I said. "I'll think about your offer." The truth, of course, was that all my money was tied up.

We drove for longer than usual, almost an hour, and this made me worried about the timing of the drama I was trying to orchestrate. In the back seat, Khajee was silent.

Finally we pulled off just north of Chambersburg, and we made our way to a mega-mall from the 80s. The parking lot was the size of a golf course, and there were a half dozen anchor stores, but all the names had been stripped from the sides. Judging from that, the cracked asphalt of the lot, and the weeds sprouting up, the place had been a ghost town for years.

We parked by a service entrance, joining a dozen or so vehicles waiting in a pack. Blalock killed the engine and I said, "So this is it, huh?"

Maybe he heard the extra emphasis in my voice meant for Khajee, but he turned to me and said, "You seem agitated. Perhaps you should gather yourself before we proceed."

I opened my door. "I'm good to go."

The three of us entered through what had once been a department store, and the inside was abandoned, dark. Every twenty or thirty feet, a battery-powered camping lantern on the floor cast an eerie glow on the left-behind shelving and racks, the nude mannequins forever holding their fashion poses. It was all damn creepy. At one point, something shuffled in the shadows and Khajee said, "Look."

Blalock and I turned to see a fox trotting calmly from behind a sale counter, its legs long and lean. He didn't seem to care about us, and he disappeared into the blackness.

"Nature abhors a vacuum," Blalock said.

We left the department store and emerged into a cavernous corridor — two stories, lined with smaller shops on both levels. Above us the glass ceiling let in some dim moonlight, which tinted the strange world a bluish gray. A few of those windows were broken, and something fluttered in the dark void over our heads — birds or bats, I couldn't tell.

Ahead of us, at the intersection of several hallway spokes, there was an oasis of bright light, and we headed in its direction. Some of the storefronts we passed were gated with bars and some weren't. A couple had graffiti spray-painted across them. We went by a twenty-foot screw in the center of the lane by some benches, then fifty feet later, an enormous extinguished cigarette. "Is this supposed to be art?" Khajee asked.

"If they were aiming for piece of crap," I said, "they nailed it."

Blalock added, "No accounting for the aesthetic of the masses."

When we reached our destination, we found a huge circular staircase looping around what had once been a fountain I guess. Now it was just a dried up concrete circle, about the same size as a wrestling mat. Just outside it, there was a row of chairs set up, but a bunch of the high rollers had climbed the ramp for a better vantage point. From thirty feet above, they leaned over the railing and waited for the spectacle.

Beaming lights hung from those same railings, and thick cables ran from them down and out, toward a distant rumble in that cavern's pitch-blackness. I pictured a gas-powered generator, though this was just a guess.

As we entered the light, Grunt stepped from the shadows and blocked our path, hands crossed at his waist, looking like some overgrown crossing guard. He eyed each of us in turn, then nodded once in recognition, allowing us to pass.

Sunday made his way over, grinning unapologetically. "The numbers are off the charts," he said. "We've already got double our previous record for viewers."

"Exceptional," Blalock offered.

Sunday fixed his gaze on me, stroked his white beard once. "And you. You're prepared to play your part?"

I nodded. "I promise you a show you won't believe."

Khajee nudged me from the side, and I reined in my smirk. "I was wondering though, how's the betting coming? What do the oddsmakers think of my chances?"

"Most figure the last fight was a fluke and Badder's due for revenge. The money is following him and he's still the favorite, paying out two to three. Don't be too upset though. At three to one you're not much of an underdog."

What this meant was that for every dollar someone bet on me, they'd get paid three if I won. In my head, I did some quick calculations. If Shrimp could get his hands on his big brother's credit card again and did like I told him, the haul would be just over $100,000. I thought about those Sunday afternoon open houses, the way the realtors always looked at me and Mom like we didn't belong. I imagined her strolling up to one in some bright newly finished kitchen and saying, "I'll take it."

Sunday slid an arm around my shoulders, pulled me away from the others. He leaned his face in close to the side of my head and said, "Listen. Everybody likes a trilogy. You know how they work, right? I've got my eyes on how the money is playing out tonight. A week from now, depending on how things go, you, me, Badder, we'll figure out how to close out your little feud and we'll all make a killing. But tonight, this plot twist works best for us if you go down fast. Like inside thirty seconds even. You with me?" Here, he gripped my neck for emphasis, and again, I was struck by his old man strength. "Just be a good boy and go down, all right Kid?"

Knowing what I knew, my real intention, it was hard to keep a poker face, but I tried to keep my expression flat when I said, "You can count on me, Mr. Sunday."

After my little pep talk, he went off to attend to other matters. While the remaining high rollers made their way in, I saw him getting them drinks from somewhere, slapping backs, shaking hands, working the crowd. Blalock stayed near me and Khajee, so I was never alone with her. She made eye contact with me a couple times in a way that seemed meaningful, but I couldn't tell for sure what that meant. Had she sent the text like we'd agreed? Was the cavalry on its way? We were so far from Camp

Hill, but if they arrived too soon, my match would never happen and there would be no payout.

The first two matches were clearly choreographed crowd-pleasers. Maddox, who still had some fans I guess, was given a sacrificial lamb from West Virginia. He worked him over for a few minutes, then dropped him with a nice uppercut. I saw the guy flatten out on the ground and looked at his eyes — clear and bright — and I knew he could rise if he wanted to. But he was following Sunday's script too, and like me, it called for him to lose. So he stayed down.

Khajee fitted my fighting gloves onto my hands, which were tender from my fight with my dad but healed enough to grapple. She pulled the straps tight. "Tiger tough," she said.

"Tiger tough," I repeated.

The second match gave Santana, head wrapped in a halo of gauze to protect that ear, a chance to pound a hulk from New York. The muscle-bound dude seemed to have the upper hand for the first couple minutes, but go figure, our saintly man somehow managed a dramatic victory with a spinning kick, one that sent the ogre tumbling over the concrete rim of the dried-up fountain, crashing right into a tripod camera. Maybe I was seeing things wrong, but everything looked fake now. The scales had fallen from my eyes.

As they righted that camera and Santana took his victory bows, the hulk's people dragged him from the combat zone. The air shifted around me. I could sense the crackling anticipation of all the fans circling the fighting pit, and all those watching from home. I stood on the edge of the fountain, framed by Khajee and Blalock. He said, "It's like the Coliseum. You make a noble gladiator."

I hadn't felt especially noble lately, but that was something I was working on.

Sunday appeared on the ramp, twenty feet up, and the mobile cameraman moved to the center of the fountain just to get a better shot. From down below like that, lit by lights above him, I'll bet Sunday came across like a god.

"Friends and fellow fight aficionados, the time has come for payback. For retribution!"

At this, Badder came bolting from the darkness across from me, as if born from its black fabric. He jogged around the mobile cameraman, throwing elbows, heaving his hands up as the crowd cheered. His face was again tattooed, and I had the strange urge to tell him his big sister did a great job for the big show. I noticed he didn't offer his signature warrior scowl, and this made him seem more serious. Beneath all the makeup and the playacting, Badder had pride, and losing to me — even on purpose — had cost him something. Tonight, he was expecting to get that back. The audience picked up on his intensity too, and they howled their approval.

Khajee stepped in front of me, slipped my mouth guard in, and I waited for her final words of wisdom and inspiration. "Kick his ass," she said.

Sunday swept a hand toward me, just in the shadow of the ramp, and the cameras' lenses followed to aim my way. "Or could this be a night of validation? Are we witnessing the dawn of a new Brawlers era? I call forth Wild Child!"

The crowd surged when I walked into the light, and I found myself smiling at how I alone interpreted Sunday's words. He pulled out that stupid gong, and as Badder and I circled each other in the fountain's center, the people grew rabid with excitement and yelled, "No mercy! Prepare! Brawl!"

Badder, who'd been tentative in our first match, shot in off the whistle that night, catching me flatfooted. He was shooting for a double-leg, but I sprawled on instinct and crossfaced his ugly mug. Still, he got a good grip on my right knee, managed to topple me to the hard surface of the dried pool. He covered quick, and mere moments into a match I had to win, I found myself flat on my back, staring straight up. Above me, through the nautilus swirl of the curling ramp, I saw for the first time a glass dome capping the open space. I imagined SWAT troops rappelling from a hovering helicopter, but this felt like fantasy to me.

Kneeling across my belly, Badder pounded down hammer fists, doing his best to bludgeon my head. But I managed to dodge those punches because he was slow and sloppy. It wasn't hard to read his increasing frustration. Finally he flattened out, draping that meaty gut across my face and tucking his head in tight so no one could see him say, "Let's just get this over with. My turn tonight, remember?"

When I didn't instantly agree, he popped a few punches into the side of my skull and said, "Don't let that last show confuse you, Baby Blue. Ain't no way you can take me."

On my back still, I worked my way up so we were face-to-face before I quietly answered. "We'll see."

Badder's eyes froze, and I planted a kiss on his cheek, just cause I knew it'd freak him out. And indeed, he sprang upright. Rather than try to escape though, I lurched up too, overshot his head, and reversed my right elbow around his neck. When I flung myself back down, I smashed his face into the concrete floor. For a second he went limp, and I rolled to the side, flipping him onto his back. I kept my hold and arched my spine, ratcheting my forearm deeper into his gullet. Like this, there was no way the man could breathe for long. He flailed beneath me, but he wasn't going anywhere. I strained and held tight and waited — either for the tap or the dead weight that meant he was passed out.

Instead my groin exploded in fiery pain. White light shot through my eyes. Must've been a knee Badder jammed between my legs, violating the one rule boys learn on every playground. The shock and pain stunned me, and Badder slid free, rose to his feet to gather his breath. I heard the crowd booing as I struggled to my hands and knees, knowing how vulnerable I was on all fours.

Badder didn't waste the opportunity. He kicked me straight in the face — no technique, nothing fancy, just a drop kick that snapped my head. I caught a glimpse of Badder grinning, then he bounced away. Groggy, I swung a lazy hand out for a leg or a foot, anything to get hold of him and bring us both to the ground, but my fingers clutched nothing but air.

Suddenly a massive weight made all four limbs shudder.

Badder was straddling my back, and he quickly coiled his thick legs inside mine, hooking his feet on the backs of my shins. This was bad. Worse still, as out of it as I was, I couldn't do much to defend a chokehold he was securing from above. Even as his arms put my neck in a vise, I locked my elbows and steadied my legs, strengthening my base because I knew what would come next. Astride my spine with that chokehold, Badder was in a dominant position. If he tumbled us to the side, got under me, then he'd be choking down instead of up, and that would be the end for sure.

So we engaged in a sort of paralysis battle, a tug-of-war with our whole bodies. He yanked and tugged and heaved from above, trying to roll us or break my stance, and below I held firm — legs like rocks, arms like Roman columns. Badder's choke was sunk deep, but Khajee'd had me in tighter locks and I'd withheld for a while, scrunching my shoulders to lift my deltoids and fortify my neck.

All in all, I'd say Badder was exerting more energy than me. But the edge of my vision was starting to go hazy, and I didn't know how much longer I could hold out. With no other option, I had to try a crazy move, something I thought under the best circumstances would push the needle right to the edge of impossible.

I reared back a little, not so much as to give him momentum, just enough to allow me to swing my right foot forward, plant it. Genuflecting now with Badder draped on my back, I began to feel just how heavy three hundred pounds could be. With some of the weight off my arms, I could reach up and take hold of his forearm, inch it off my neck to let a little oxygen slip in. I took half a breath, but it felt like plenty.

A few in the crowd realized what I was thinking, and I heard somebody yell, "No. No. No freakin' way!" I didn't care much for the vote of no confidence.

Badder still had legs in, and he was committed to this choke, so he didn't realize how vulnerable he'd be if I could pull off this stunt. I leaned into my planted foot, drove forward slowly, igniting every muscle in my lower back, and made just enough space to bring my left foot forward. Now I sat in a sort of squat with my opponent essentially piggybacking me. Badder yanked backward, and I teetered, fought forward, teetered back again. This was the spot, this was the moment balanced on a pin when everything would be decided.

On my first attempt to stand, nothing happened. I strained and tried to rise, but the weight was crushing, and I stalled like an engine. Badder snickered in my ear and tightened his grip on my throat. The darkness clouding the edges of my vision pulsed and began to swarm toward the center. Soon I'd be cast into blackness. I had enough in the tank for one more try, but I was so tired, and the old notion of being a failure weighed me down. But where my mind was failing, my body stayed strong. My muscles remembered all those hours in the gym, squatting with a bar bent across my shoulders, the stink of sweat and the clanking of the weights, the gritted teeth, and the forehead veins I'd see bulging in the filthy mirror.

When I first heard the sound, I didn't recognize my own voice. It came out of me, half scream and half roar, a battle cry from my soul's depths. All I can compare it to is the sound women make giving birth in movies, and that feels right, because something was coming alive that night. Holding Badder's forearm, I slowly rose. On shaky knees with trembling thighs, I rose. With a pressure in my head that threatened to pop the eyes from my skull, I rose.

Maybe the crowd went wild, I don't know. I didn't hear them. And all I saw was Khajee's tiny face, right there thirty feet ahead of me. Her eyes were open wide, but still she seemed calm. She knew what I was up to, and she nodded, just once.

If that had been a regular wrestling match, the instant I got to my feet the ref would've blown his whistle and tapped the back of his head, indicating "potentially dangerous." There's a damn good reason for this, as Badder was about to find out. Maybe he could've saved himself just by trying to work a foot down, but I'd bargained that he wouldn't surrender the hold he had, and given how wobbly my legs were, it seemed a good bet that I'd collapse any second.

Instead of collapsing though, I leaned forward, gathered myself. Clutching his forearm around my neck with both hands, I then sprang back, picking my feet up high as we plummeted. Imagine someone doing a backward flop off a high dive.

We slammed into the concrete with a thud, a five-hundred-plus-pound bomb impacting on Badder. He made a whumpf! sound, followed by a groan, and the audience gasped as one, then went stone silent. Badder's arms were instantly limp, and I flipped around to face what I was sure was an unconscious opponent. I was shocked to see him looking up at me, stunned but still awake enough to make that wide-eyed, tongue-waggling face one final time.

"You ain't eating me today," I said, then I hammered a right that snapped his head sideways. His eyes rolled to cue balls, and the crowd erupted.

I staggered to my feet, and the guy with the shoulder-mounted camera charged in to get a close-up, and all around me the applause seemed amplified. It took some effort to lift my weary arms, but I thrust them up to better absorb the glory I'd earned. For a few seconds, I basked in their adoration, catching my breath and scanning the faces of the fans. There was Blalock squinting through his thick lenses, perplexed. And Maddox and Santana and even Dominic, reluctantly clapping with odd smiles on their faces. Grunt looked at Sunday, unsure how to react it seemed, but Sunday locked his expression on me, daggers flashing in both eyes.

This is when the lights went out.

To be clear, not every light was extinguished. The camera right in front of me must've had a battery pack, because its twin bulbs stayed illuminated, radiant in the inky void. But all the others hung above us on the curving ramp went dead. For an instant, I felt suspended in a glowing white sphere.

"What the hell?" somebody asked.

There was a sort of general chaos, as for a few seconds everyone seemed to speak at once. Then a bullhorn voice, loud and distinct, cut through the cacophony. "Police! Stay where you are!"

This cry came from down the dark cavern where those

power cables led, and it didn't take a genius to figure the cops had cut the juice. Now they were charging toward us from that direction, two dozen bouncing beams of light in the pitch dark. Of course, in the history of law enforcement, the demand to stay where you are has only had one traditional response, and our group was no different: Everybody freaked.

The fans, the brawlers, all of us scattered. Thanks to the cameraman's light, I could see people scurrying back and forth, crashing into each other, and Khajee made her way to me through the stream. She yelled, "Now what?"

The police were storming toward us, I imagined in heavy gear with guns drawn. Somewhere in this assault was Harrow, the recipient of my third fateful phone call, but of course I couldn't see her. "Down! Down! Down!" the bullhorn voice demanded.

The cameraman got to his knees and his light was doused. And I was about to comply too, exhausted and willing, ready for an end to all this. But some of the guys — maybe a couple of the high rollers, maybe their bodyguards — had other ideas. Their gunshots rang out from the curling stairway, echoed in the central chamber. The police returned fire, and Khajee and I crouched low in the fountain for cover. But then she tugged my hand and said, "Mac. Look!"

Down the corridor we'd come up earlier, a single glowing light danced in the darkness. Somebody had snapped up one of those lanterns and was fleeing along the dimly lit path, making a break for the cars. Khajee said what I was thinking, "Sunday," and as one, we got up and raced after him.

Following the lanterns on the ground, we pursued the fleeing light past the same stores we'd come by earlier, past the humongous extinguished cigarette. But as we neared the abandoned anchor store with its army of mannequins, the lantern we were chasing suddenly paused, a hundred feet ahead of us. Beyond it, strobing red and blue lights flickered, and it was easy to picture police cruisers in the parking lot. That lantern suddenly reversed course, coming right back at us. "Hide!" Khajee whispered. "Into the shadows!"

We leapt from the illuminated path, got low behind a bench, but before the lantern reached us, it veered to the side and disappeared. I wondered if Sunday had just turned the darn thing off, but Khajee snapped up a lit lantern of her own, and we rushed to the area where we last saw Sunday's. She located a door, and when she lifted her light it shined on the words, "Staff Only."

"Maintenance hallway," she said. "This runs behind all the stores. There's got to be an exit. C'mon."

Together we charged down a dim concrete hallway, coming quickly to an intersection. It felt like we were in a labyrinth, complete with the threat of a Minotaur. "Which way?" I asked. She shushed me. In the silence, deep down the darkness to our right, we heard mumbling.

Quiet as we could, we headed in the direction of the voice. There was a loud banging, muffled curses. After a left at the next crossroads, we saw a glow around the bend just ahead. Khajee squeezed my hand, released it, then brought a finger to her lips. She extinguished our lantern, which I thought was pretty smart.

We crept ahead and peered around the corner. Forty feet ahead of us in the lantern's shine stood not just Sunday but Grunt, who was slamming his big shoulders into a locked door. They were totally distracted, and we snuck toward them, all but on tiptoes. Grunt battered the door but it didn't budge. Sunday said, "Enough. Try shooting the damn lock."

With this, the two of them stepped back. Grunt yanked a pistol from his beltline and leveled it at the door. The report was loud and sharp, a flashing burst of white and a deafening pop that echoed down the corridor. Khajee gasped. In the silence that followed, Sunday said, "You hear that?"

He turned toward us, not twenty feet away, and lifted his lamp. The safety of the corner was twenty feet behind us, but we didn't run for fear of giving ourselves away in the dark.

Grunt humphed and shrugged his shoulders, lazily lifting his gun in our general direction.

"No," Sunday said. "Cops would've announced themselves. Could be some of our esteemed guests. Just hang on." With that, he turned off their lantern, dropping us all into absolute black.

In the next extended instant, I recognized the lightless void, knew it like a childhood nightmare, and I waited for the phobia that always followed. The terror that would swallow me and whisper in my ear:

You're small.

You're weak.

You can't help.

But that voice never came. Instead, I was visited by the craziest vision I'd ever had. A prophetic flash that seemed to freeze time, and when I came back, I knew what I had to do.

Noiselessly, I eased Khajee against one wall, lifted the unlit lantern from her hand, and pressed my back against the cool of the opposite wall, across from her. Ahead of us, Sunday declared, "We know you're there. I'm guessing you want to get out same as us. Speak up."

Khajee and I held our silence, and I could just make out the shush of Sunday's voice as he whispered something to Grunt. A few heartbeats later, another shot burst the stillness with a pop and a white flash. That tiny flare made my target as I bullrushed forward, heaving the lantern ahead of me and hollering to Khajee, "Run get help!"

My aim must've been true, because there was a clattering crash and something skittered along the concrete beneath me. Totally blind, I sprinted in behind my projectile, following it like a lead blocker, and I dipped my shoulders and prayed I wouldn't plow headlong into that door. That night, my prayers were answered.

When I rammed into Grunt, he was totally unprepared. I knocked the air out of him, and we slammed into the locked door. He pounded my back as we tumbled onto the floor, and I swung a fist up at where I thought his face might be. I connected with something, his thick chin or the side of his skull. One of his massive paws found my head, and he snagged a handful of hair, drove my face sideways into the wall. As he yanked me back for another shot, I spiked an elbow deep into something meaty, maybe his gut. He let loose an "oomf" and released his grip.

I scrambled to my feet and suddenly light flooded the world. Sunday held up his lantern, and its glow illuminated his shocked face. "Kid?" he said.

Next to him, Grunt was on one knee, frozen and gawking too. I didn't know if he was paralyzed for a second by sheer surprise or just trying to gather his breath, but his eyes didn't even lock with mine. They floated lazily over my shoulder, widened at something.

I spun to find Khajee, holding the gun in a two-handed grip, aimed squarely at Grunt. To my total surprise, Grunt spoke in a raspy voice, like broken glass. "You sure you know how that thing works, little girl?"

Unshaken, Khajee took one step closer and tilted her face, sighting an eye along the barrel. "I know which end the bullets come out," she told him. "And the trigger's not a mystery."

Grunt, still genuflecting, seemed like he was trying to weigh his options, and I decided to narrow them. Pivoting at the hip, I jabbed my leg out and launched my foot forward, driving my heel deep into his jaw. It hurt like hell but his face cracked back. The big man teetered for a moment, wobbled, then collapsed in a heap.

I turned to Sunday, my fists raised and ready. But he slowly set down the lantern, shook his head, and meekly lifted his palms.

Khajee said, "Okay. Turns out maybe I was wrong about your front kick."

I eased from my fighting stance and asked, "So am I worthy of the Tiger Claw secret now?"

She smiled, and I had the only answer I needed.

Over Khajee's shoulder, voices called out "Police!" from the far end of the maintenance maze. Lights flashed down the hallway, and the sound of boots echoed toward us. I pictured Harrow and her team. Surely they'd been summoned by the gunfire and were racing to save us, not realizing that Khajee and me, we'd already saved ourselves.

EPILOGUE

It turns out that crazy vision I had in the dim corridor was my last one ever. After that, my power left me for good. And really, that final time, I didn't glimpse the actual future. I didn't see the bond that would form between Khajee and my mom, or all that would come to pass during my days at Fort Indiantown Gap, which Quinlan arranged just like Harrow and I talked about on that third call. Truth be told, I didn't miss the gift of prophecy. Just like the past isn't something that can be fixed, the future isn't something we're supposed to see. It's something we're meant to create, here in this moment, one move at a time.

What came to me when Khajee and I appeared to be trapped in that maze, the memory I still recall from time to time when things seem hopeless, is this: the presence of some future self, an older Eddie, reaching back to me through the years in that frozen moment. His grizzled face is lined with age, and he settles a thick and calloused hand on my chest as he smiles and says, "Don't worry. You got this." In a blink, he vanishes. I take one steady breath, then another, and in that darkness, I'm not gripped like I'd always been by the fear my father might find me, that I'd forever be nothing more than a slobber-crying failure. Instead, I see then that I'm neither a sheep nor a wolf. Not Brute Boy or Wild Child. Not my father. I'm just me, Eddie MacIntyre. At last, I'm okay with that, and it doesn't suck to feel that way.

ACKNOWLEDGMENTS

I'd like to first thank my former editor Cheryl Klein, who years back brought me an idea about a troubled high school wrestler and then gave me the space to make the story my own. When the project was handed over to Nick Thomas, I was skeptical anyone could fill Cheryl's shoes, but his steadfast optimism, perceptive eye, and stalwart intransigence on key aesthetic elements have proven invaluable. He got this book into fighting shape.

I'm in debt to Natnaree Junboonta, Michael Jerryson, and Dan Fethke for their expert insights into Thai culture and Buddhist tradition, as well as Julie Francisco of the Kalpa Bhadra Kadampa Buddhist Center of Harrisburg for her wisdom and generosity of time and spirit. For sharing their keen understanding on matters of meditation, I thank Toru Sato and Tomoko Grabosky.

I drew inspiration from many individuals I met through my involvement with wrestling and judo, among them Dave Holmes, Hachiro Oishi, my nephews Jerrod and Brian, and my brother John. A special nod to his son Keegan, whose combination of ferocity on the mat and gentle kindness outside the arena struck me as an interesting character core long ago.

This book was helped greatly by a sabbatical from my teaching post at Shippensburg University, and I should like to thank the committee and administration. I must also note the support of my colleagues, among them Nicole, Kim, Rich, Shari, and Sharon.

I also need to give a shout-out to Chris Naddeo, long-time reader, for his unreasonable encouragement of my writing and his impenetrable defense to a tai otoshi.

Finally I'm grateful beyond words to Beth and our boys, for continually giving me reason to write.

NEIL CONNELLY is the author of seven critically acclaimed books, including four YA novels with Arthur A. Levine Books. The most recent was *Into the Hurricane,* which *Kirkus Reviews* called "thoughtful and provocative." He teaches creative writing at Shippensburg University and lives in Camp Hill, Pennsylvania, with his wife and their sons. You can find him on the web at neilconnelly.com.

This book was edited by Nick Thomas and designed by Phil Falco. The production was supervised by Rachel Gluckstern. The text was set in Electra LT Std Regular, with display type set in Blunt Con it. The book was printed and bound at LSC Communications in Crawfordsville, Indiana. The manufacturing was supervised by Angelique Browne.